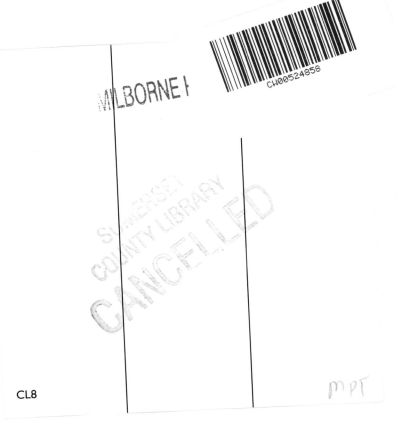

MILBORNE I

CW00524858

CL8

мрт

To my husband Ashley,
who has to put up with all my
book-related meltdowns!

TEN YEARS AGO

'Michael! Sadie!' the voice the other side of the bathroom door shouted. 'We know you're in there. Just hurry up already.'

The voice startled Michael, and he swore as he struggled to sort his clothes out. The girl, Sadie, was watching him from under her fringe as she did up the buttons on her blue-and-white checked shirt.

'What?' he said to her. The word came out sounding far harsher than he meant it to, but the guilt was beginning to set in and he was angry with himself.

'Aren't you going to say anything to me?' she asked.

Michael took a step towards her, but he swayed drunkenly. He reached out to steady himself, but what he thought was a solid surface turned out to be a shower curtain and he almost fell over. For a moment the image of himself falling into the shower filled his mind and he let out a stupid giggle, then he looked at the girl again. She'd finished dressing now and was watching him uncertainly. She smoothed down her shirt, fussed briefly with a beaded bracelet around her wrist and then said, 'I'm going home now.'

Michael stared at her. What should he say? What was a normal thing to say? Should he offer to walk home with her, or would she rather he left her alone? His mind wouldn't work fast enough, and he ended up saying the worst thing possible. 'Don't tell Rae,' he said.

Sadie looked as though she'd been slapped, then her eyes flashed with anger and she strode past him towards the door in a swish of sandy hair and a waft of some sort of sweet smell. *Strawberries?* Michael wondered. *No,* he told himself, *what adult woman would smell of strawberries?*

He reached out for her arm. 'I'm sorry,' he said, 'I'm sorry...' He struggled for her name. 'Uh...'

'Sadie,' she said. 'My name is Sadie.'

Michael nodded. Whoever was outside started knocking on the door again. Most of the people at the party knew his girl-friend, Rae. That was all he could think about. They all knew Rae, and they all knew that he'd come upstairs and gone in the bathroom to have sex with someone else. He made an absurd giggling sound again. There were four bedrooms in the house and all of them had been occupied with other couples. It had to be the most hormone-fuelled party he'd ever been to. It was as if everyone was taking one last chance to act crazy before they headed off to whatever their future was now the exams were over. He turned towards Sadie, meaning to say something nice – or at least coherent – but instead his mouth hung open and no words came out. Sadie pushed past him, and she looked upset. 'Sadie,' he said, 'hey, wait—'

She unlocked the bathroom door and ran out. He thought he heard her mutter something as she left. It sounded like, 'I'm so stupid.' He watched her pushing through the queue outside the door, and then she was gone. Some of the people were laughing, and someone said, 'At last.' Michael tried to follow her but he couldn't get through the crush of people. The hallway began to spin in front of his eyes so he slumped down on the carpet. He must have passed out then, because for a time he forgot everything.

...

The guilt began to set in again as Michael staggered home a few hours later. All he could think about was Rae. Would she find out what he'd done? She *couldn't* find out. If she found out she'd be devastated, and it would be so pointless for her to be devastated over something so *meaningless.* Yes, he and Rae had been arguing a lot recently. And yes, he wasn't quite sure if he loved her any more, but he didn't want it to be *over,* did he? He certainly hadn't meant to find Sadie, or to cheat on Rae with her. He paused at the side of the road and a surreal feeling washed over him as he remembered it. He took a few steps forward and then stopped again. It had been so good. The thought of it had been good, the moment he'd realised Sadie was actually up for it had been better, the reality had felt like – he struggled with his thick, drunken mind to find the right word. Flying: It had been like flying, he decided, even if he'd been too drunk to *fly* very well.

Michael looked at the time on his phone. He had to hold it about five centimetres from his face before he could read it, and even then the numbers danced before his eyes: 05:40. He started walking again, and for a while he lost track of his thoughts. When he drew near to his house he felt relieved and started to walk faster. He wanted to be home now. If he could crawl into bed it felt like it would all go away. Then only a few more days and it would be the end of university altogether, and he'd have a whole summer while he helped out in his parents' musty old furniture shop to try to put right what he'd done. A solitary car passed by, making a whooshing sound in the thin layer of drizzle on the tarmac. Michael shivered. He had barely noticed that it had begun to rain.

His house was within sight as he passed a small, dark side road and heard movement behind him. He turned, but before he could see what was happening his head exploded with pain. He cried out, and was dimly aware of a woman screaming. He realised he was being dragged from the pavement and away from the main street. Feeling weak and stunned, he tried to fight, but he couldn't. When the next blows came he stopped being aware of them as the world fell away, and he slipped into blackness.

PART ONE

TEN YEARS LATER

One

'Not again,' Sadie said, 'please, not again.'

Michael looked down at the pregnancy test in her hand, and saw that it was negative. He sat down beside her on the bathroom floor, and put his arm around her awkwardly. 'Sadie...' he said.

'No!' she shouted, the suddenness and loudness of her voice taking him aback. She shoved his arm away. 'No,' she said again quietly.

Michael gave up. He knew how desperate she was for a baby and never had a clue what to say when she got a negative result. When he tried to talk to her he usually ended up putting his foot in it and making things worse. Sadie put the test down on the floor and rested her forehead on her knees, her hair falling forward and brushing her bare legs. It was six-thirty in the morning and she'd done the test the second she got up, so she was still wearing a baggy old t-shirt of his that she wore in bed. When she'd called him into the bathroom to wait for the result she'd looked glazed with sleep. He watched her as she slowly lifted her head again, took a deep breath and let it out in a long sigh. 'I'm all right,' she said. 'I'm going to be all right. Just give me a minute.'

Michael left her and when she appeared half an hour later she was dressed and ready to go out. 'Come on,' she said when she found him in the living room eating a bowl of cereal in front of the TV, 'we're going to the shop today, aren't we? You wanted to go in early before it opens—'

'You don't have to come,' he said. 'If you can't face it I can go on my own—'

'What would I do here? I don't want to rattle around the house all day. I want to be busy.'

'Sadie—'

'Please. Let's just go.'

It was a cool, misty morning and Sadie shivered a little as they stood outside Benton's Furniture. Michael struggled to unlock the old door, which always seemed to catch and get stuck, swelling up or shrinking according to the weather. Most things in the shop had been old when Michael had taken it over from his parents. They were retired now, but it had taken a good couple of years before they'd trusted that they could leave him to it without the shop falling to pieces in their absence. The new stock that Sadie had come in to help him arrange was the first step in the sweeping changes he had planned for the store.

Once inside, Michael felt daunted at the size of the task. Spread over two storeys, the shop floor was like a rabbit warren, packed full of far too many items that were badly displayed and made him feel claustrophobic. It would take weeks if not months to get it all sorted out. But Sadie was in her element. Completely unfazed she jumped in immediately, suggesting where he should place furniture and lamps and cushions, roping all the other staff in to help, until by the time they got home they were both exhausted.

'Oh. God,' she said as they walked through the front door.

'What is it?'

'We've got to go out tonight,' she said, 'Emily and Andy invited us round for dinner. I'd forgotten about it.'

'That's tonight?'

'Yeah.'

'Sadie, we should cancel, after the news we had this morning—'

'No,' she said, 'I won't cancel because of that.'

'But—'

'It's not Emily's fault that she's pregnant and I'm not. I refuse to take it out on her.'

Michael sighed. 'Okay,' he said, 'if you're sure.' He gave her a look. 'I don't know why she had to tell you the second she found out,' he said.

'We've been through this. She thought it would be easier for me if I had a bit of warning rather than finding out when they do their big announcement in a couple of months. She was thinking of my feelings.'

He sighed. 'Yeah, I guess.'

'It's been a year, Michael,' she said after a brief pause. 'We've been trying for a *year.*'

'I know,' he said. 'Let's try not to think about it right now. Let's just get through tonight.'

Two

Emily and her husband Andy lived in an old Victorian terrace, which they'd stripped back to the brick and then done most of the renovations themselves. In fact, Michael and Sadie had helped out a few times with the decorating in exchange for as much beer and takeaway pizza as they could manage. Personally, Michael hated the cutesy country cottage look that they'd replaced the peeling wallpaper and woodchip with, but he liked Emily and Andy well enough, even though they were really Sadie's friends, not his. Emily had been Sadie's closest friend at university, and he knew that made it even more painful that Emily had recently had the news Sadie was so desperately hoping for.

It was late by the time they finished eating and Sadie went off to help Emily clear up in the kitchen, so Michael found himself left at the dining table with Andy. A small, quiet man with a mop of dense, dark hair and thick eyebrows, Andy had never been somebody Michael found it easy to talk to. In fact, most of the time Andy seemed quite content to be in the shadow of Emily, who was far more personable and sometimes even spoke for him. However, they managed to keep up some small talk for a minute or so, and then Michael found himself asking the question he probably least wanted to hear the answer to.

'So,' he said, 'you looking forward to being a dad?'

Andy looked a little unsure. 'Yeah,' he said, 'I mean, kind of scared too. I don't really know what to expect.'

Michael was about to speak but he noticed Andy was giving him an odd look.

'What?' Michael said. 'What is it?'

'I just remembered… you must already have a bit of experience of it.'

Michael laughed. 'I never have anything to do with kids,' he said. 'I have a little nephew, but I don't see very much of him – my sister doesn't live round here.'

Andy frowned, 'I must have got mixed up,' he said.

Michael began to feel uneasy. He wished he could drop the whole conversation, but he knew he'd feel troubled until he understood what Andy was talking about. 'Mixed up about what?'

Andy began to look intensely uncomfortable, but he must have realised he couldn't get away without some sort of explanation so he tried his best to give one. 'Emily said something about you having a baby with an ex-girlfriend,' he said, 'but I must have heard her wrong.' He quickly got up and started clearing the remaining glasses from the dining table while Michael watched him in astonishment, his skin beginning to prickle. *Rae*, he thought to himself, remembering his ex-girlfriend for the first time in years. *He's talking about Rae.*

...

Although Michael was desperate to find out more, the last thing he wanted to do was bring it up in front of Sadie and upset her, but he found he could think of little else. Neither, apparently, could Andy, because as they all sat in the living room Emily turned to them both and said, 'What's going on with you two?'

'Nothing,' Michael said. 'I've had a bit of a long day, that's all.'

Emily looked at Sadie, then back at Michael and Andy again. 'You look kind of *guilty*,' she said. 'What have you been talking about?'

In a bid to get Sadie away from the house before the conversation went any further, Michael quickly said, 'Sorry, Emily. Thanks for the dinner and everything but I think we're going to have to head home—'

He stood up abruptly and Sadie gave him an odd look. To his relief she disappeared off to the bathroom before leaving, and Michael managed to take Emily to one side.

'What is it, Michael?' she asked, 'what's wrong?' Her tone was friendly enough, but he could see a line between her eyebrows and her blue eyes were flicking unnervingly about his face.

'Did...' he said, not sure how to word it, 'Andy said something to me about Rae having had a baby—'

Emily's face turned pale. She reached up to her throat where a thin silver chain nestled, and rubbed it briefly between her fingertips. 'Oh,' she said, 'oh, God. He shouldn't have told you that.'

'Is it true?'

Emily looked around as if she was trying to find a diversion, but when she failed she said, 'Listen, Michael, I don't really know.'

'Where did you hear it from? Or have you... you haven't known all this time, surely—'

'No! No, of course not.' She was silent briefly, as if gathering

14

her thoughts. 'I went to a hen night a little while ago for someone I knew at uni. It ended up being a kind of crazy night. Anyway, there was someone there called Alice – I'm sure you must know her, she shared a house with Rae. They were close friends, I think.'

Michael nodded.

'Well,' Emily went on, 'when Alice was drunk she blurted out something about Rae being pregnant at the end of university. Apparently Rae had stayed with her for a little while because... well... you were in hospital after the attack, and she'd found out about you and Sadie. She had nowhere else to go. I don't know all the details, Alice just said that Rae was pregnant and then she disappeared.'

'Disappeared?'

'That's what she said. I don't really know Rae, or Alice, so I can't tell you any more than that. But some of the other people there who were friendly with Rae back at uni said they never heard from her again either.'

A sense of foreboding began to spread through Michael's body. He'd never heard from Rae again, but having cheated on her he hadn't seen anything unusual in that. He'd assumed that she'd gone back to live with her family after university since he wasn't aware of her having a job lined up. However, when he had woken up in hospital, he had found one message from her on his phone – the last thing she'd ever said to him. And what she'd said had made it very clear she considered their relationship to be over. In fact, he could remember the words at the end of the message perfectly even now, ten years later. They had always stuck with him. They had read:

You will never see me again.

Three

The conversation was cut short when they heard Sadie making her way down the stairs. Michael was quiet as they said goodbye, unable to take his eyes from the innocent smile on Sadie's face as she hugged Emily and Andy, thanking them for the dinner and talking about meeting up again soon. A sick feeling of guilt began to settle in his stomach as he thought about what he'd learned and how much it would hurt her. He lurched out of the house in a daze and ended up having to make a grab for the wall. Sadie laughed at him. 'Bloody hell Michael,' she said, 'how much did you drink?'

He shook his head and tried to laugh with her, but she was already making her way over to the car and paying little attention to him.

That night, he barely slept. His tossing and turning was keeping Sadie awake, so he went downstairs to the kitchen and sat at the table by the window, his laptop and a mug of tea in front of him. He'd thought about Rae a lot when they'd first parted because he felt ashamed about what he'd done and he had worried about her, but gradually he'd moved on and almost forgotten. Now the things he'd heard from Andy and Emily threw his relationship with Rae into sharp focus again. She'd never exactly been the most stable person, in fact he'd heard the word "mental" used many times in the past when he overheard people gossiping about her, though it always made him angry to hear her talked about so cheaply and offensively. He supposed that maybe it was arrogant to think that his actions might be enough to send her over the edge, but nevertheless he did wonder what his betrayal had done to her, and he hoped that wherever she was she was okay.

There had been times in the first year or so after their breakup when he'd thought about trying to get in touch with her, but her presence online seemed to have vanished, her profiles deleted, any trail that could lead easily to her hidden or destroyed. He'd never wanted to delve any further than that. Trying to pursue somebody who had gone to such lengths not to be found seemed like a violation, but now he found himself opening the laptop and trying to search for her again.

He tried harder this time. In the past he'd spent no longer than a few minutes, maybe half an hour at most, but this time he didn't give up so easily. When he finally stopped his online search and looked at the time, he realised he'd been sitting there for almost two hours and his tea was stone cold. The screen suddenly seemed very bright in the dark room and he closed his eyes. *A baby,* he thought to himself, a *baby.* He opened his eyes again and let the screen come back into focus. He couldn't believe it had happened. And he couldn't believe that Rae hadn't told him. Perhaps Alice had been lying or confused. Or perhaps *Rae* had cheated on *him,* because given how difficult he and Sadie were finding it to make a baby, it seemed far-fetched that a pregnancy could just happen to a girlfriend of his by *accident.*

He rubbed his eyelids and sat back in the chair. His searches had been hopeless. He'd turned up no new information about her. Everything he found when he searched for the name "Rae Carrington" was either about somebody else or referred to her ten or more years ago, back when he'd known her. He remembered Emily telling him that nobody else had heard from her, and his mind began to turn to some darker thoughts about what may have happened to her. He shook himself. He couldn't start thinking like that.

He decided he needed to approach things differently. He wasn't friends with Alice online but he managed to find her profile and send a message. After all, she was the last person he knew of who had seen Rae, and she was the most likely person to have some idea where she'd gone next.

…

He didn't get a reply that night. Nor the next day, or the next. Before he knew it almost two weeks had stretched by and Sadie was beginning to notice how nervy and distracted he was.

'Is it because we were disappointed again?' she asked him. 'By the pregnancy test, I mean. I understand. I do. But it's better to try to focus on other things.'

He'd come up with some empty words to reassure her, but his guilt washed over him in a wave. He hated keeping it secret from her, but he could see no point in telling her and upsetting her when it was little more than a rumour. He needed to talk to Alice. Then he'd have a better idea what it actually was that he needed to tell Sadie.

Once a few more days passed, Michael began to lose patience and phoned Emily.

'Do you have any contact details for Alice?' he asked her. 'Email address, phone number—'

There was silence for a while, and then she said, 'I have her email address. It was on a group email about the hen party.'

'Can I have it?'

'Yes, of course. Michael, listen, I'm sorry I didn't tell you about this when I first found out. I shouldn't have tried to keep it secret. I *was* going to tell you at some point, obviously, I just—'

'Sadie.'

'Yes. I don't want her to get hurt. This baby stuff, she's finding it so hard.'

'I know.'

'And I have no idea if what Alice was saying is even true. She was so drunk. I'm sure it's all a big misunderstanding.'

'Yeah,' Michael said, 'you could be right.'

She read out Alice's email address to him, and he made a note of it.

'Thanks, Emily,' he said.

'No problem. I hope that this all works itself out. You know, in a good way.'

'Yeah,' he said, 'so do I.'

...

Later that day, Michael sent Alice an email. It was short and to the point, asking her whether the rumours he'd heard were true, saying how helpful it would be if he could talk to her, or at least if she could tell him that Rae was okay. He was left to stew for a couple more days but finally, to his relief, a message came back:

*Wasn't sure whether to reply to you or not. It's hard for me to think about talking to you after seeing the state you left Rae in all those years ago. I think it would be easier if we met face to face, but I'll say now that I don't know where Rae is, and I haven't heard from her for years. I don't have much to tell you and what little there is you might not want to hear. I don't know if she had the baby, but she **was** pregnant and I'm as sure as I can be that the baby was yours.*

Alice.

Four

Michael arranged to meet Alice a couple of weeks later, on a Saturday afternoon. Sadie was meeting friends and he managed to rearrange some shifts at the shop to free himself up for a few hours. He couldn't help but keep thinking about the baby – well, it would be a *child* now. Almost ten years old. It was so surreal he couldn't begin to get his head around it.

It was just over an hour's drive to get to the café Alice had suggested, so he'd had plenty of time to work himself up into a state. No matter which way he looked at it, there was a chance the outcome could be life-changing. He was excited in a way, but mostly he wished the past had simply stayed in the past, because he liked his life the way it was. The idea of change unsettled, and quite frankly, scared him.

The café was small and humid, the windows steaming up on the chilly February afternoon. Michael thought he was the first to arrive, but then he spotted a woman sat on her own in a booth in the corner, and he eventually realised it was Alice, though her chestnut-coloured hair was longer, and she had glasses, which he'd never seen her wear in the past. She noticed him looking at her and gestured for him to come over.

'Did you find the place okay?' she asked as he sat down.

'Yeah,' he said. He awkwardly started pulling his jacket off, trying to hide his nerves. The way she seemed so calm was flustering him, but he finally managed to pull himself together. 'You look well,' he said.

She nodded slightly and said, 'Thanks.' Apparently she couldn't bring herself to say the same about him, and instead she adjusted the bow at the top of the floral blouse she was wearing. 'I don't have very long,' she said. 'I have to pick my girlfriend up from the airport in a couple of hours.'

'Oh,' Michael said, 'yeah, that's fine. Have you been together long?'

'About a year.'

'Cool, that's—'

'You married Sadie,' Alice said, with a pointed glance at the ring on his left hand.

'Yeah—'

'Congratulations,' she said flatly.

'Does…' Michael said quietly, 'does Rae know?'

They were interrupted when a teenage girl in a baggy white

shirt came to take their order, and once she'd left again Alice sighed as if she had no idea where to begin.

'I know,' Michael said. 'You don't know where Rae is or what happened to the baby.'

'No. And I certainly don't know whether or not she knows you married Sadie. For her sake I hope she doesn't, because if the state she was in when I last saw her was anything to go by, I'm not sure she'd be able to handle the knowledge that you married the woman you cheated on her with.'

Michael didn't know how to answer, and they sat in silence for a minute or two, until their tea arrived – in a leaky metal teapot that left puddles on the table when they tried to pour it.

'Alice,' Michael said, 'you knew Rae better than anyone. What happened to her after that night? After the night that I—'

She nodded. 'I'll tell you, Michael,' she said. 'Just let me think how to start.'

...

For the next few minutes Michael listened in horror as Alice explained quite what a mess Rae had got herself into after finding out about him and Sadie.

'You're sure about what you saw?' he said. 'Around dawn on that morning after the party I was at with Sadie, you were woken up by a sound outside and when you looked out of the window Rae was getting out of a car?'

'A nice-looking car as well,' Alice said. 'I don't know makes or models or anything, but it's not the kind of car you have unless you're doing well in life.'

'But you didn't see the man's face?'

'No. The door opened and Rae started getting out. But it was like she didn't really want to. Then it looked like the man pushed her, and she stumbled out onto the pavement.'

Michael's anger surged, and he took several gulps of tea to try to swallow the feelings back down. He was hoping by going through it again he could get every last bit of detail, and uncover some clue about where Rae was now.

'Was she hurt?'

'I couldn't see her very well. She ran back inside and into her room. I knocked on her door but she didn't answer. She didn't come out until late the next morning, then that night she didn't come home at all. When she finally turned up again the next day she looked dreadful, like... I have no idea how to describe it. She wasn't making any sense.'

'Do you think she'd been with the same man again?'

'I don't know. She started packing her bags, but when I asked her what her plans were she said she had nowhere to go. Then she blurted out that she was pregnant. I had to argue with her for a long time before she agreed to let me help her. I had a flat sorted out that I was about to move into, but she said she'd only stay there with me if I swore not to tell anyone where she was, especially you. But it was a nightmare. I was flat-sharing with someone I worked with and Rae was on the sofa. She tried to find temporary work but she couldn't seem to manage it. She just couldn't get her head together – she'd turn up for interviews or ask around for work dressed in last night's clothes, or hung-over—'

'But she was preg—'

Alice held up a finger. 'Don't even think about judging her for drinking.'

'I'm not—'

'She was so messed up by what you did, Michael!'

Alice's voice had grown loud, and a couple of people looked round at them.

Michael waited for her to collect herself. He didn't know what to say.

'I tried to get through to her,' she said at last, 'but she kept rambling about all sorts of strange things, I could hardly under-stand her.'

'What things? What did she say?'

'Michael, most of it I can't remember clearly and what I can remember I don't really want to repeat. I mean, you know what she was like. Even at the best of times she didn't make a great deal of sense—'

'Alice, please, anything could help.'

Alice gave him a long look. 'It was a lot of stuff about how she wasn't Rae,' she said finally. 'How she was somebody else, or needed to be somebody else.'

Michael took a second to think about it – to go through every-thing Alice had told him again – to try to find any gaps, or anything he could press her for more detail on.

'So she didn't stay with you for long?' he asked. 'She left?'

'I asked her to leave. She stole some money from my flatmate, and sometimes she'd bring people back, and we weren't comfort-able about it.' She looked up at Michael. 'Like I said, she was in a bad place. I wanted to help her but it was becoming impossible.

Me and my flatmate didn't feel safe with the random people – men – she'd bring home, and then when she stole the money I couldn't have her staying there after that. She said that the money was for some "documents". I have no idea what she was talking about. I suggested that perhaps she should go back to her parents. I thought it was a sensible suggestion.'

'What did Rae think?'

Alice closed her eyes briefly, then turned her head to the side and lifted her hair, and Michael saw a jagged scar running just in front of Alice's ear.

'What? She did that?'

Alice let her hair drop back down. 'She went absolutely mad when I suggested it. Screaming at me. She smashed a bottle and… well…' She gestured towards her face.

'My God,' Michael said. 'Alice, I'm so sorry—'

'Are you?'

'Yes, I can't believe she—'

'Well, after that she left,' Alice continued, cutting him off abruptly. 'That's the last time I saw her. I have no idea why she reacted like that when I mentioned her parents. I think… No. I don't know. Maybe she was on something. She certainly didn't look right that night. Her eyes… they were… It was weird. I try not to think about it. But that was the point when I had to stop helping her. I think I did all that anyone could. If I'm honest, I don't care what happened to her after she did this to me. I feel sorry for what she went through, but there's no excuse for this. Especially when I was trying to help her.'

'You didn't report what she'd done to you?'

'No. Perhaps I should have done, but I was just relieved she was away from me and I wanted to forget the whole thing. Or try to, anyway.'

Michael tried to think of something sympathetic to say, but gave up and decided to move on. 'But you don't know where she went?' he asked.

Alice finished the last of her tea. 'I'm sorry, Michael,' she said. Her voice was businesslike all of a sudden, and he realised their conversation was over. 'I know it's not what you were hoping for, but that really is all that I can tell you.'

'Wait,' he said, as she leant down to pick up her bag. 'Before you go, do you know why she didn't tell me she was pregnant? I mean before what happened between me and Sadie. Why didn't Rae tell me while we were still together? She must have known—'

'I can't tell you what was going on inside her head.'

'I know, but…'

Alice sighed. 'I guess she was waiting for the right time,' she told him. 'She was only five or six weeks along when she told me, it's not like she'd been hiding it from you for ages.'

'I wish she had told me.'

'Because you wouldn't have slept with Sadie?'

'I would have wanted to be involved.'

'Perhaps that's not what she wanted. It was her choice. And whatever happened with the baby was her choice too.'

'Are you saying you think she got rid of it?'

'I have no idea. Maybe. And now I really need to get going.'

She picked up her coat and bag and began to make her way through the crowded café. Michael wanted to leave himself, but his body didn't seem able to move. He sat for several more minutes, letting her words sink in, until finally he got to his feet with one thought in his mind: *I've got to tell Sadie.*

Five

Michael wanted to tell Sadie about what had happened as soon as he got home, but she was still out and messaged him to say she wouldn't be back until late, so he sat on his own all evening, turning it over and over in his mind. She finally came home at about midnight – too late for him to try talking to her – and she went to bed and fell straight asleep. Michael was wide awake so he went back downstairs to watch TV. He must have eventually dropped off because he was woken at around six-thirty by Sadie coming into the lounge.

'Michael?' she said. 'Couldn't you sleep?'

He shook his head, and was about to try to say something, but Sadie was distracted. 'It's time again,' she said.

Michael's heart sank and it must have shown on his face.

'Fine,' she said. 'I guess you can stay down here if you're not interested.'

'No, I am,' he said, 'of course I am.'

He followed her upstairs and waited while she went in the bathroom to do a pregnancy test. A few minutes later, when he hadn't heard anything, he knocked on the door.

'It's not locked,' she said quietly.

He stepped inside, and found her sat on the floor again.

'Negative?' he asked.

She nodded and he sat down beside her.

'I guess…' she said, 'I guess we need to face that it's not happening.'

Michael looked down at the test in her hand. She was gripping it so hard that her knuckles had turned white, and he gently took it from her. 'Sadie,' he said, 'I need to—'

'I feel like we're cursed,' she said, cutting him off.

'What?'

'The night we got together, you were beaten so badly you nearly died,' she said. 'What is that if it's not a sign?'

'A sign of what?'

'That perhaps we shouldn't be together,' she said softly.

Michael didn't reply. He knew she didn't really mean it.

'Do you ever think about it?' she asked suddenly, 'about how close you were to dying?'

'Not really,' he said. It wasn't completely true, but he did make an effort not to dwell on it. The police had never caught the attacker, and though he told himself he had to move on, he wasn't sure he would ever truly be free of it. He realised that Sadie was still speaking, and he tried to listen. 'Perhaps…' she was saying, 'perhaps we don't deserve to have children. I mean, I don't know what we could have done that was so wrong, but—'

'Sadie, there's something I need to tell you,' Michael said abruptly.

She looked round at him. Her sadness made her eyes look dull and glazed, grey rather than their usual green. A little crease formed between her eyebrows as she realised he was about to say something big. 'Michael,' she said, putting her hand on his arm. 'Michael, you're scaring me. What is it? What's wrong?'

He waited just a little longer. He felt frozen, sick, like someone was telling him to jump out of a plane. 'Sadie, I'm sorry,' he said.

Her eyes began to fill up with tears, 'Michael!' she said, 'Michael, what? Are you *leaving* me? Is there someone else? What is it? Please—'

'I think…' he said. He swallowed painfully and then drew in a deep breath. 'I think Rae might have been pregnant when me and her broke up.'

He'd said the words into his lap, and when he looked up he saw that the colour had drained from Sadie's cheeks and she whispered, 'What?'

Six

'I only recently found out,' he hurried to explain. 'Andy said something when we went to his and Emily's for dinner. Emily had seen Rae's old housemate Alice—'

'*Emily* knew?'

'No,' Michael said, 'I mean yes. But only for a couple of months—'

Something dawned on Sadie. 'We saw them a month ago!' she said. 'You've *known,* all this time—'

'Not for sure. I was trying to get in touch with Alice in case it was all a misunderstanding. I finally saw her yesterday. She confirmed it.'

'Yesterday,' Sadie said, 'while I was out. You were off finding out about your *baby*—'

'Sadie—'

'At least we know something now,' she said.

'What do you mean?'

'We know it's not you.'

'What are you talking about?'

'It's not you!' she said. '*You're* not the one who can't make babies! Not if you managed to make one with *her*. By *accident*—' She suddenly hit out at him with her hands, catching him on the arm. 'How could you?' she shouted, 'how *could* you be so irresponsible? Why weren't you being careful?'

'Sadie, we were,' Michael said, 'every...' he thought about it and corrected himself, 'I mean, there might have been once or twice, when we didn't—'

'You stupid man!' Sadie screamed. She stood up. 'I suppose you're going to go and find her now,' she said. 'You're going to go and play happy families with her, because God knows you can't with me.'

She started towards the door and Michael grabbed her. 'Stop it,' he said, 'listen to me. All I know is that Rae was pregnant when me and her broke up. Alice doesn't know what happened after that. She doesn't know what happened to Rae. Nobody does. And she doesn't know what happened to the baby. When Rae was staying with Alice after university it sounds like she was in a right state, partying, drinking, she sounded like she'd completely lost the plot.'

'While she was pregnant.'

'Sadie, you can't let what we're going through at the moment colour how you think about decisions Rae made. You'll drive yourself mad.'

'Mad?' Sadie said. 'You want to know who's mad? That fucking ex-girlfriend of yours—' Sadie stopped abruptly. She never usually swore, and it had taken both of them aback. She started to push Michael out of the way. 'Leave me alone,' she said, 'let me go, Michael. Let me go.'

Michael released her arm and although he wanted to follow her he could see she needed some space, so he stopped himself. He leant against the wall in the bathroom and closed his eyes. It was a nightmare. A total nightmare.

...

After shutting herself in the bedroom for half an hour or so, Sadie came out and told Michael she couldn't be around him. She drove off somewhere, leaving him to face an anxious few hours waiting for her to come home. When he saw her car pull into the drive, his heart leapt and he opened the front door for her.

'Sadie, I'm sorry,' he started to say. 'I'm so, so sorry.'

She held her hand up to stop him. 'I know,' she said, 'and I'm very shocked and hurt. But we need to put all that aside right now. The fact is, you may well have a son or daughter out there, and no matter about you, or Rae, or your history together, your *child* deserves us to all be adults about this.'

'I don't think Rae wants me to find her. I don't think she wants anyone to find her. I tried to look her up after we saw Emily and Andy, but there is nothing out there. She's deleted all her profiles online, there's no trace of her. It's like she's disappeared from the face of the earth.'

'Perhaps she wanted to hide straight after it all happened,' Sadie said, 'but a lot of time has gone by and maybe she would like it if you took some responsibility.'

'Sadie, if I had known, I would never have *abandoned* her. Even if it was over between me and her, I would have made sure I did my bit.'

'I know,' she said, 'I know that. And I know that no matter how much I'd like it if this whole thing just went away, you would never forgive yourself for not trying to find her. And I don't think I'd be able to get it off my conscience either.'

Without saying anything further she went upstairs, and came back down with some paper and marker pens.

'What are you doing?' Michael asked.

'You said you can't find Rae online. Well, we're going to have to try harder. We'll need to get organised, write down everything you know about her.'

'Sadie,' he said, 'not right now. Not *today*— '

She waved his protest aside. 'Yes, right now,' she said. 'I don't want to sit and speculate. I want to *act.*'

She went through to the kitchen and sat at the table. Reluctantly, Michael joined her. 'What you said,' he told her, 'about it not being *me* who can't make a baby…'

Sadie glanced up at him, a warning look in her eyes.

'I don't want us to think about it like that,' he continued. 'It's not your *fault,* or mine. If one of us can't have a baby, it means that *both* of us can't. But it's too early to even say anything like that yet. We haven't even spoken to anyone about it…'

Sadie thrust a marker pen into his hand. 'Please, Michael. Just write down what you can remember about Rae.'

Seven

Despite her insistence that she needed a distraction, Sadie seemed unable to start work straight way, and she disappeared upstairs again. The sudden rift between them made Michael feel sick. They'd never really argued before, not properly. They'd had little spats – more in the past few months – but it had never been like this. By the time she surfaced again it was evening. Michael had filled a couple of sheets of A4, and had some reasonable leads. Sadie plonked herself down next to him, and cast her eye over it.

'Rae's mum,' she read, 'Sue Carrington. Enjoys pottery.'

'Yes.'

Sadie pulled the sheets closer to her. 'And Rae is from Frinchford-on-Sea.'

Michael nodded. 'I can't remember her dad's name. She has two brothers as well: William and James Carrington.'

'Her parents may well still live in Frinchford-on-Sea,' Sadie said. 'Along with her mum's name, that's a good starting point.'

She shoved the papers away again. 'You know, I find it hard to imagine Rae having a family,' she said.

'What do you mean?'

'I don't know exactly,' she said. 'I always found her so strange. People were drawn to her because she was dramatic, and exciting, and she had this kind of charisma, but she always left me feeling cold. I can't really describe it, but I felt like she had this *veneer*. I could never get my head around who she actually was. I can't imagine her having a family because she never quite seemed real, not the few times I saw her. I just imagine her springing up out of nowhere.'

Michael had to admit he knew what she meant. Rae had always been a bit showy and over-the-top. She'd been loud and theatrical and glamorous, like a whirlwind that scooped people up and then spat them back out. He'd thought that was what she'd do with him, and there had been days when he'd go without so much as a text from her until he felt wretched with the thought it was over. Then she'd turn the full force of her attention onto him again and it was like basking in the sun. He'd loved her, and he was sure she'd loved him, but it had begun to feel like trying to grab hold of mist. There had been no substance to anything: her stories about her past were vague and exaggerated, she'd never let him meet her family. In the end he had felt he didn't really know her at all. He felt it again now as he tried to write down notes on her. There were huge gaps in his knowledge, and he'd written down precious few hard facts, mainly just odd fragments of things she'd told him and random observations.

Michael turned to Sadie, wanting to thank her for helping him when it must hurt her so much, but it was as if she knew what he was about to say. 'I'm doing this for the sake of yours and Rae's child,' she said, 'but I'm finding it very hard.'

'Me too,' he said.

She gave him a small smile. 'So what will you do now?'

'Like you said. Her parents have got to be the place to start.'

She nodded slowly. 'Okay,' she said. 'Okay. Well, I'm here to support you, Michael. If you need me.'

He put his arms around her and hugged her. 'Thank you,' he said into her hair.

Eight

It only took a small amount of research for Michael to pick up the trail to Rae's parents. A woman named Sue Carrington had recently opened up a pottery studio in a village near to Frinchford-on-Sea, and he was confident that she was Rae's mum, since it all tied up so nicely with what he'd written down about her. Initially he planned to phone her, as Frinchford-on-Sea was a ten-hour round trip, but when he told Sadie what he planned, she said, 'Let's go there.'

'Are you sure?' he asked. He was surprised she wanted to get involved.

'Yes. I'm owed some time off work, and I'm sure you could sort something out at the shop. I feel fed up here. I know this is about finding Rae, but maybe we could have some fun. Like we used to. We could pretend for a while that we're not trying for a baby, that we're just me and you.'

The rain misted down as they made the journey a couple of days later, and by the time they reached their destination it was pouring, making the tired seaside town look dismal, the streets grey and deserted.

The bed and breakfast they'd chosen was small and friendly, and although he could tell Sadie was trying to put on a brave face, she seemed genuinely won over by the cheery room with its view of the battleship-grey sea.

'I like being at the seaside in the rain,' she said. She threw herself down onto the bed, and smiled at him. 'I think things will be okay,' she said. 'Whatever happens, we'll always have each other.' She giggled at her cheesy line, but when Michael didn't join in she sat up again. 'You're worried about her, aren't you?'

'I worry about what Alice said.' He'd told Sadie all about it on the drive, and she'd tried to reassure him, but he hadn't been convinced. 'Michael, I'm sure it's not as bad as it sounds.'

'I'm just so *angry*,' he said.

'Angry about what? That she was dealing with everything on her own? That she didn't tell you she was pregnant?'

'Not just that. Lots of things. Like what happened to her that night, after she found out about us, and what Alice said about her getting out of a guy's car. Being *thrown* out, by the sound of it, once he was done with her. How could—'

'Michael, don't upset yourself. You don't know what happened—'

'What if he hurt her?' The possibilities kept pouring into his head. 'What if he made her—'

Sadie put her hand on his leg. 'Michael,' she said gently, 'you told me Alice said Rae was reluctant to get out of the man's car. If he'd hurt her, I think she would have wanted to get out as fast as she could.'

Michael shook his head and tried to calm down. 'What if this is all hopeless?' he said. 'Nobody has heard from her, Sadie, nobody. Perhaps the reason I can't find any trace of her is because...' His voice turned harsh as he said the thing that had been preying on his mind for weeks. 'Maybe it's because she's dead.'

'You can't think like that,' Sadie said. 'Be positive. That's the only way to do this. Be open-minded, and be positive. There is no reason to think the worst. None at all.'

...

Michael woke up early the next morning and left Sadie sleeping while he showered and dressed. They'd decided it would be best for Michael to visit Sue alone, while Sadie stayed behind to put her feet up, or maybe go for a stroll along the beach. They ate breakfast together in a tense silence, then Michael left, his stomach churning.

He reached the pottery studio at around ten o'clock. It was inside a large brick building that housed lots of little shops and studios selling all sorts, from handmade jewellery to wedding cakes to antiques, and it was quiet at this time of day. When he arrived at Sue's Ceramics there was a sign on the door saying "back in ten minutes", so he stood outside looking through the window at the array of seaside-themed plates, bowls and mugs. After about five minutes he saw a slim, neatly dressed woman who he estimated to be in her late fifties looking at him curiously as she walked towards the shop. She was carrying several shopping bags and precariously gripping a takeaway coffee.

'Sorry,' she said as she struggled to open the door. 'Have you been waiting here long?'

Michael stared at her for a moment, trying to see a resemblance to Rae, but where Rae's hair was thick and almost black, Sue's was fine and blonde, and while Rae's eyes were dark and her features sharp and defined, Sue was fair and her face soft. Kind. Not that it meant anything, really. People didn't always look exactly like their parents. Michael helped her with the door, mumbling that he hadn't been waiting long, and followed her inside.

Sue dumped her shopping at the back of the shop in her work space, and then joined him at the front with another curious glance. 'If you don't mind me saying, you look like you have a lot on your mind.'

He nodded. 'I'm trying to find someone,' he said. 'You are Sue Carrington, aren't you?'

'Yes,' she said, frowning slightly. 'Who are you trying to find?'

'Rae Carrington,' he said, 'your daughter. I don't know if she ever mentioned me. I was her boyfriend back when she was at university. We lost touch and—'

Sue interrupted him, 'I'm sorry, uh... what did you say your name was?'

'I didn't. It's Michael.'

'Michael,' she said, 'I think you must have come to the wrong place. You see, I don't have a daughter.'

Nine

Michael stared at her. 'What?' he said stupidly. He couldn't believe it. He'd been so *sure.*

'I have two sons,' she said, 'but I don't know of any Rae Carrington. You must be mistaken.'

'No,' he said. 'Rae said you're her mother, she said she grew up in Frinchford-on-Sea, that she has two brothers, William and James Carrington, that her mum enjoys pottery—'

Sue looked uncomfortable. She put her coffee down on the counter and looked squarely at Michael.

'Look, I'm sorry but I don't have a daughter. I don't know who you've been talking to—'

'Rae told me about you herself. But I must have got it wrong. I'm sorry.' He turned to the door and Sue took a step towards him, her expression softening. 'I'm not sure what's happened here,' she said, 'but those things you just said, they do seem to refer to me. Why don't we go and get a coffee and talk this over.'

'You already have a coffee.' Michael gestured towards the paper cup on the counter.

'I'll get another one,' she said. 'Come on, you look like you could do with sitting down.'

Michael followed her out of the shop, grateful for how understanding she was being. He found himself feeling comfortable with her, and when they sat down in a sprawling café area in the middle of the collection of shops, Sue smiled at him and said, 'Why don't you start at the beginning?'

'Are you sure you don't need to be at the shop—'

Sue waved his words away. 'A few minutes won't hurt,' she said. 'Take your time.'

Michael took a deep breath, not sure where to start, but once he did he found himself telling her almost everything; all that Rae had told him about her past, what he'd discovered from Alice, and how Rae had been pregnant when they'd parted. He was too ashamed to say he'd cheated.

'Well, Michael, I don't think there's much doubt that Rae knows who I am,' she concluded. 'But if I ever met her, I don't remember it. She would have been a child, I suppose. Or a teenager.'

'Yeah, I guess so.'

'I need to give it some thought,' Sue said. 'There must be an explanation. Are you happy to give me your number? I'll call you if anything occurs to me.'

Michael quickly wrote his number on the back of their drinks receipt and gave it to her. 'Thank you,' he said, 'thank you so much. For listening.'

'It's no problem,' she said, 'and I hope you do find her. It's never too late, you know. To make things right with somebody.'

They said goodbye and Michael walked slowly back to his car, still feeling shaken by the revelations. Sue Carrington was not Rae's mother. So why on earth had Rae ever said that she was?

...

Michael filled Sadie in on what had happened while they sat on a wall at the seafront, eating fish and chips with wooden forks. The weather was much improved from when they'd arrived. It was still chilly, but the rain had cleared to make way for weak sunshine, and Michael would have felt relaxed but for the fact he was so confused by what he'd discovered. He checked his phone every five minutes in the hope he'd hear from Sue.

'Michael, she'll call you when she's ready,' Sadie said. 'She probably wants to take a few hours to think it over.'

'It's just so weird,' he said. 'Why would Rae pretend someone else was her mother?'

Sadie stabbed a chip. 'Maybe Rae wasn't pretending. Perhaps Sue is her mother.'

'What do you mean?'

Sadie put her fork back down. 'You said that Rae went mad when Alice mentioned her parents. Maybe she had some sort of falling out with them that was so terrible that Sue disowned her.'

Michael stared at Sadie. 'No,' he said, 'no, I don't think that could be right. Sue was such a *nice* woman, I can't believe that—'

'People aren't always who they seem,' Sadie said. 'Even if she is a lovely woman, everyone has limits. Perhaps something happened with Rae that made Sue reach hers.'

Michael fell silent and watched a couple of dogs playing on the beach. At his side Sadie carried on eating, occasionally swinging her legs out in front of her, then resting them back against the wall.

'Rae's surname really is Carrington,' he said after a while. 'If it wasn't, I would have seen her actual name written on things... letters, official stuff. There's no way she could have had a different surname and nobody noticed. Even if she somehow kept it from me, her housemates would have realised if she ever got any post. It was – no,' he interrupted himself. 'Her essays. I read through a couple of them, to check for spelling and grammar and stuff. Her name would have been on them—'

Sadie ate her last chip and stretched her legs out. 'I think you have your answer, then,' she said. 'If Rae's surname really is Carrington, and everything else she told you matches up, then this Sue must be her mother, or at least a relative. It's not a common name, and after all, why would Rae lie?'

'She never let me meet her parents, though. Perhaps it was because she was lying.'

'Yeah, but she wouldn't let you if she'd had some massive bust-up with them either, would she? She possibly just didn't want to talk to you about whatever happened. Maybe it was still a bit raw.'

'It's all so *strange*.'

'I know,' Sadie said, 'but let's try to forget about it for now. Sue will phone if and when she's ready. Until then, there's really nothing more we can do.'

Ten

The call came at around four in the afternoon, and Michael practically fell over himself to answer it. He listened as Sue Carrington explained that she'd talked it over with her husband, and after initially being completely bewildered, the two of them had had an idea about how Rae might have met them. She said it was a long shot, but it was the only idea they had, and that if Michael was free he was welcome to come round and talk to them.

'Bring your wife too if you like,' Sue said. Michael had told her that Sadie was with him. 'Save her hanging around on her own.'

The Carringtons' home was about a twenty-minute drive away. It took them a little while to find the exact address, but when they did they found themselves outside an attractive stone house with a large, neat garden wrapped around it. Michael and Sadie walked up to the door hand in hand, and it opened before he had a chance to ring the bell.

'I saw you through the window,' Sue told them. 'Do come in.'

They stepped inside, and found themselves in a square hallway dominated by a huge vase of flowers on a table underneath an ornate mirror. He thought it looked like something out of a magazine. He followed Sue through to the sitting room, where a quiet, studious-looking man with greying hair stood up and greeted them, introducing himself as David. Michael felt awkward being in their house but the Carringtons seemed completely at ease and happy to have them, and he quickly relaxed. Sue started chatting away to him and Sadie, telling them how she'd recently met her first grandchild, and then she said, 'How about you two? Do you have any children?'

Michael and Sadie looked at each other.

'Not yet,' Sadie said. 'One day, I hope.'

'The first eighteen years are the worst,' David Carrington said, and Michael and Sadie laughed politely. But Sue seemed to realise she'd hit a nerve, and she tactfully moved on.

'We'd better tell you what we think may have happened,' she said. She looked across at her husband and then back at Michael. 'Are you sure that Rae's surname was really Carrington?'

'Yes,' Michael said.

Sue frowned a little, but continued. 'Well, that makes all this seem even more far-fetched, because she must have changed her name…'

'We think that your ex-girlfriend might have been a child involved in a charity we support,' David Carrington explained. 'For many years, almost twenty in fact, we've been assisting a youth charity in Frinchford-on-Sea. Financial help, that is. We don't get involved in the running of it, but we visit every now and again, and many of the children and teenagers there would recognise us.'

'You think that *Rae*—'

'Sometimes the children there haven't had the best lives,' Sue continued. 'It certainly wouldn't be out of the question for one of them to tell a few lies about what is going on for them. You know, pretend things are okay when they aren't, put a brave face on. The idea that one of them would actually start telling people that David and I are her parents might sound a bit bizarre, but it wouldn't be out of the question.'

'Hold on,' Michael said. 'So you're saying Rae met the two of you because you support a charity that she was involved with, and that she was so taken with the two of you that she *changed her name*—'

'I know it sounds unlikely,' Sue said, 'but over the years there have been some children there who found themselves in very sad circumstances, and making things up could be a way of coping.'

'Rae said she had a wonderful childhood!' Michael said. 'She was always talking about holidays to exotic places, big parties with family and friends…' He trailed off as he realised what he was saying. Even at the time these stories had sounded a bit hollow. But was *everything* about her a lie? Could she really have changed her name? It seemed so extraordinary.

'We're not saying that's definitely what happened,' David said, 'but Rae does seem to have given you our names and the names of our sons as her family. It's hard to think of any other explanation.'

'I…' Michael was so bewildered he found himself blurting it out before he could stop himself. 'Are you sure you haven't just disowned her?'

David and Sue looked stunned, and Michael was about to apologise, but Sue laughed. 'I'm afraid our life isn't nearly so dramatic as you're imagining. In fact, I think you turning up is the most intriguing thing that's ever happened to us.'

'Sorry,' he said, 'I'm sorry. It's just that I don't know what to make of it—'

'Michael, I can't tell you why she did this. Like I said, we

don't know Rae. But this was the only thing we could think of.'
   Michael rubbed his forehead and looked helplessly at Sadie.
   'I'm never going to find her,' he said, 'it's hopeless.'

Eleven

As Michael and Sadie left, the Carringtons both said that they wished they could have been more helpful, and Sue asked Michael to let her know if he found Rae, because otherwise she'd always wonder. Michael assured her that he would, but with a heavy heart because he thought there would never be any news to tell.

Just as they were leaving, Sue had an idea. 'Wait,' she said. 'There's a lady who works for the charity. Her name is Pattie – she's been there years and years, I'm sure as far back as when Rae would have been there. I could call her and explain who you are. I'm sure she'd be happy to talk to you. It's really very unlikely she'd be able to tell you anything, and even if by some incredible chance she knew how to contact Rae, she wouldn't be able to share that information with you. But if you think speaking to her might be of some use...'

'Yeah,' Michael said, though he didn't feel very optimistic. 'Thank you. I would like to speak to her, if she's happy to see me.'

'Okay,' Sue said. 'I'll call her tomorrow morning, and let you know what she says.'

Back in their hotel room that night, Michael and Sadie were reeling from what they'd heard. Michael kept thinking the whole thing sounded insane, almost like some sort of joke, but then he'd remember how cagey Rae had been about her family, how idealistic the picture she'd painted of her childhood was. They went to bed early but neither of them could sleep for a long time.

The next morning Michael got a call from Sue, saying that he and Sadie could meet Pattie at the Frinchford-on-Sea youth centre that afternoon. They spent the morning walking on the beach. Michael thought Sadie seemed a bit distracted, but it was a strange time for both of them, and he didn't think too much of it.

...

The youth centre was based in what appeared to be an old church hall or community centre, built from red brick with tall panelled windows. It looked completely closed up, but when they tried the front door, it opened and they stepped inside.

'Be there in a sec,' came a voice from somewhere inside, and moments later a woman around the same age as Sue appeared in the entrance foyer. She was dressed in jeans and a grey hoodie, and her hair – dyed a dark plum purple – was held in place by a silver crocodile clip that had let several strands escape around her face. 'You must be Michael and Sadie,' she said. She started back inside before they had a chance to answer, saying, 'Come in, come in.'

They followed her through to a small office at the other end of the building, where Pattie sat down at a cluttered desk and gestured for them to sit down on a couple of chairs along the wall. 'Very strange thing,' she said, 'this girl you're trying to find. Sue and David think she must have met them when she used to come here?'

'That's right.'

Pattie stood up again, even though she'd only just sat down. 'Tea, coffee?' she said.

Michael said he was okay but Sadie asked for a tea, so they sat in silence as Pattie went off to make it.

'What do you think?' Michael whispered to Sadie. 'Surely this is going to be a complete waste of time.'

'I don't know,' she said, 'but she agreed to see us, so perhaps she does know something.'

Pattie came back a few minutes later and handed Sadie a white-and-pink spotty mug before sitting back down at the desk with her own, which had "paws off my mug" written on it in big red lettering.

'I don't know how much I can tell you,' she said, which made Michael's heart sink, but then she added, 'I must have met her, though. It sounds like she would have been here about fifteen, twenty years ago, which is, believe it or not, after I started here.'

'Sue said she thought Rae may have made up a lie about who her family is because she didn't like the truth.'

'Yes...' Pattie said. 'Well, it does sound unlikely, but then again I never stop being amazed by some of the things I hear. You'd think after this amount of time I'd be unshockable, but you never know what's around the corner.'

'It seems that she legally changed her name to Rae Carrington,' Michael said, 'so I guess she wouldn't have been called that back then. But I don't know what her real – her *original* name was. I'm really worried about her. Nobody seems to know where she is.'

'Changed her name,' Pattie said, after considering what he said. 'Well, she must have changed her second *and* first name, because in all the years I've been here there has never been a girl called Rae. I'm good with names and faces so I'm sure I would remember.' She was thoughtful for a moment longer. 'Always seems such a strange thing to me, changing your name. Surname is one thing, but suddenly having a different *first* name—' She stopped as she suddenly remembered something. 'There was a girl here once whose name was Kitten. That's one name I'll *never* forget. Kind of cute, really, in its way, but it certainly did her no good. Yes, Kitten. She was a tiny little thing, big dark eyes and straight black hair. She looked younger than her age. She got bullied, partly because of her name, but it wasn't just that. The other kids found her odd. I remember that, they said she always *made things up.*' Pattie stopped talking abruptly and looked up at Michael.

'When was that?' Michael asked quickly. 'When was that girl, Kitten, here?'

Pattie considered it. 'I couldn't tell you exactly,' she said, 'but it probably was between fifteen and twenty years ago.'

'Do you have any photos or anything? Do you still keep—'

'From that long ago? You know, we probably do. Somewhere.'

Michael looked around the large, untidy office. 'Please,' he said, 'if you could look it would mean a lot to me.'

Pattie seemed unsure, but eventually she nodded and went across to a cupboard by the door. Inside Michael could see rows of organised and dated files, as well as papers stuffed in higgledy-piggledy, but Pattie seemed to know where to look, and after a surprisingly short time rummaging she pulled out a newspaper clipping.

'I thought I remembered this,' she said. 'The kids were all involved with the reopening of a park in the town centre. They helped with the improvements and we had a barbecue to celebrate.' Pattie studied the photo. 'That's Kitten,' she said, showing Michael a blurry photo. 'And there's Sue and David too.'

Michael looked at the picture – a group of children and a handful of adults standing smiling in the middle of the revamped park. He recognised David and Sue, and Pattie as well, but his attention was consumed by the face Pattie was pointing to – a girl who looked to be somewhere between the ages of eleven and thirteen, with a long fringe and curtains of dark hair over her shoulders. He couldn't be absolutely certain – it was so long ago and Rae had looked very different by the time he met her – but he couldn't deny the resemblance, and as he stared into the little face, his skin broke out in goosebumps.

Twelve

Michael just about managed to read Kitten's full name, "Kitten Tiler", in the caption underneath the photo before Pattie took the picture away again. She seemed almost uncomfortable with what she'd revealed to them.

'That's really all I can tell you,' she said. 'I remember very little about her, or her family. In fact, I think she only came here a handful of times.' She looked at Michael with an unusual expression: sympathy mixed with unease. 'I hope I've been some use,' she said. 'But even if Kitten is your Rae, I'm still not sure how much that's going to help you to find her.'

'It does,' Michael said. 'Thank you. Thank you so much.'

It took no more than a couple of hours searching online before they turned up some more information about the Tiler family in Frinchford-on-Sea, though sadly it wasn't very good news. Rae's – *Kitten's* mother had died several years earlier, and they could find nothing about her dad. However, they did discover a sister, Star Tiler, who still lived locally, and whose address was listed when they did a directory search online.

Michael drove there straight away, but before he got out of the car, Sadie touched his leg. 'I need to tell you something.'

Michael took his hand away from the door handle and studied her face. She looked pale, and was clutching her hands tightly in her lap. 'Sadie?' he said. 'What is it? You don't look well—'

'I'm fine,' she said. 'I'm more than fine. I was going to wait and tell you back home, but...' She opened her handbag and took out a pregnancy test. Tentatively Michael held his hand out for it. He wasn't sure what was happening. She'd already done this month's test; did she just want to show him another negative result? He wasn't sure he could bear going through that again right now.

Sadie placed it gently in his palm and he looked at it.

It was positive.

'What?' he said. 'I don't understand.'

A smile started to creep across Sadie's face. He could see tears in her eyes. She gave him another test from her bag. 'I did two,' she said, 'this morning. I don't think there can be any doubt.'

'But...' Michael said, looking from the tests to her face to the tests again. 'But you did a test a few days ago. It was negative.'

'I did it early,' she said. 'It was one of those ones you can do a few days before your period is due, but they're not so accurate when you do that. I... you know I normally end up doing a few tests each month – I was determined not to do that this time, but when my period didn't start yesterday, I began to wonder—'

Michael threw his arms around her. He could feel tears in his eyes and he kissed her hair. 'I can't believe it,' he said. 'I can't believe it, Sadie.'

It took a few minutes for them to calm down. Michael wondered what he was even doing now – his hunt for Rae was no longer central in his mind, and felt almost irrelevant.

'Come on,' Sadie said. 'I know it's difficult to think of anything else, but we still need to find Rae.'

'I can't believe you've known all day!'

Sadie smiled. 'I hope you don't mind me not telling you straight away. I liked having a few hours to think about it on my own, to gather my thoughts.'

'I think I need a few hours to gather mine.'

Sadie squeezed his hand. 'I feel more able to face all of this now,' she said. 'So let's find out what it is we need to face.'

Thirteen

Michael got out of the car, feeling fired up again and keen to get some answers, but it wasn't to be. When he knocked on the door to Star's house nobody answered, so he had to turn around and get back in the car, and they ended up waiting another hour or so without anyone turning up.

'This is hopeless,' Michael said. 'Let's go and get something to eat and we'll try again this evening before we drive back.'

Just at that moment he saw a family walking down the pavement; a man, a woman, two small children running in front of them and a third being pushed in a pushchair. As soon as he saw them his pulse raced. He wasn't sure why but he felt convinced that the woman was Rae's sister, and as they approached the terraced house and filed inside, he felt a mixture of nerves and inevitability, like fate had intervened and brought them all together.

He gave the family a few minutes to get inside and then he walked up to the house again and knocked on the door. He could hear vague sounds of Star and the children, but it was the man who answered, and he looked at Michael suspiciously.

'I'm looking for Star Tiler,' Michael said. 'Does she live here?'

'Who wants to know?'

Michael tried to look past him into the house, but it seemed the children and their mother had gone right inside, and he could hear the sound of the television. He felt uncomfortable talking to Star's boyfriend, or husband or whoever he was. He hardly knew where to begin explaining himself.

'It's about her sister, uh, Kitten. I was her boyfriend several years ago and...'

The man turned around and called into the house. 'Star!'

'What?' she shouted back.

'Just come out here.'

Several seconds went by, then finally Star stepped into the hall. She was dressed in jeans and a tight white jumper, her hair pulled back so tightly into a ponytail that it looked almost painful and made her forehead seem too big for her face. She ignored Michael completely and waited for the man to explain what was going on.

'Some guy wants to talk to you about Kitten,' he told her.

She was visibly startled, and she took a step towards Michael, watching him suspiciously. The man stayed hovering there for a moment, and then he disappeared into the house.

'I'm looking for your sister Kitten,' Michael said, and he started explaining who he was, but Star cut him off.

'I'm not talking,' she said, 'I don't know you. You could be some sort of stalker.'

She began to shut the door. 'No!' Michael said, 'please. I'm not a stalker. She was pregnant when we broke up. I just want to know—'

Star narrowed her eyes. She stopped trying to close the door but she stood firmly in the way of the entrance, one hand against the door-frame and the other on the door handle. 'When was that?' she asked him.

'Ten years ago.'

'You had a baby with her ten years ago but didn't bother doing anything before now?'

'I only recently found out she was pregnant.'

Star looked at him as though she didn't believe him, but she didn't speak.

'I've heard some worrying things about her,' Michael continued. 'She's changed her name – when I knew her she was called Rae. After we split up it seems like she got involved with some other man, and then she disappeared. I was hoping you and her are in touch, because none of her university friends—'

'Her *university friends,*' Star said. 'Don't even get me started. Silly little cow always thought she was too good for us. God knows how she ever managed to get the grades because she never seemed anything special to me. I always reckoned she was shagging a teacher.'

Michael must have looked horrified, because she laughed at him. He took a moment to collect himself, realising she had said it deliberately to make him uncomfortable, and then said, 'Please, do you know where she is?'

Star looked him up and down. 'Me and Kitten were never close. We weren't even brought up together, and she's never had any time for me. The last time I saw her was at her wedding. She was calling herself *Tamsin.* It was a fucking joke.'

It was growing dark, and Michael was beginning to give up, but at these revelations he felt a surge of hope.

'When was the wedding?' he asked quickly. It must have been since their break-up, in which case that meant she was okay – she was with someone. She was *alive.* And if she was going by the name Tamsin, perhaps he could use it to track her down.

Star thought about his question. 'Why are you so interested?'

'Because you're the only person I've spoken to who has seen her more recently.'

She didn't answer and Michael wondered if he'd got all he could. 'Look, I'm sorry I bothered you,' he said. 'Thanks for—'

'You are a stalker, aren't you?' she said. 'I had a boyfriend like you once. I broke up with him and he went round everyone trying to find where I was.'

'I'm not like that.'

'Well, if Kitten wanted you, believe me she'd have let you know. Kitten always gets what she wants. If you ask me, you're better off well out of it. Kitten's selfish. She's selfish, she's stuck-up, and she's a nasty piece of work. If she had your baby, it's the first I've ever heard of it. There were no children at her wedding.'

Michael's mind was racing. Did that mean she'd never had the baby? Or was the child just not at the wedding – perhaps she'd got somebody to babysit for the day? He wanted to ask more but he heard the man yell, 'Star!'

'I've got things to do,' she said. 'Are we done here?'

'I...' he tried to form a question, but realised his time was up. Star was clearly itching to slam the door in his face and he thought the man might come back out any second to get rid of him. 'Could you pass a message to her?' he said.

Star didn't answer.

'I can give you my phone number, and my email address. Please tell her I'm looking for her. My name is Michael Benton. She doesn't have to see me face to face, not if she doesn't want to, but if she could just get in touch—'

Star began to push the door shut. 'Wait, I'll write it down!' he said.

The door closed firmly in his face, so Michael ran back to the car and wrote his details on the back of a scrap of paper. Then he slipped the paper through Star's letterbox and made his way more slowly back towards the car. It was dusk now, and the streetlights were coming to life, casting their orange glow onto the pavement. He had no idea what to conclude from his meeting with Star – if anything it had made him more confused. But at least he'd heard some evidence that Rae was alive and well, he had some new information to work with, and hopefully if Star could bring herself to contact Rae – Tamsin – and pass on his details, then he might hear something from her soon.

PART TWO

Fourteen

Michael woke with a start. He lay still, breathing rapidly, trying to calm down before he disturbed Sadie, but he was too late. She seemed to have turned into a light sleeper since becoming pregnant, and the second she awoke she moaned softly and said, 'I'm so uncomfortable.' She threw the covers off. 'And I'm so hot.'

Michael reached out and touched her arm. 'Sorry,' he said, 'I think it was me who woke you up.' He tried to get his head together. It all became mixed up in his mind when he was dreaming – the things he'd discovered about Rae, his thoughts about the baby she may or may not have had, her name changes, her marriage. Months had passed and Michael had heard nothing from her. He'd tried to look her up using the name "Tamsin", but without knowing when or where she got married, let alone who she was married to, it was like trying to find a needle in a haystack. His mind was often preoccupied with the thought of the little girl Kitten; her pale face with its frame of unruly hair invaded his thoughts and dreams. Why had she changed her name – not just once, but twice? It seemed that her life was a recurring pattern of trying to be someone she wasn't. Was she ashamed of her past? Star seemed to think Kitten wanted to hide her background, but why? It was obvious to him now that her family hadn't been as wealthy as she'd tried to make everyone believe – in fact it seemed they were probably the opposite – but he struggled to imagine that it was all to do with that.

He settled back against the sheets, but he couldn't sleep and now neither could Sadie.

'You keep thinking about her, don't you?' she said.

'Yes. I just want to know—'

'But perhaps you never will. Rae doesn't want to be found. Star passed on your details and she hasn't called you—'

'Maybe Star never passed them on.'

'What?'

'She wasn't exactly warm and welcoming to me.'

Sadie sighed, but when she spoke again her voice was soft, sympathetic. 'What else can we do? We could hire a private investigator, I suppose, if you're really—'

'No, I don't want to do that.'

'Then I don't know what else to suggest.'

Michael rolled over and put his hand on Sadie's little bump.

'I'm trying to put it out of my mind for now,' he said. '*You* are my priority. The two of you, it's just...'

'It's just that you may already have a child.'

Michael let go of Sadie and lay back against the bed again. He didn't know how to answer her. 'Is the baby awake?' he asked. 'It starts kicking around this time, doesn't it?'

'It won't be an "it" by the end of next week,' she said. 'Hopefully not, anyway. Do you think the hospital will be able to tell us the sex? I hope they can tell us.'

She pulled and kicked at the duvet a bit more, trying to get comfortable. '*It* is asleep at the moment,' she said, 'but *I'm* not.' With a sigh she threw her legs out of bed.

'Where are you going? Do you need anything?'

'I'm going for a wee.'

'I'll get you a glass of water.'

'I'm not thirsty—'

'I'll get it anyway.'

Michael got out of bed and wandered downstairs to get Sadie the water she didn't want. He felt sorry for her because she'd never coped well with lack of sleep. Sometimes when she got home from work she was so exhausted that she'd sleep on the sofa while he cooked dinner.

In the kitchen he didn't get the water straight away. Instead he checked his phone for probably the hundredth time that day in the hope that Rae had emailed or phoned him, but there was nothing. He put the phone down again and rubbed his eyes. The whole thing was so frustrating. He knew there was no point in pretending to Sadie that he didn't think about the son or daughter he may already have, or even that he didn't think about Rae – or Tamsin as she was now called – but he just didn't know what to do. Also, he had to admit to himself, there was a limit to what he *wanted* to do. His life was full already, and right now Rae and her problems felt like the last thing on earth that he needed.

Fifteen

'A girl!' Sadie said. It was eight days later, and they were having their twenty-week scan. 'I said I thought it was a girl, didn't I? I had that dream about buying dresses—'

She stopped talking as she realised Michael was staring fixedly at the image on the screen, watching as the baby moved its arms and legs like it was dancing. She reached out for his hand. 'Michael, are you pleased?'

'Yes,' he said, 'of course I am.'

Sadie gave him a meaningful look, but didn't say much else while measurements were taken and checks carried out. At the end, when she sat up and wiped the excess gel from her stomach, she said quietly, 'You need to find out what happened.'

Her words took him aback. 'Sadie, this is *our* day.'

'I know, but...' She trailed off with a glance at the sonographer, and manoeuvred herself carefully from the bed. 'We can't pretend it never happened,' she said as they left the room. 'I can't stop thinking about it, and I know you can't either. You *have* to find her, Michael. Please. *Please*, put this to rest.'

'I thought you said we may never find her.'

'I know. But we can't leave it like this. We have to try harder. We have to try *everything*.'

He frowned, surprised at her sudden determination but her mind seemed set. With few other options, Michael decided he would go to Frinchford-on-Sea to visit Star again. He asked Sadie if she wanted to come but she said she'd rather stay home, so Michael drove up late after work, stayed overnight and then made his way to Star's house early the next morning, hoping to catch her before the day had properly got going.

When she answered the door, she was wearing pyjamas and had a mug of tea in her hand. She took one look at him and said, 'I don't believe this. What the hell are you doing here?'

'I just want to find Rae—'

'Jamie!' she yelled into the house, 'Jamie—'

'I'm not trying to cause any trouble,' Michael said, but it was too late. The man who had answered the door to him before came out into the hall and Michael could see that if he didn't leave of his own accord he was probably going to be made to. He couldn't understand why Star felt so much animosity towards him, but he didn't want to stick around and question it. 'I'm going,' he said, 'I'm going.' He'd written his details down again, and he managed to thrust them into her hand. 'Please,' he said, 'if you are able to contact Rae... I mean Tamsin, please tell her I'm trying to find her. Please, Star—'

The door slammed in his face.

...

Another couple of months passed. Michael and Sadie got to work making the small third bedroom in their house into a cosy nursery, and they were both on tenterhooks again waiting for Rae's call. But there was nothing but silence, and by the time Sadie was thirty weeks pregnant all their thoughts were on their imminent new arrival.

It was after one of their antenatal classes that Michael noticed a missed call on his phone. He ignored it to begin with, but once they got home and Sadie went upstairs to have a bath he grew curious and called the number back. It went straight to a standard answer-phone message, with no mention of the name of the person who had tried to call.

The next day Sadie came to help him in the shop for a few hours. A big clearance sale had shifted a lot of the old stock, and Michael was pleased with the new modern ranges he'd brought in. Sadie spent most of the time sitting in the office on the comfy armchair, working through a punnet of strawberries she'd bought from a market stall down the street.

When it was quiet Michael came and sat at the desk, watching Sadie laugh as she balanced the punnet on her bump where she said the baby was kicking at it. He was about to go over and feel the kicks for himself when his phone rang, and he quickly answered it, thinking the number looked a little like the one he'd missed the call from.

'Michael,' a concise, confident female voice said, 'is that you?'

'Yes,' he said, but he struggled to even get the word out. He felt like his heart had stopped as he recognised her voice. 'Is it you... Rae?'

In the corner Sadie was frozen with one hand on her bump, the other holding a strawberry in mid-air. She mouthed, "Is it her?" and Michael nodded.

On the phone, Rae laughed. 'Oh, that takes me back,' she said. 'It's been years since I've had anyone call me Rae. Didn't Star tell you the name I go by now?'

'But it is... it is you?' he asked, even though he knew it was already.

'Yes,' she said, 'it is me, Michael. It's Rae. But I'd rather you called me Tamsin. Tamsin Quinnell.'

Sixteen

When Michael got off the phone, he was still reeling with shock. She'd told him almost nothing, just that she was okay – she was married and had a daughter who was a few months old. Michael tried to ask about what had happened to his own baby but she avoided the question. She said she'd talk to him in person and that she'd email him her address, then before he could ask anything further she hung up.

The email came through not long after. Michael looked up the address and was pleased to discover it was only around a ninety-minute drive away. Tamsin gave precise instructions that he should come the very next day, at two p.m.

Sadie watched in silence while he looked up the address, and then she said, 'What if you go there and the... *child* is there?'

Michael's pulse raced. He didn't know what he'd do, that was the truth.

'I'm beginning to think it's unlikely,' he said. 'Star said she knew nothing about a child, and Rae... Tamsin... wouldn't say anything to me on the phone.'

'But...' Sadie said, her eyes boring into him, 'but it's possible.'

'Yes,' he said, 'I suppose it's possible.'

...

The drive to Tamsin's house was a pleasant one – or would have been if Michael had been able to pay attention to it – the journey taking him down country roads of increasing narrowness, bordered by fields lush and green in the summer haze. He ended up getting to her address a few minutes early, and looked at the house she lived in with awe. He double-checked the email, sure he must have arrived at the wrong place, but he hadn't. The email said "Waterhill, East Street, Maybrooke". He was in the village Maybrooke, and he'd seen the street sign that read East Street, and now he was stopped at a smart grey sign bearing the name Waterhill. He looked again beyond the sign, where, sat at the top of a sweeping gravel driveway, was an imposing Georgian house that must have cost a small fortune. It was painted white and adorned with sprays of vivid green ivy, and set in generous grounds – there was a small terrace off to one side with a wrought-iron table and chairs, while on the other was a neat round pond, with grass sweeping away behind. Michael parked his car but didn't get out straight away. He still felt sure he'd got it wrong. Or perhaps Tamsin was playing some sort of trick on him, sending him off on a wild goose chase for her own amusement.

It seemed that the noise of his car had alerted whoever lived in the house, because the front door opened. For one daft moment he considered driving away again, but he began to prepare himself to explain his mistake to the owner of the house before getting on his way. Then he saw her, and he froze. The woman coming towards him really *was* Rae. He couldn't help but stare at her – after his difficult search over the past months, the idea that he would ever see her in the flesh had begun to seem far-fetched, and he felt as though she might dissolve before his eyes.

He quickly got out of the car, very aware of his dishevelled appearance compared to hers. She looked every bit a woman who would live in such a lovely place, dressed in high-waisted taupe trousers that moved around her legs like a kind of fluid, her long hair freshly brushed and falling in a spray of black across her crisp white shirt, a subtle sparkle at her throat from a small diamond necklace that nestled there. When she smiled at him her teeth were very white, and her lips were a warm red. That was one thing that really reminded him of the Rae he'd known – her lips had been a new colour every day, anything from the softest baby pink to a purple so dark it was almost black. She'd always dressed dramatically, rarely in colours but usually in black, white or grey. This woman, *Tamsin,* she was like Rae, but a softer version, a very *sophisticated* version. When she spoke, he thought that even her voice had adjusted itself a little.

'Michael,' she said, giving him a quick look up and down, 'come inside. I can't leave the baby.'

She turned without a second glance at him and started back towards the house. He followed her obediently, ending up in a country style kitchen, with a sage-coloured dresser on the wall full of china and glasses. Michael immediately spotted the baby in a pink bouncer, reaching out towards some toys that hung above her. He felt a nervous flip-flop in his stomach at the thought that his own child could be somewhere in the house, might suddenly walk into the room.

'Her name's Madeline,' Tamsin said, breaking the silence. She reached down and lifted the baby from the bouncer. 'I've just made her a bottle. Let's go and sit in the living room.'

'She's beautiful,' Michael said as he followed Tamsin back

through the hall. It was true – the baby had thick, dark hair and a cute round face. 'How old is she?'

'Four months.'

'Congratulations,' Michael said. 'My wife is pregnant.'

Tamsin looked briefly over her shoulder at him.

'You mean Sadie?'

Michael nodded, feeling a mixture of surprise and relief. He'd been wondering how to break it to her, but it seemed she already knew.

'You're not the only one who can go digging, Michael,' she said. 'It seems like you put a lot of effort into finding out about *me,* so I decided I'd look you up too.'

'Rae, I'm sorry.'

'My name is Tamsin.'

Michael fell silent. He found it almost impossible to stop thinking of her as Rae, but he tried to force the old name out of his head and the new one in. Tamsin stopped suddenly. 'I've been wondering how on earth the two of you ended up as a couple. I mean, from what I've heard you weren't exactly courteous towards her at that party. But perhaps she's one of those women who like that sort of thing.'

'She came to see me in hospital,' Michael said, 'after she heard I was attacked. I think...' he stopped, not sure where he was going, but then he carried on. 'She'd liked me for a while, apparently. That's what she said. I...'

Tamsin suddenly laughed, a high, pealing sound that took him aback. 'Oh, for God's sake, Michael,' she said, 'why are you telling me this?'

'I don't know.'

She carried on walking and he found himself in the living room, a bright, airy, stylish space with two pale green sofas facing each other across a glass coffee table. There were a few baby toys on the floor, and Tamsin kicked a rattle out of the way before settling herself on the sofa with Madeline. Michael couldn't help but be fascinated by the baby, which made him imagine what it would be like when he and Sadie had their little girl, and he stood watching for a second too long so that Tamsin looked at him curiously and said, 'You can sit down.'

Michael plonked himself down quickly, and Tamsin picked up Madeline's bottle of milk from the coffee table and gave it a shake.

'I wasn't sure whether to get in touch with you,' she said. 'When Star first told me you'd visited her I did nothing. Then she said you'd been back. I was going to ignore you again, but I thought you might go back a third time. Star's partner Jamie has quite a temper on him. I thought that having been beaten half to death once, you probably weren't eager for it to happen again.'

'Uh...' Michael said, not sure how to react, 'well, thank you. For getting in touch.'

Tamsin shrugged his thanks away. 'What do you think of the house?' she asked.

'It's beautiful.'

'Paul, my husband, bought it for me as a wedding present. Well, for the both of us.'

Madeline didn't seem too keen to drink her milk, and Michael thought he saw a flicker of anger or pain cross Tamsin's face, but it was gone again so quickly he wasn't sure it had really been there.

'What does Paul do?' Michael asked. He longed to just ask about his baby, but he didn't feel able to, somehow.

'He's an investor.'

'What...'

'Don't ask me any more than that,' Tamsin said, as Madeline finally settled down to drink quietly from the bottle. 'He goes and sees people, he invests in things, he seems to make a lot of money out of it.'

'That... uh... that's good.'

Tamsin smiled. 'You're nervous, aren't you?'

'I just want to know about my – our – baby.'

'Not about me then?'

'And you,' he said quickly, 'of course I want to hear about you. I've been worried, especially after I spoke to Alice—'

'Oh yeah, *Alice,*' Tamsin said. 'I bet she had a good story to tell. Did she say how I came back that night in some random guy's car? I'm sure she did, because she never let me hear the end of it, asking who he was, if he'd "done something to me".'

'Did he?'

'No!' Tamsin said. 'He was Paul. My husband. Turns out the same night that you were shagging your future wife, I was doing the same with my future husband.'

Seventeen

For a while the only sound was Madeline drinking her milk, and an occasional soft thud as the baby kicked her feet against the sofa arm.

'You did me a favour, really,' Tamsin said. 'I could hardly have had the life with you that I have with Paul. You're running that funny little furniture shop, aren't you?'

'I took over once my parents retired.'

'Doesn't it drive you mad?' she said. 'Stuck inside with all that stuffy old furniture.'

'It's as good as any job.'

'I daresay,' Tamsin said.

There was silence for a while.

'Paul divorced his wife to be with me,' Tamsin announced. 'He'd been with her nearly fifteen years.'

Michael took a moment to process this piece of information, and she immediately picked up on it.

'You're wondering how old he is,' she said, 'to have already been married that long when he met me.'

'I wasn't, actually—'

'Everyone is always so perversely obsessed with age gaps, don't you think?' she said. 'He's fifty-seven, if you have to know. For his fifty-fifth birthday we went to Easter Island. I didn't even know there was such a place, did you?'

Michael struggled to keep up. And he had to admit that now she'd drawn attention to it, the age gap did surprise him. Tamsin was only thirty-one.

'I didn't marry him for his money,' she said casually.

'No,' Michael said, 'no, of course not...' He trailed off. He really just wanted to know about his baby before they talked about anything else, but Tamsin clearly had other ideas.

'Don't look so sheepish,' she told him. 'Everyone assumes it's about money. Even more so when they know I was never really Rae Carrington. That I was Kitten Crystal Tiler. I didn't grow up in a beautiful house with wonderful, generous parents and exotic holidays, I grew up in a filthy little apartment with a mum who hated me so much she gave me a name that made me sound like a cross between a porn star and something you put on your bathroom wall.'

'It's not *that* bad, the name—'

Tamsin laughed. 'You have no idea.'

'So tell me. Tell me why you lied to me about your family.'

Madeline had finished her milk and Tamsin sat her up, rubbing and patting her back. 'It has its advantages, being with an older man,' she said. 'Paul is a very accomplished lover.' She looked at him mischievously. 'Accomplished,' she said, 'but with the sex drive of a man in his twenties.'

Michael tried to let it wash over him. Time had made him forget the way she talked, but now he could be right back there again listening to her eleven years ago. He was just relieved that it was Paul and not him whose sexual exploits – real or fictitious – she related to all and sundry.

She stood up, holding Madeline close to her chest. 'I'll give you a tour of the house if you like. There's lots to show you—'

'Stop,' Michael said. 'Just stop. Tell me what happened to our baby.'

Tamsin kissed Madeline on the top of her head. 'She's gone.'

Michael felt a surge of emotion, both at the fact he now knew it was a girl, and at the word "gone". He stared at her. 'What do you...'

'Adopted,' Tamsin said, 'I had her adopted, Michael. As soon as she was born.'

…

'So,' Michael said finally, his voice seeming to come from a long way away, 'you did have her?'

'Yes,' she said. 'Do you want a drink?'

'What?' Michael said.

'Tea, coffee.'

'I...' he was so surprised by the change in the conversation that he couldn't even think. 'Can't we talk about—'

'I only drink black coffee or green tea,' Tamsin said, 'but we do have normal tea. White with one sugar, that's how you used to have it.'

'Yeah,' he said, 'yeah, that's still—'

Tamsin plonked Madeline down in the middle of a round pink play mat. 'Keep an eye on her for a minute,' she told Michael, and then she left.

Bewildered, he sat down next to the baby, who gave him an expression of cool disinterest. He reached out his finger for the palm of her hand, and she curled her fingers around it. He smiled at her. 'Hello,' he said. To his surprise Madeline suddenly smiled back, her face transformed by the cheeky grin that showed one small bottom tooth. He found himself feeling charmed by her. He picked up a rattle and shook it, and she held out her hands towards it.

When Tamsin came back, she placed a tray down on the coffee table with two cups of tea – they really were cups too, smart china cups and saucers decorated with a delicate pattern of pink and gold blossom. She sat next to him on the floor.

'What was she like, Tamsin?' Michael asked gently. 'Our daughter.'

Tamsin shrugged. 'She was a baby.'

'Well, did she have hair like Madeline's? What were her eyes like?'

Tamsin reached across to the tray, and picked up a photo. 'Here,' she said, handing it to him, 'I dug this out for you this morning.'

He looked at the picture. A tiny little newborn baby wrapped in a white blanket. She was all pink and wrinkly, and had a tuft of dark brown hair.

He stared at it for a long time, and he could feel tears beginning to fill his eyes. Tamsin was watching him. 'You can keep that,' she said. 'I have another one upstairs.' She carried on looking at him. 'And don't *cry*!' she said sharply, 'or I'll take it away again.'

Eighteen

Michael hoped she'd say more while they sat and drank their tea, but she refused to be drawn on the subject. He accepted her offer of a house tour, and she walked around with Madeline in her arms, showing him room after room. 'I won't show you all the bedrooms,' she said when they got upstairs, 'but this is mine and Paul's.' She pushed the door open and Michael found himself in a glamorous room with grey walls, white furniture, a mirrored dressing table and a black chandelier hanging from the ceiling. Madeline stared intently at the dressing table and Tamsin said, 'Madeline likes mirrors. She thinks there's another baby in there looking at her.'

As they walked down the hall, Michael looked out of the window over the garden, where he saw a studio at the bottom of the lawn. 'Paul had that built for me,' Tamsin said, 'for my art.'

Michael nodded. He could remember her doing paintings and drawings at university, where she'd studied art history. 'That's all of it,' Tamsin said as they went back downstairs. 'Unless I show you Paul's study. Which I will, because it's quite something.'

She opened a door off from the hallway. Michael looked inside and was confronted with walls full of books – many of them ancient looking – and by the window a heavy wooden desk.

'A lot of these books were his dad's,' Tamsin said. 'And his dad may even have had them passed down from his dad. It's not like he ever reads them... Paul, that is. Not the really old ones. They're just decorative.' Michael looked at Tamsin. She seemed engrossed in what she was saying.

'Can our daughter come and find us?' he asked. 'When she's older?'

She whipped her head round and frowned. 'You know what you do, Michael?'

'What?'

'You *pick,*' she said, 'you find a wound, and you pick, pick, pick at it.'

'You mean you don't want to talk about it?'

'Our daughter is gone. She'll be nearly ten now.' Tamsin laughed. 'Ten,' she said. 'I was only a couple of years older than that when I started fucking.'

She looked at his face and laughed. 'Oh, for God's sake, Michael, don't look at me like that.'

On that note, she seemed to decide she'd had enough of him.

'Paul's coming home soon,' she said. 'I guess we've said everything there is to say.'

Michael stared at her in astonishment. He felt they'd barely scratched the surface. She started ushering him towards the door but he refused to move. 'No,' he said, 'I'm not leaving until we talk properly.'

'And I told you that my husband is due home.'

'Tamsin, stop,' Michael said firmly. 'Talk to me.'

'What about?'

Michael pulled the photo of their daughter from his pocket and thrust it at her. 'This,' he said. 'Our baby! Talk to me about our baby!'

'What do you want me to say?' she asked sweetly, and his anger boiled over.

'Why didn't you tell me?' he said, 'why didn't you tell me you were pregnant? Why didn't you let me support you?'

'You made your decision. You had sex with Sadie. You showed me exactly how you felt about me.'

'I had a right to know—'

'No!' she shouted. In her arms Madeline started to cry. 'You've upset my baby,' she said. 'I think you should go.'

'Not until you let me tell you I'm sorry!'

Tamsin bounced Madeline in her arms and looked closely at Michael. 'Go on then.'

Michael's eyes flicked from her to Madeline, then down at the photo in his hand. 'I'm sorry about what happened with Sadie. I'm sorry things worked out the way they did, and I wish I could have been there for you.'

Tamsin reached down and tickled Madeline's feet, and the baby girl kicked out happily at her fingers, her earlier upset seemingly forgotten.

'Please,' Michael said, 'can you really tell me nothing else about my daughter? Isn't there anything you want to say to me?'

Tamsin's eyes glittered darkly. 'I didn't want you,' she said, 'I didn't want you to know about our baby, and I didn't *want* you to find me.'

Michael watched her silently, hoping she'd say something else. 'Okay,' he said finally. 'Okay, Tamsin. I'm sorry I bothered you. I'll go.'

'She had a funny little cry,' Tamsin said suddenly, as he turned for the door. 'Like a kitten. And in my head I named her Scarlett.'

Michael looked back at her, but before he could speak he

heard a car pulling up outside.

'That's Paul,' she said. 'I told you he'd be back any minute.'

Nineteen

When the door opened, Michael found himself face to face with Tamsin's husband. He was smartly dressed, and very well groomed. When he saw Michael he seemed to flinch, but his face showed little emotion. An air of steady self-assurance settled around him instead, and Michael noticed how tranquil Tamsin was in his presence. She seemed to glow now that she was standing beside him. Paul turned to Tamsin, but before he could ask what was going on, she explained it to him. 'This is Michael Benton,' she said. 'He found out that I was pregnant and came to find out what happened to his baby. I told him about the adoption.'

Paul's eyes narrowed briefly, but he didn't say anything.

'Michael is going now,' Tamsin continued.

'Yes,' Michael said, 'thank you for the baby photo, Tamsin, and for agreeing to see me.' He turned to Paul. 'Sorry to just show up like this—'

'I invited him,' Tamsin said.

'Yeah,' Michael said, 'well, I'll leave you to it.'

'I'll walk you to your car,' Paul said.

Michael felt nervous as he stepped outside with Paul, convinced that he was going to get an earful or at least some sort of stiff warning, but to his surprise, as they walked down the gravel drive towards his car, Paul was perfectly friendly and conversational.

'So you only recently found out that Tamsin was pregnant?'

'One of Tamsin's university friends blurted it out at a party recently, and the information got back to me.'

'That must have come as a shock.'

'Yeah, it did. Anyway, I'm glad I've spoken to her now. I'm so pleased she's happy here, and that she's okay. How long have you and her been married?'

'Nine years.'

'Oh,' Michael said. It was longer than he expected, and he quickly did a calculation. 'So she was only twenty-two—'

'I probably asked her sooner than I should have,' Paul said. 'But I loved her – I *love* her – very much. I didn't want to wait.'

'No,' he said, 'yeah, like I said. I'm happy she's happy.' In truth it wasn't anything about her age that had taken him aback – at twenty-two she was surely able to decide what she wanted her future to be – but what struck him was how soon it was after his break-up with her. He'd thought it would have been a few *years* at least before she got married. He shook the idea aside. He felt stung, but it had been over between them. She'd had every right to move on, just as he had.

They reached the car and Michael unlocked it but Paul put his hand on the door to stop him getting inside. Michael's heart sank. He'd obviously been right to feel nervous. 'Paul,' he said, 'I didn't come here to upset her, I really just wanted to—'

'To find out about your child,' he said, 'yes, I understand. Anyone would do the same.'

Michael frowned. 'I'd better get going…'

'Michael, Tamsin is not okay. She's very far from okay. I know what you did – cheating on her – it's not like you're the first person in the world to ever do that to somebody. But Tamsin isn't very resilient. She's never got over it.'

'I told her I'm sorry—'

'I'm sure you did. I don't want to be heavy-handed about this, but I'm going to have to tell you not to come here again. And not to contact Tamsin.'

'I wasn't planning to,' Michael said quickly. 'I would have liked to hear more about the baby, but Tamsin has said all that she wants to, and I've got no reason to bother her any more.'

Paul smiled and touched Michael briefly on the shoulder. 'Good man,' he said, and then he turned and made his way back towards the house.

…

When Michael got home, it was early evening and he could see the light on in the kitchen. Sadie rushed to greet him as he walked through the door, the smell of some sort of tomatoey sauce following her. She was wearing an apron that had a thin spray of red droplets across the front, and she was visibly shaking. He could see the waiting and the uncertainty had taken its toll on her – she looked as if she might actually collapse. 'Michael,' she said, 'tell me. Don't try to break it gently, just tell me, is there a child?'

He wanted to speak, but his chest tightened and although he opened his mouth it was like all the emotion of the afternoon began to overwhelm him and he couldn't get the words out.

'Michael!' Sadie said, and she rested her hand against the wall to steady herself. 'Michael, tell me! What happened to the baby? What happened—'

There were tears in her eyes, and he forced himself to speak. 'Girl,' he said brokenly, 'adopted.'

Sadie took a great gulp of air. Some tears spilt out from her eyes. She took a step towards him, then another, and he held her in his arms.

Twenty

Tamsin sighed contentedly and snuggled closer to Paul. They'd just made love, and she could see a thin film of sweat across his forehead. His eyes were closed, but he pulled her in closer to him, and she rested her head on his chest.

'Quite a day you had today,' he said to her.

'Mm,' she agreed.

They fell silent again. Then Paul asked the question she'd been waiting for ever since he got home.

'Tamsin, why did you tell Michael you had the baby adopted?'

She didn't reply. She felt comfortable and relaxed, and didn't really want to talk about it.

'Tamsin,' he said firmly.

She looked up at him. 'Do you mind me having seen him?' she asked.

'I'd be lying if I said I was happy about it,' he told her, 'but I knew there was a chance he'd find out about the pregnancy, and that if he did he'd come looking for answers. I just hope that you've got rid of him.'

'I think I have,' she said. 'He married Sadie, you know. She's pregnant.'

'Is that right?'

'I told him he did me a favour, because otherwise I wouldn't have ended up with you. And I told him—' she giggled childishly '–I told him that you are a "very accomplished lover". You should have seen his face.'

To begin with she thought Paul was irritated, but he smiled, seemingly despite himself. He almost never got cross with her. It was as though being with her kept him in a sort of warm bubble, where anger and upset were soon dispersed and replaced with a pleasant, quiet companionship. She was certainly in no doubt that he did love her company, and that he loved *her*. Since she'd married him she'd felt more secure than she ever had in her life.

'Should I be flattered?' he asked her, 'or were you saying it to make him feel embarrassed?'

'Both. You're better in bed than *he* was, anyway,' she said.

She thought that might make him smile, but instead he said, 'You haven't answered me.'

'Hm?'

'Why did you tell him the baby was adopted?'

Tamsin began to feel irritated. 'Oh, God, Paul, I don't know,' she snapped.

'Tam—'

'Do we *have* to talk about it?'

'I don't like it when you do things and then say you don't know why. You need to keep your head together. *Think* before you start telling people things like that.' He looked at her closely. 'You do know what actually happened with the baby, don't you, Tam? You remember.'

'Yes,' she said. 'Of course I remember.'

'And I assume you didn't tell him how we met? How long I've known you for?'

'I said I met you the night he cheated with Sadie.'

He didn't reply but she felt him nod as she snuggled back against him, so she assumed he was satisfied with her answer. 'Paul,' she said sleepily.

'Yes?'

'I love you.'

'I know you do. And I love you too. That's why people don't need to know all the details about everything. Other people would never understand. But you should have told him the truth about his baby; there was no reason not to.'

Tamsin closed her eyes. It seemed he was about to say something else, but she was thankful when he didn't and she fell asleep quickly and peacefully, her head still resting on his body.

Twenty-One

At around half-past four, Sally Cornish arrived at the Quinnells' house and parked her car next to Tamsin's. She went there most afternoons to drop something off for them to eat, and as always she felt pleased at the thought that Tamsin would eat some decent home cooking. Although she was Paul and Tamsin's house-keeper, so not a friend as such, she had a soft spot for them both. She had a special fondness for Tamsin, who seemed so young, and who ate like a sparrow – the most bizarre things too – ice-cream for breakfast, a handful of peanuts for lunch, or sometimes just coffee or juice, or no food at all.

She reached across and picked up the tea-towel-wrapped dish from the passenger seat. It was a cloudy day outside, but very warm, the air close and humid. Sally slightly regretted her choice of making a casserole for the Quinnells' tea on such a hot day, but there were only so many different meals she could give them to reheat later on. When she looked up again she saw Tamsin standing at the window in the hall with Madeline in her arms, and she waved to her. Tamsin didn't wave back, but she smiled.

Tamsin opened the door for Sally as she approached the house. Sally thought she seemed a bit distracted, but she was used to Tamsin's moods being random and unpredictable.

'Hello Tamsin,' Sally said. She cooed at Madeline, who reached her chubby hands out towards the dish she was carrying. 'Do you like the pattern?' she said, referring to the flowery tea towel around the dish. 'It's pretty, isn't it?' She walked through to the kitchen, and Tamsin followed her. 'Guess what happened yesterday,' Tamsin said.

Sally laughed. 'I don't think I'll be able to.'

'Scarlett's dad came here.'

Sally was so startled she almost dropped the dish. She opened the fridge and carefully set it inside. When she turned, Tamsin was putting Madeline down in the baby bouncer on the floor. Sally knew she needed to tread carefully.

'Wow,' Sally said, trying to keep things light. 'I wasn't ex-pecting you to say that.'

'He contacted me a while back – at least, he found my sister and she called me. I wasn't sure whether to bother talking to him at first.'

Tamsin sat down at the dining table, and Sally sat opposite her. 'So,' Sally said, 'that's the first time you've seen him for a long time?'

'I told him the baby had been adopted.'

Sally nodded. 'I see,' she said.

Tamsin's eyes flashed. 'Don't judge me!'

Sally blanched a little and all the heat went out of Tamsin's face as suddenly as it had flared up. 'Sorry, Sally,' she said. She looked towards the window. 'I think I might take Madeline for a walk, and clear my head.'

'That's a good idea,' Sally said quickly, glad of the change of subject. 'Make sure you take something in case it rains, though. It feels thundery out there.' She stood up. 'I'll let you get on, then,' she said. 'Do you want me to take any washing?'

Tamsin nodded. 'Madeline's things,' she said. Sally went back out to her car and collected a big laundry bag, and then she nipped upstairs to Madeline's room, where she took the dirty clothes from the laundry basket and stuffed them into the bag. She checked a couple of other rooms too – Tamsin was haphazard about where she left things. When she got back downstairs, Paul had surfaced and was helping Tamsin open out the pushchair. 'I think I'll walk to the farm shop,' Tamsin told them both. 'Madeline likes to look at the stuff in there.'

'Good idea,' Sally said. She thought really it was Tamsin who liked looking at the things there. Sally had been amazed, when she'd started working for the Quinnells, to discover Tamsin's absolute lack of understanding about food. In fact, she didn't even recognise an onion. Sally had been so surprised that she'd laughed. Hadn't her mum ever cooked at home, she asked – which was probably a bit rude, but she couldn't help herself. She'd never forgotten Tamsin's answer. "Cooked?" Tamsin said. "There were days I felt lucky when I found something to eat in the kitchen bin." She laughed after she said it – a weird, high-pitched, false-sounding laugh, and the whole thing shook Sally to her core. But that conversation was years ago now, and Sally had been careful to keep mentions of Tamsin's childhood to a minimum since then.

Sally went to check in the living room for any more bits and pieces of Madeline's that might need washing, and she left the house around the same time Tamsin and Madeline did. The next day, she really wished she'd paid more attention to everything that had been taking place while Tamsin was getting ready to go on her walk, but she couldn't possibly have known how important it would be.

Twenty-Two

The farm shop was about fifteen minutes away from the house, and Tamsin set off at a brisk pace. It wasn't the best walk to do with a pushchair – there was a section of road without pavement and people drove fast down the country lanes, not expecting a woman with a baby to be just around the corner. It was only a short section, though, and then she could cross the road and the pavement started up again on the other side.

It was near closing time when she reached the rustic, yet large and well-stocked shop, but the woman behind the counter made no attempt to rush her and Tamsin was glad, because she was enjoying being away from the house for a while. She walked past the vegetables in their wicker baskets, making a show of looking interested, but she had no idea what to do with the majority of them. Once when she'd come in the winter there had been a celeriac, and she'd been so startled by the rooty, alien-looking thing that she'd bought it just so she could take it home and show it to Paul.

Today she didn't buy much, just a jar of honey and some bread and milk. Madeline made gurgling and hooting sounds as they began the walk home, and Tamsin looked up at the sky, where the thunderclouds had turned a dark, angry grey. She was glad she'd brought her coat and the rain cover for Madeline's pushchair with her. She was very careful about things like that. In the months since Madeline had been born, her memory seemed to have become terrible. Of course it was normal for new mums to feel overwhelmed and get a bit mixed up from time to time, but with her it seemed to be constant. She'd think she had Madeline's milk bottle then get home and find it still sitting in the kitchen, or she'd need to change Madeline while she was out and find she had no baby wipes, or no nappies, or no spare clothes for her – even though she could swear she'd checked before she left the house. Other times she'd be absolutely certain she had turned the baby monitor on but then Paul would go upstairs and tell her Madeline was screaming away, and it would turn out it was off.

Tamsin shook her head to try to clear the thoughts. She'd been stressed ever since Star had called her and told her about Michael, that had to be it. She hadn't really *felt* stressed – it wasn't a feeling she ever really experienced – but perhaps it had just been simmering away. That's what her emotions usually seemed to do. Then they'd come out at weird moments – things she didn't even know she felt.

When the first fat drops of rain began to splatter down, she was still a good five minutes away from the house, so she quickly bent down to grab her coat and the rain cover from the storage basket underneath the pushchair. She couldn't feel anything with her fingers so she knelt down and looked inside it. It was empty.

'What?' she said. 'What? No.'

She scrabbled around inside it again. The rain was getting heavier. 'No,' she said out loud, 'I put it in here. I don't understand.'

At that moment the heavens opened. There was a crack of thunder and the rain came down in a sheet, soaking her and Madeline. 'Shit!' Tamsin cried out. She started to run down the road. *Paul is going to be so disappointed with me,* she thought, *he told me to get my head together.* The rain carried on pouring down, plastering her hair to her face, and she thought back to the moments before she left the house. She *had* put the coat and rain cover in. She really had. She could remember it. She tore down the lane and up the drive to the house, crashing in through the front door and slamming it behind her. Madeline was screaming, her little powder pink summer dress so wet it was translucent and stuck to her body. 'Paul!' Tamsin cried out, 'Paul, could you come and help? Madeline... Madeline's—'

She heard him coming from the kitchen, then her eyes fell on the hall table. There, beside the lamp and the glass dish where they put their car keys, were the rain cover and her coat. She frowned at them, and then looked down at Madeline, who was screaming and shivering in her chair. She'd taken the coat and rain cover with her. She was *sure* she'd had them with her. She was so sure that she rubbed her eyes and looked at the table again, but they were still there.

'Paul,' she said, as he quickly pulled Madeline from the pushchair and held her close to him to warm her up, 'I don't understand how this happened...'

'Get a towel for her.'

'But I was so careful, Paul. I'm so careful to remember things...'

'Just get a towel for her, Tam. We can talk about this later.'

'I don't understand why this keeps happening to me!'

Paul put his hand on her shoulder, gripping Madeline with his other arm. 'Calm down,' he said, 'everyone's all right. Let's just get Madeline sorted, okay?' He looked at her wet clothes and hair. 'And you, as well,' he said.

...

After dinner Paul cleared the plates away while Tamsin stayed sitting listlessly at the dining table. They'd talked on and off about what had happened with Madeline, but Tamsin didn't know what to say any more. There had been so many conversations like this since the baby had been born, where she insisted she'd done this or that, or remembered to take such and such a thing out with her and Paul would implore her to listen to reason, insisting that she'd just forgotten.

He brought over two fresh glasses of wine when he'd finished tidying the kitchen and sat down opposite her again. 'Tamsin,' he said, 'sweetheart, listen to me—'

'I don't want to,' she said. 'Either you believe me or you don't.'

'I believe that *you* believe you took those things with you.'

Tamsin took a gulp of wine and narrowed her eyes at him. 'That's not saying much. In fact, I think that's worse than if you said you thought I was lying.'

'Fine,' he said. 'You know what, let's forget about it, can we, please?'

Tamsin did as he asked, in that she stopped talking about it, but she had no intention of forgetting about it. She'd drop it for the evening, try to get a good night's sleep, and perhaps tomorrow things would be clearer. Maybe then she would be able to work out what was going on.

Twenty-Three

As soon as she walked into the house the next day, Sally could sense an atmosphere. Tamsin was icy and Paul seemed distant, so Sally tried to keep her head down and get on with some cleaning. But when she needed to move some toys and asked Tamsin where she wanted them to go, Tamsin suddenly erupted.

'I'm surprised you bother asking!' she shouted. 'You don't normally, when you go meddling in mine and my daughter's things!'

Sally was so taken aback that she froze, but Paul had overheard and quickly came into the room, placing his hand on Tamsin's arm. 'Tam,' he said, 'calm down, it wasn't Sally—'

'How do you know that?' she asked, spinning to face him. 'Because it was *you?*'

'Tamsin,' Sally said gently, 'what is it you think I've done?'

Tamsin stared back at her, looking like a caged animal with her dark eyes glittering viciously. She opened her mouth to answer, but before she could Paul took charge of the situation. 'When Tamsin went out yesterday with Madeline, they got caught in the rain, that's all,' he said. 'She was just wondering if you took her coat and rain cover out of the pushchair for some reason.'

Tamsin glared at Paul. 'Don't say it like that!' she said. 'You're making me sound like a crazy person! One of the two of you took those things! It's been going on for months! I've been over and over it. It's the only explanation.'

Sally took a step towards Tamsin. 'These things happen—'

'Madeline was soaked!' Tamsin said. 'She was *freezing—*'

'But she's fine now,' Sally said. 'I saw her when I arrived, and she looked as happy as anything.'

'No!' Tamsin pointed her finger at Sally and Paul in turn. 'One of you. One of you is doing this!'

'Sally, I'm so sorry,' Paul said, 'it was a real shock for Tamsin to see Madeline in such a state—'

'Don't talk about me as if I'm not here!' Tamsin screamed, and then she ran from the room, slamming the door behind her.

'Sally,' Paul said, 'I don't know what to say. She—'

'She's had a difficult time with the baby. I understand, but...'

'What?'

'It's just that this isn't exactly the first time things like this have happened. Ever since that little girl was born—'

'I'm dealing with it,' Paul said, 'but she shouldn't shout at you. I'll make sure she doesn't do it again.'

'No, let me speak to her,' Sally said. 'Perhaps she might find it easier to talk to me.'

Sally went upstairs slowly. She wasn't sure where Tamsin was, and she didn't want to startle her by bursting in where she wasn't welcome. She felt sorry for her, and for Paul, because it was obvious what a great strain the baby was putting on the family. Ever since Tamsin had been pregnant, it was like a kind of sickness had spread through the house. Sickness was an odd word for it, she knew, but it was the most accurate one she could think of. When she reached the top of the stairs, she found Tamsin sitting on the window seat on the landing, her legs crossed, staring straight ahead. Sally sat down next to her. 'I've had four boys,' Sally said, 'so believe me, I know a little bit about what you're going through.'

Tamsin turned to face her. 'Did your boys scream when you came in the room?' she asked. 'Did people stare at you when you were out because the boys were crying but you never seemed to have brought with you what they need, and you think it's a one-off but it happens over and over and over and all anyone can say is that it's in your head?'

Sally took a deep breath. 'Tamsin—'

'They didn't, did they Sally?' Tamsin said, 'because you were just *able* to do it. But I can't.'

'Well, you are. You're doing it. And Madeline is a happy baby.'

'Is she? Sometimes I feel she'd be better off without me. Sometimes I feel like I'm losing my mind.'

Sally was silent for a moment as she considered how to respond. 'Tamsin,' she said gently, 'have you thought of speaking to somebody about this? About how you feel?'

'I talk to Paul.'

'I mean someone other than Paul. Your GP, or your health visitor. Or other mums, maybe?'

Tamsin ran her fingers through her hair, seeming calmer all of a sudden. 'They'll say I'm mad. People always do.'

Sally patted Tamsin's hand. She didn't know all the ins and outs of it, and she didn't like to make assumptions, but she was fairly sure that even before the baby, all had not been well with Tamsin. It was as though there were many different Tamsins, and negotiating the unwritten laws of how to communicate with her in each of her moods was difficult, if not impossible.

77

'Paul didn't want me to have a baby,' Tamsin said, 'and he was right. So now perhaps he wants me to fail.'

'Paul loves Madeline, and he loves you.'

'Sally, are you *sure* you didn't move those things?'

Sally shook her head. 'Why would I?'

'You were looking for Madeline's washing. Are you sure you weren't checking in the pushchair?'

'No, I...' Sally tried to remember. 'I was in the living room. Weren't you out there in the hall with the pushchair? You would have seen me.'

'Not while I was getting Madeline from the kitchen.'

Sally sighed inwardly. 'Tamsin, you're probably exhausted. Some people can cope with the sleepless nights better than others. Lack of sleep can do funny things to you.'

Tamsin looked at her. 'Sally,' she said, 'I know I sound irrational. And I know everyone forgets things sometimes, and it seems like I'm overreacting. But it's happening too often. This isn't just human error, I'm so, so *sure*...'

'But Tamsin, *why* would anyone move things around, or do any of these things you worry about? I wouldn't, and neither would Paul. And nobody else comes here—'

'Yes,' Tamsin said, 'I'm sorry, Sally...' She trailed off as she uncrossed her legs and got up from the window seat. 'Maybe you're right,' she said quietly, turning as she reached the top of the stairs. 'Maybe it is just lack of sleep.' Sally watched her make her way slowly downstairs. She thought she'd never seen anyone look so defeated.

Twenty-Four

For the next couple of days, things were more settled, though not much better. Madeline frequently seemed to cry when Tamsin entered the room, and however much Paul reassured her that it meant nothing, it continued to wear her down. She loved the little girl, but she'd begun to feel increasingly numb and disconnected from her, exhausted by how hard things seemed to be. To make matters worse, Paul had to go away on a business trip. She always hated it when he went away overnight, but since having Madeline she found it almost unbearable. She'd spend the evenings drinking glass after glass of wine, and the days looking after Madeline while feeling like a zombie, sometimes barely even noticing the little girl's cries, and feeling confused and a little surreal.

Finally after four nights, it was the day that Paul was due home, and Tamsin felt more optimistic as she spent the morning in the dappled shade of the fruit trees at the bottom of the garden with Madeline. Around eleven o'clock Sally came out holding a huge bouquet of roses and lilies. 'These just came for you,' she said.

Tamsin took the flowers and read the card, which said: *I've missed you so much Tam, I can't wait to be reunited with you later. Paul. xxx*

'He's very romantic,' Sally said. 'It's almost worth him having to go away when you get things like that!'

Tamsin slipped the card back into its envelope. 'It's not worth it,' she said. 'I hate him leaving.'

'Yes, I know,' Sally said. 'I was only joking.'

Tamsin looked down at Madeline, who had rolled over onto her side on the blanket and started playing with a crinkly fabric book. Every time Paul left, Tamsin went into a kind of fog, her emotions strange and frightening, the security she felt when Paul was with her suddenly shattered by his absence. On a few occasions earlier in their marriage, she'd gone out to try to distract herself and ended up having one-night stands. She always confessed to Paul what she'd done and he'd tolerated it, until one of the men continued trying to pursue her. He'd turned up at the house demanding to see her and Paul had lost his temper and broken the man's nose. After that she'd avoided getting herself in the same situation again, even though she was sometimes tempted. "It's a sickness," Paul had said to her. "I know you can't help it. But if these guys decide to start calling you, or turning up at our house, then I can't help what I end up doing either."

Tamsin lifted the flowers to her face and smelt them. She was looking forward to being reunited with Paul too. She knew it sounded a bit stupid, but the only reason she lost control the way she did when he was away was because she loved him so much, and his absence sent her into a panic, and a kind of vicious anger towards him too, a horror that he would abandon her like that.

As the day dragged on into evening, Tamsin grew more and more impatient for his return. She opened a bottle of wine, and poured herself a glass, but to try to deter herself from drinking more she left the bottle in the kitchen rather than taking it through to the living room. Nevertheless, she found herself continually creeping back into the kitchen to get herself a refill. In the end it was almost twelve when Tamsin finally heard Paul's key in the door. She had just gone into the kitchen to open a second bottle of wine, when he came into the room and stepped up behind her.

'Tamsin,' he said, 'I'm sorry it's so late.' She turned around, and stumbled a little.

'Are you drunk?' he asked her.

'A little bit.'

He smiled and kissed her on the forehead. 'Let me go upstairs,' he said, 'I'll get changed and look in on Madeline. Then I'll have a glass with you.'

'Okay,' Tamsin said.

She opened the new bottle and poured a glass for herself and for him, but then he came running down the stairs again. 'Tamsin,' he said, 'I think we'll have to forget the wine. Madeline's wet through; her sleepsuit, her sheets, everything. Did you not change her when she had her evening milk?'

'I...' She frowned. 'I'm sure I did.'

He glanced meaningfully at the empty wine bottle on the kitchen counter, but then he said, 'Come on, we'll sort her out together, it won't take so long that way.'

Tamsin followed him upstairs, and together they changed Madeline's night clothes and cot sheets. Then Paul went off to unpack his things and get ready for bed.

For some reason Tamsin couldn't quite account for, she picked up the bundle of wet laundry from the floor, and smelt it. With a frown, she put it back down again. It certainly didn't smell of urine. In fact, if she didn't know better, she'd say it was as if a cup of water had been poured all over Madeline while she slept, and the little girl hadn't wet herself at all.

She shook her head, and went over to comfort Madeline, who was whimpering as she tried to go back to sleep. 'I don't know what's going on, sweetheart,' she whispered, 'but I don't think I'm cut out to be your mummy. I think it's making me ill.'

Twenty-Five

The next week or so was tough going. Tamsin felt exhausted and strangely disconnected, just going through the motions because she had no choice. She tried to take it all in her stride, to not take any of it personally when Madeline was difficult, but in fact it seemed to hurt more every day.

She tried to talk about it to Paul one evening. They were sitting in the garden, enjoying the last of the day's sun. Madeline had not long gone to sleep, and Tamsin knew in a few hours she'd be up again, but for now she had a bit of peace.

'Paul,' she said, 'I don't feel right.'

Paul touched her hand briefly. 'I know,' he said.

'No, I mean about Madeline.'

This time Paul turned around to face her. He looked very serious, and she watched him curiously. 'Tam, I've been thinking,' he said, 'and I know it sounds a bit radical, and I'm not trying to hurt you, but…'

'What? What is it?'

'Hold on a minute,' he said, 'wait here.'

He disappeared back inside the house and Tamsin waited patiently, watching the glow in the sky over the fields that backed on to their garden. She felt very peaceful, looking at the view, watching how the landscape changed through the year. Often she painted the fields when she was in her studio, and she thought she was at her very happiest when she was doing that.

When Paul came back outside, he put down some printouts of information he'd found online. He pushed them across the table to her and she picked them up.

'I…' she said, reading the title. 'Adoption?' Her breath caught in her throat. 'You think—'

'Like I said, I'm not trying to hurt you. I don't want to push you into anything. It's just hard for me to see you struggling so much, and God knows you never had any role model in your own mother.'

'No!' Tamsin shouted. 'Stop it, Paul, stop it! I'm not like her! Are you saying I'm like her?'

'Tamsin—'

She put her hands over her ears, and Paul pulled them away. 'Listen to me,' he said. 'Your mother wasn't fit to even be called that. All I meant is that if you had such a difficult relationship with her, perhaps it's going to be hard for you to have a proper bond with Madeline. Not for want of trying,' he said quickly, 'you do your absolute best, anyone can see that. And I know you love her—'

'Do *you* love her?' Tamsin asked.

'What?'

'You didn't want me to have her. You tried very hard to persuade me not to.'

'I thought it was for the best,' he said. 'I told you I didn't want children, and I thought it would be too much for you. The thing is, Tam, when I married you I was looking forward to the rest of my life being easy, and pleasant. But instead... I mean, for God's sake Tamsin, I'm too old! When Madeline's twenty I'll be getting on for eighty! I'll probably be dead,' he added bluntly.

Tamsin shot him a look. She hated it when he started talking like that. 'Madeline doesn't like me,' she said. 'She just doesn't like me.'

'Tamsin, you have to think about what's best for all of us.' He moved the papers away from her again. 'But don't worry about this now. Not if you don't want to. I was probably being a bit hasty.'

'Perhaps I need a change of scenery,' she said. 'Maybe if you could look after Madeline for a day, I could just go somewhere. Get my head straight.'

'Okay,' he said. 'I don't have anything on tomorrow. Why not do it then?'

...

The next day Tamsin woke early. She showered and dressed, and drank a black coffee while she flicked through a glossy magazine. By nine o'clock, she was heading out of the door to her car. As she sat behind the wheel she wondered where she should go, and then a smile crossed her face as an idea occurred to her. She started the engine, and sped away down the gravel drive.

Twenty-Six

She wasn't sure what it was that made her think of driving to Benton's Furniture. It was true that her meeting with Michael crossed her mind from time to time, but she had no strong feelings about it and until this moment no inclination to have any further contact with him, so she was surprised by how much she was looking forward to seeing him all of a sudden.

She wasn't very impressed with the shop from the outside. It looked like it was midway through being overhauled, with signs reading "clearance", and an odd mixture of old-fashioned and modern furniture inside. Checking her reflection in the shop window, she fussed with her hair a little before making her way in. She strode straight up to the first salesperson she saw and asked for Michael. Something about her tone must have been commanding because the young man scurried off, looking a little intimidated, and a few minutes later she saw Michael coming towards her from a collection of dining tables at the back corner of the store. When he saw it was her he froze, and then carried on walking at a slightly faster pace, looking surprised, confused and, she thought, a little concerned.

'Rae—' he said, then he stopped and said, 'Sorry, Tamsin. What are you doing here? I didn't expect to see you.'

'Are you pleased?'

He looked uncertain, but he held an arm out, gesturing towards the back of the store. 'Come on,' he said, 'we'll talk in the office.'

She followed him into a musty, airless room with one window high up on the back wall, and shelves full of files, catalogues, and all sorts of paperwork that age and dust had turned a uniform shade of yellowy-browny-grey. She sat down on an old armchair in the corner, crossing her legs delicately, while Michael took the desk chair and turned to face her. He was wearing a suit, and she found it strange because she wasn't sure she'd ever seen him in one before. It wasn't a particularly nice one, either: it looked a bit cheap and shiny, and his tie was an unpleasant shade of green.

'Well,' she said, 'this place is like a time warp.'

He laughed, a little guardedly. 'My parents kept records of everything going back decades,' he explained. 'All on paper, of course. I'm planning to sort it all out one day but, well, you can see how much of it there is. It's pretty daunting.'

'Mm.'

Michael was looking at her closely. 'What?' she said.

'It's just... sorry, Tamsin, I'm just wondering why you're here. Is something wrong?'

'No.'

'Okay. The thing is I'm working at the moment, and I'm not sure—'

'I just wanted to see the shop. See what your life is like now. You've seen my life, after all.'

'Well, this is it,' he said, gesturing around him.

Tamsin nodded slowly. 'He warned you off, didn't he?' she said.

'Who's that?'

'Oh Michael, stop it. You know exactly who I mean. Paul. When he spoke to you he told you to leave me alone, didn't he?'

Michael didn't answer straight away, then he sighed. 'Tamsin, he might have a point. Of course I'm happy to talk to you, but I know I really hurt you...'

'He told you I'm not over it,' she said, 'that I'm all *messed up.*'

'He cares about you, that's all.'

'I know he cares about me,' she snapped. 'He's a fantastic husband. I love him more than anything.' It was true, but Michael looked startled and she realised that she had said it rather ferociously. 'So you're not going to talk to me because you're scared of my husband?' she said.

'I'm not *scared* of him.'

'Sounds like you are.'

'I just don't want to upset you.'

She stretched her legs out and looked around the drab office again. On Michael's desk there was a huge elastic-band ball, and she could just imagine him sitting at his desk messing around with it. 'My life didn't begin and end with you, Michael,' she said casually. 'Whatever Paul told you, he's blown it out of proportion. I mean, when I'm with him *sparks* fly. In bed, I mean. Whereas what you and me had, that was never much more than a fizzle.'

Michael didn't answer for a long time. She began to feel bored, then he said, 'That's not how it felt to me.'

'Really?'

'No. And you know that. You know I really loved you.'

'Yes. Well. You had a funny way of showing it.'

Twenty-Seven

Michael stared at Tamsin, trying make sense of it all. She was dressed in a casual grey shirt-dress with a pair of large, showy sunglasses pushed up into her hair and she looked incredibly out of place, though she seemed perfectly relaxed and at ease, settled into the old blue-and-white striped armchair like she'd been coming to the shop for years. But what was she here for? As far as he could tell she'd come for no particular reason and had nothing of any great urgency to say. He wondered briefly where Madeline was, but assumed she must be with Paul.

'I'll have a coffee,' she said suddenly. 'Black. You do have proper coffee here, don't you?'

'No,' he said, 'just instant.'

'Oh.' She stood up. 'We'll go and get one then. And something to eat. I'm hungry.'

'Tamsin, I can't just leave.'

'Oh, come on,' she said, 'people aren't going to think anything of it. And you're the boss, aren't you? Surely there are some advantages?'

'That's not how I do things.'

'Okay, fine. I'll go and then I'll come back.'

She started towards the door, so Michael stood up too. 'All right,' he said, 'I'll come with you. But I can't be gone long.'

They walked to a bakery a few doors down and both got coffees and bacon sandwiches. Michael suggested they walk for a while to find somewhere pleasant to sit, so they made their way through a few narrow streets until they came to a small park in front of a church. They sat on a bench in the shade and Michael watched as Tamsin tucked into the sandwich ravenously. He'd always noticed that about her – she could go for long periods without eating at all and seemingly not being aware of her hunger, and then when some food was in front of her she'd wolf it back like she was scared someone would steal it away.

'I'm finding it strange,' he said.

'What's that?' she said with her mouth full.

'Adjusting. To the news about the adoption.'

'Oh,' she said. She seemed completely uninterested, like she'd forgotten about the whole thing.

'The thought that she's out there somewhere—'

'Why worry about it?' she said. 'She'll never be able to find you unless *I* tell her who you are. Your name isn't on her birth certificate.'

'No,' he said, 'I realise that.'

'How'd Sadie take it?'

'Same as me, I guess. It's a shock.'

Tamsin took another huge bite of her sandwich and a gulp of coffee.

'Tamsin,' he said, 'could I ask you something?'

She shrugged her shoulders.

'Was Paul there? At the birth?'

Tamsin swallowed abruptly and faced him with an eyebrow raised. 'What a peculiar question,' she said.

'Is it that peculiar? I was just thinking that you and him must have been close by then, you married him not that long after we broke up—'

'As soon as his divorce came through.' She peered at him closely. 'Why do you want to know about the birth? Do you not like the thought of another man being there or something?'

'The opposite,' Michael said. 'I don't like the thought of you being alone.'

'Mm. Well, Paul was there. He was there for me through everything.'

Michael nodded. 'I'm glad.'

Tamsin finished eating and screwed the packaging from the sandwiches into a ball. 'So,' she said, 'what do you think of him – Paul?'

'I…' Michael struggled for an answer. There had been nothing wrong with Paul, as such, but he couldn't say he'd instantly warmed to him. 'I don't really know him, Tamsin,' he said. 'I was only with him a couple of minutes.'

'How long is it they say it takes to make a first impression?' she said. 'A couple of seconds, or something?'

Michael smiled. 'He seems like he really loves you.'

'That's the only good thing you can say about him, is it?'

'It's the only thing I'm interested in. Let's face it, I'm never going to be friends with him, am I?'

'You know, I told Paul the baby was his to begin with. I went after him to try and get some money out of him.'

'What?' Michael said, staring at her in astonishment. 'You did what?'

'Well, we had sex in the back of his car on the night I met him – the night you had sex with Sadie – but the condom broke.'

'So… you…'

'I wanted him to let me stay with him, that night, because I didn't want to go back to the house, or face anyone, but he told me not to be so stupid. He said he'd give me some money if I really had nowhere to go, and he made me promise him I'd get the morning after pill, but, well, I was already pregnant. I didn't tell him that. I gave him my address, and when we got there he gave me the money, quite a lot of money. I could see he didn't really understand why I needed it when I'd asked him to drop me at my house, but he just wanted rid of me. Anyway, when he opened his wallet to give me the cash there was some sort of gym membership card in there that was sticking out a bit so I could read his name, and the name of the gym. You know how good I am at remembering names and faces when I want to. I bet once he left he thought there was no way I could track him down. But I'd filed the information away.'

Michael frowned at her. 'Tamsin, why are you telling me this?'

'Why not?'

'I'm not sure I want to hear it. You said Paul cared about you, but now you're telling me he treated you badly—'

'Oh, grow up, Michael! Me and him just used each other for sex that night. What would you have had him do, propose to me first?'

'Okay,' he said, 'fine. How did you and him come to meet each other, anyway? You were at home that night, you felt too ill to come to the party – that's the whole reason I was there alone.'

'Morning sickness.'

'What?'

'That's what I was ill with.'

'So why were you out? Did you go out on your own—'

'I don't remember, all right! Someone who was at that bloody party sent me a photo of you with your face stuck to Sadie's. They said you'd gone upstairs with her. So I got drunk. I guess I went out, I don't remember…'

'Yet you remembered Paul's name and the name of the gym he went to?'

Tamsin narrowed her eyes. 'What are you saying?'

'I'm just trying to understand.'

Michael watched her carefully. She was tapping her foot rhythmically on the ground and until he'd started questioning her she'd been rattling the story off like it was rehearsed. He wasn't sure what it all meant, but anything that happened straight after their break-up was something he was interested in. 'So, why did you decide to track him down again?'

'Well. I'm sure *Alice* filled you in on everything that happened while I was with her. When my stay there became... untenable... I had to figure something else out. I changed my name to Tamsin. I felt that I couldn't be Rae any more. Paul didn't live locally. I had to get a train ticket. And I went to Paul's gym.'

'I knew it was a long shot,' she continued, 'I went in, and there was just this one young man on reception. I think he was only about eighteen. I asked him to give me Paul's address. He refused. So I told him I'd make it worth his while.'

'Tamsin...'

'He said he'd write down the address for me and hand it over outside when his shift finished. I guess he wanted to make sure I fulfilled my side of the bargain. I gave him a blowjob round the back of the gym, and he gave me the address.'

Michael didn't say anything, but he felt angry with her that she'd do all of this to find Paul when she could have just come to him for help.

'So, the next day,' Tamsin went on, 'I took three buses and walked several miles to get to Paul's big fancy house, and I watched and waited. I saw his wife go out, and then I marched up to the door. He was furious. He pulled me inside out of sight and asked me what the hell I thought I was doing. He was trying to scare me, but I think *he* was even more scared of *me*. He seemed like the kind of guy who'd throw some money at a problem to make it go away, so I told him I was pregnant. Then I made him an offer. I told him how much I wanted and said if he didn't give me the money I'd tell his wife.'

Michael just stared at the ground, letting it all wash over him. 'Tamsin,' he said, 'I wish—'

'He didn't believe I'd tell her,' she said. 'He just laughed at me. Said I was a stupid little girl, or something like that. I'm not sure he really believed I was pregnant. He told me to get lost. He said there was no way in hell I was getting a penny from him, and he threw me out.'

She stopped, so Michael said, 'Then what?'

Twenty-Eight

Tamsin finished the last of her coffee. She could see her account of how she'd met Paul was making Michael feel uncomfortable and guilty, so she carried on.

'Well, I didn't really leave. I walked off down the road so he thought I was gone, but then I came back. I waited until I saw his wife come home. From a shopping trip it looked like. I went straight up to her and told her that her husband had got me pregnant. She didn't even say anything to me. She just looked me up and down and went inside the house, and I stayed hanging around outside. When Paul came out his face was white with anger. He grabbed me and shook me. He was calling me names. I thought he might actually kill me—'

'Tamsin, this is your husband! The man you're telling me you love so much—'

'He never hurt me,' she said. 'He was just cross. I was pleading with him, telling him I had nowhere to go. He said he didn't care. But then, it was weird. All of a sudden he started laughing. He said it was worth all the money the divorce was going to cost him if he could get rid of the miserable bitch he was married to. He went inside and left the front door open, so I crept closer and I could hear them yelling, then he came back out again with a bag. He grabbed me by the arm and pushed me into his car, then he got in himself and he drove off. He asked me if I really was pregnant, and I said that I was. I just sat there. I had no idea where he was taking me, but then we turned up at a hotel. He opened my door and asked me if I was coming, so I followed behind him. I had…' she laughed, 'I had all these bags with me. I forgot to say that. All that day I'd been lugging around pretty much everything I owned in a couple of carrier bags. It was ridiculous. The whole thing was ridiculous.'

'Tamsin, could you really not have gone to your mum? Or Star? I mean, it couldn't have been worse than—'

She cut him off mid-sentence. 'When we got to the room he tried to have sex with me, but he had to stop because I fainted. I think he was really scared. As I came round he kept asking what was wrong with me, and I managed to tell him that I couldn't remember the last time I'd eaten. He ordered some food for me. I ate it in about five minutes flat, then I fell asleep on the bed.'

'My God, Tamsin.'

'What?' she asked. She thought Michael looked a bit ill.

'Why did you go anywhere with him? What if he *had* killed you? You said you thought he might—'

'Then my problem of having no money and nowhere to live would have been over, wouldn't it? It was win-win.'

'You can't mean that.'

'We stayed in the hotel for a week,' she said, continuing her story. 'He looked after me. I was happy. Then one night he sat me down and said we had to start thinking about the future. He got a flat and we moved in together. Not long after he asked me to marry him.'

She looked at him. 'And, well, here we are,' she said abruptly.

Michael seemed shell-shocked for a moment. 'So, when did you tell him the baby was mine?'

'Oh,' she said, with a wave of her hand. 'I can't remember exactly. But I got around to it eventually.' She sat back on the bench and looked up at the trees above their heads, the leaves bright green as the sun shone through them.

'I'm not sure what you want me to say,' Michael said.

Tamsin sat up straight again. 'Every day since he's done nothing but look after me,' she told him. 'He hated his previous marriage. That's why he had sex with me that night of the party. I guess that's why he was on such a short fuse when I tracked him down. He was unhappy. Trapped.'

'It doesn't make me very comfortable when you say you thought he was going to kill you.'

She laughed, 'I was probably exaggerating,' she said. 'And I do get on people's nerves. My mum always said I had a face that's asking for a slap. And no matter what you think about Paul, he's the only person who has ever stuck by me. He's treated me with nothing but kindness since that night at the hotel.' She was quiet briefly. 'You know,' she said, 'I thought I had a life as Rae, with you. And I thought I had some friends. Not many *true* friends, but some, like Alice. But even she threw me out in the end. It was like all of a sudden everyone turned their backs.'

'Tamsin, she told me you cut her face.'

'Only on the side,' she said. 'Her hair covers it up.'

'You're lucky she didn't press charges!'

'Going to prison wouldn't scare me at all,' she said. 'I am not who you think I am. I never was.'

'Tamsin,' he said, 'please. Tell me. Why did you come here to see me today? Why are you telling me these things? Do you need something from me—'

'I'm trying to work it out,' she said.

'Work what out?'

'Whether I can ever be a good mother to Madeline,' she said, 'or whether I should give her up.'

Twenty-Nine

Immediately after she said it, Tamsin stood up. 'I guess I should go,' she said.

Michael looked at her in astonishment. He felt overwhelmed. 'Don't *go*,' he said. 'You can't say something as massive as that and then walk off! Why do you think you're not a good mother?'

'I'm going, Michael.'

She started to walk away so he followed her, but she wouldn't say anything right up until they got to her car. Then she stopped, leant against it and said, 'Would you have sex with me?'

Michael's surprise must have shown in his expression, because she laughed at him. 'I don't mean I want to,' she said. 'I mean hypothetically. If you knew you wouldn't get found out. And if I was up for it.'

'I'm not answering a question like that.'

'Why not?'

'Because we're not teenagers.'

'Oh, come on, Michael. Don't take everything so seriously.'

'Okay,' he said, 'if you want to play this game, no, I wouldn't.'

'Why not?'

'Tamsin, listen to me. I care about you because I loved you, and because you had my baby, but I don't think we should have an ongoing relationship with each other.' He watched her. She seemed disinterested, and he didn't know what to make of it.

'I guess I'll go then,' she said.

'I didn't mean you have to go right this second.'

'I know when I'm not wanted.'

'Tamsin—'

'Perhaps you'll see me again,' she said. 'I am warming to your little shop. Seems like a good place to hide away, just so long as you remember to leave before you turn into an old fossil.' She jabbed her finger at him. 'That's what *you* are, Michael. You're old before your time. Do you even remember how to have fun?'

He ignored her insult. 'Tamsin,' he said, 'you can't just turn up at the shop—'

She got into the car, and as she drove away she held her hand up and waved goodbye over her shoulder.

...

That evening, as he and Sadie cleared up after dinner, Michael decided he should tell her about Tamsin's visit.

'She just showed up at the shop?' Sadie said as she scrubbed at a burnt patch on a frying pan.

'Yeah.'

Sadie nodded slowly. Michael had told her pretty much everything Tamsin had said. Even the distasteful question at the end by her car.

'Michael, I'm really unhappy about this,' Sadie said.

'I told her I didn't want to keep seeing her. I think I made it pretty clear—'

'You know what Rae... what *Tamsin* is like,' she said. 'She just makes up her own rules. If she fancies coming to see you again, she'll come.'

'I don't know what to do.'

Sadie finished with the frying pan and put it down by the sink. 'Listen,' she said, 'sit down, Michael.'

They sat at the table by the window, and Michael closed his eyes briefly and rubbed his eyelids. He felt exhausted.

'I'm worried that Tamsin is latching on to you again.'

'Latching on?'

'I don't know how else to describe it. That long story she came out with about her and Paul, I think she's manipulating you. She wanted it to sound unpleasant because she wants you to feel guilty—'

'You think she made it up?'

'I don't know. I wasn't the one there listening to her. What she said isn't out of the realms of possibility, I guess, but...' She frowned. 'I don't know. It did all sound a bit strange, how she met him and everything.'

'But she must have met him somewhere, somehow,' he said. 'I can't really imagine why she'd lie about it.'

Sadie was quiet for a while, but her forehead was wrinkled with worry.

'Sadie,' he said, 'what is it?'

'Well, there is a reason she might lie about how she met him.'

He waited expectantly.

She shook her head. 'No,' she said, 'just forget it. I don't want to stir things.'

'Sadie?'

She didn't speak, so he carried on looking at her until she caved in. 'All right,' she said, 'I'm not saying this to upset you but, Michael, perhaps she lied because she already knew him.'

Michael stared at her. 'You mean...'

'I'm sure I'm wrong,' she said quickly.

'But if she was seeing him while she was with me, that could mean the baby may not even have been mine.'

Sadie took his hand. 'Michael, I'm sure I'm adding two and two and coming up with five. And the baby... I know she's not the most reliable of people but I'm sure she wouldn't say the baby was yours if she had any doubts.'

Michael looked down at her hand over his and sighed. 'This is such a bloody mess,' he said.

'No,' she said, 'I'm sure it isn't. But just be careful. Don't let her get to you. You've told her you're sorry, and yeah, perhaps that is too little too late, but what more can you do? It's kinder to let her get on with her life – no good is going to come of her involving herself with you again.'

Thirty

After seeing Michael, Tamsin decided she would spend the afternoon walking along the river near her house. The path went through fields and she wanted to change her clothes first, so on her way home she bought a couple of bits and bobs, planning to tell Paul she'd spent the morning shopping.

When she got home the house was quiet, and she found Paul in the kitchen eating a sandwich and reading the paper. She dumped her shopping on the floor.

'Madeline's having a nap,' Paul said. 'I thought you weren't getting back until later?'

'I'm going out again,' she said. 'I'm going for a walk.'

'Oh,' he said, 'that's a nice idea.' He nodded towards the bags. 'Did you get anything much?'

'Not really. Some make-up, and a book and some clothes for Madeline. I'll show her the book later.'

'Do you want some lunch? I can make you something.'

'No,' she said, 'I'm all right. I'm just getting changed, and then I'll go.'

...

It was a pleasant walk along the river. The sun danced on the water, and insects buzzed all around, but they didn't bother her. Once she got through the fields she came to an area of shorter grass, and sat underneath a tree. It was lovely and warm even in the shade, and she decided she'd lie down for a while, but when she did she fell fast asleep, and didn't wake for almost an hour.

By the time she got home again, it was late afternoon. She could hear Paul and Madeline upstairs in the nursery, so she grabbed the book she'd bought and went upstairs to join them. She thought Madeline would enjoy the book, which had different textures on each page for her to feel, and lots of bright colours. When she went into the nursery she saw Madeline on Paul's lap, and he was encouraging her to play with a rattle. As she stood in the doorway, watching, she saw Madeline suddenly stare at the rattle intently, having previously ignored it, and then grasp it uncertainly and give it a few shakes.

'Look, Madeline,' Tamsin said, stepping into the room, 'mummy got a new book for you.'

Madeline looked up at her, and then all of a sudden, the little girl screamed and began to cry.

...

'She hates me,' she said to Paul later. 'You saw her, she hates me.'

'Maybe you startled her, or something.'

Tamsin was lying on the sofa, and Paul knelt by her side, stroking her hair. Tamsin kept reliving the scene and felt guilty at how she'd responded to Madeline screaming. She'd thrown the book on the floor and shouted at Madeline that she was so ungrateful, that Tamsin had never had a mum who bought her presents, and that she thought daddy had better read the book since Madeline loved *him* so much.

'I yelled at her,' Tamsin said. 'I yelled at a four-month-old baby.'

'Don't be so hard on yourself.'

Tamsin closed her eyes.

'Sweetheart,' Paul said, 'all this, it doesn't have to be this way. There are so many couples out there who would love to have a little baby like Madeline—'

Tamsin opened her eyes and stared at him. 'But she's *ours,*' she said, 'she's mine and yours. How can you not want her? She's your *blood,* Paul—'

Suddenly he was angry. 'Blood?' Who gives a fuck about blood? Was it worth all the years you spent in that disgusting flat with your witch of a mother because she was your blood?'

'Paul—'

'Well, was it?'

Tamsin sat up abruptly. 'Why do you compare me to her?' she shouted at him. 'How can you say this is anything like the same thing? I *feed* Madeline! I dress her, I make sure she's warm, I make sure she's safe, I don't let random fucking people in here to mess the place up and do God knows what while she's sleeping in her room—'

Paul grabbed her hands. 'Of course you don't,' he said, 'Tamsin, I didn't mean to make a comparison. I really didn't. I don't mean that I'm concerned about Madeline's safety or anything like that, it's *you* that I worry about. And me. I mean, do you remember what it was like before? When we'd go away on long weekends whenever we felt like it? When we'd go to shows, and art galleries, and get drunk at lunchtime if we wanted and then have sex for hours.'

'You want our daughter gone so you can get drunk and have sex whenever you want?'

'Well, I'm not going to get any more chances, am I?' he said, 'Tamsin, I've said this to you before. You're young, it's different. But by the time she's not consuming every moment of our lives, *I'm* going to be too old to take advantage of the freedom.'

'You've had the whole rest of your life to do what you wanted.'

'And I don't want to suffer now.'

'You really find having Madeline makes you *suffer?*'

'Not as much as you suffer,' he said. 'I can see it in your eyes, Tamsin, it's taking it out of you. You can barely hold things together, accusing me and Sally of things, flipping out every five seconds – it's not normal.'

'I don't want to talk about it any more.'

'Okay,' he said, 'I'm really not trying to hurt you. I want you to be okay.'

'Having sex for hours,' she said randomly.

'What?'

'You said you miss getting drunk at lunchtime and having sex for hours.'

'Yeah.'

Tamsin lay back down again and closed her eyes. 'Well, you and I both know you can't have sex for *hours* any more,' she said. She opened one eye to watch his reaction.

'Are you teasing me?' he said.

She giggled and he gave her shoulder a little shove. 'Well, you didn't have *baby fat* when I married you,' he told her.

He started to tickle her so she picked up one of the scatter cushions from the sofa and gave him a playful whack with it. She pushed what he'd said about Madeline to the back of her mind. Within an hour or two, she'd probably forget he'd said anything at all.

Later, she checked on Madeline before she went to bed. Paul was in the bathroom, and she heard him look in on Madeline himself a few minutes after she had. Then she heard him cry out. She ran into the nursery, where she saw him moving a blanket away from Madeline's face. 'Oh God,' she screamed, thinking the baby had been suffocating, 'oh my God!'

'She's okay,' Paul reassured her, as all the noise and commotion was making Madeline whimper in her sleep. 'She's absolutely fine.' He handed her the blanket, which was a knitted one, with holes in it as part of the pattern, and she felt relieved as she realised Madeline had probably been able to breathe fine for the short time she'd had it over her. She realised Paul was staring at her. 'Tamsin,' he said, 'you were in here a minute ago.'

'Yes!' she said. 'She was fine then! She was fine—'

He walked over to her and put his hands on her shoulders, '*You* were in here.'

'I know,' she said, 'and she was…' She realised what he was thinking before he said it.

'Tamsin,' he said slowly, 'why did you do this to our daughter?'

Thirty-One

Sally arrived at the Quinnells' house at about ten the next morning, to be greeted by the sound of Madeline crying somewhere upstairs. Initially she thought nothing of it, but when she stood at the foot of the stairs, she couldn't hear any sounds of Tamsin, only the baby. Tentatively she made her way towards the little girl's bedroom. She didn't want to interfere and imply that Tamsin couldn't look after her baby properly, but perhaps she was in the shower or otherwise occupied and would be glad of the help.

She hesitated a while, torn with indecision, but she found it heart-wrenching to leave Madeline screaming, so she went into her room, scooped her up out of her cot and gave her a cuddle.

'Shall we see if we can find your mummy?' Sally said. She walked around the landing, listening for any sounds, but Madeline was still crying and she gave up trying to hear. Then she looked out of the window and her eyes fell on Tamsin's studio in the garden. 'I bet that's where your mummy is,' she said. 'She'll be doing her art. I expect she just forgot to turn the baby monitor on, hmm?'

Madeline's cries subsided a little, and she reached out for the gold chain around Sally's neck and started playing with it.

'Yes,' Sally said, to reassure herself as much as anything, 'she'll be in the garden. That will be it.'

Sure enough, Tamsin was in her studio, and when Sally opened the door she jumped in fright, her eyes flicking nervously towards her daughter. Then they filled with anger.

'What are you doing?' she asked. 'Why do you have Madeline?'

'Oh, it's no trouble,' Sally told her. 'She was crying. I thought you must be down here. Did you forget to turn the monitor on?'

'Of course I didn't,' Tamsin said, 'it's right there—' She pointed towards it and Sally saw it on the floor by the door. It was off. Tamsin ran across to it. 'It was on,' she said, 'it was *on!*'

Sally could see Tamsin was getting upset, and she tried to calm things down. 'Perhaps the battery died,' she said.

'No. It beeps when the battery is low.' Tamsin pressed the on/off switch, and the monitor came to life in her hand.

'Well, there's no harm done, is there?' Sally said, 'I think she's ready for her milk, that's all. I can make up her bottle if you want.'

Tamsin stood staring at Sally, and Sally noticed all of sudden how disturbed she looked. She had purplish-red shadows blooming around her eyelids, as though she hadn't slept all night; her hair was unbrushed; and she was wearing jeans but with a silk and lace camisole, which Sally thought she must have had on in bed. Tamsin moved suddenly, trying to grab the baby from Sally's arms. 'Give her to me,' she said.

Sally handed Madeline over, and tried to put Tamsin's behaviour down to lack of sleep. 'I know how tiring it is,' Sally told her. 'Let me go and make up her bottle for you.'

'I'm perfectly capable of doing that myself.'

'Okay, well, if you're sure, I'll leave you to it. I'll get started on the beds.'

Sally turned for the door, but then Tamsin said, 'You think I'm a bad mother, don't you?'

'No,' Sally said. 'I think you do the best you can—'

'But it's not good enough, right?'

Sally noticed that Tamsin was clutching Madeline against her very tightly. The little girl had started to cry again.

'I was about to say that that's all any of us can do. Nobody's perfect at being a parent.'

Tamsin narrowed her eyes. 'I don't trust you,' she said. 'Have you been talking to Paul?'

'No,' Sally said, 'I haven't seen him. He's out all day at meetings, isn't he?'

Tamsin was silent again, then she flipped. 'Get out!' she said. 'Get out of my house! Get out!'

Sally quickly backed out of the studio and she started towards the house at a near run. Despite hearing Tamsin slam the door, she was afraid that any second she'd hear angry footsteps behind her. Sally knew Tamsin had strange moods – she'd been there long enough to witness all sorts of bizarre and erratic behaviour from her. But Tamsin had never behaved quite like this. When Sally got to her car, she took her phone from her pocket and called Paul. She waited impatiently for him to pick up, and she was relieved when she heard his reassuringly calm voice.

'Sally?' he said, 'is everything okay?'

'Not really,' she said. 'It's Tamsin.'

'Is she all right?'

'No,' Sally said, 'not at all. She just yelled at me to get out of the house, she… she—'

'I'll be there in five minutes. Can you stay there until I arrive?'

...

As soon as Sally saw Paul's car coming up the driveway, she rushed over to greet him. He took a big bag of groceries from the passenger seat and she followed him inside. 'I thought you were at meetings today,' she said.

'I cancelled them because I thought Tamsin might need me. I just popped out for some food. Where is she?'

'She was in the studio with Madeline.'

'Okay,' Paul said, 'what happened, exactly?'

She explained as quickly and calmly as she could and Paul nodded when she was done.

'Sally, I'm really sorry about this,' he said. 'Last night Tamsin had a bit of a scare. She went into the baby's room and Madeline had got all tangled up in her blankets. Tamsin thought she was hurt, but she was fine. It really frightened her, though. She didn't sleep a wink all night.'

'I understand,' Sally said, 'I do. And I have sympathy for her but...' she sighed, 'Paul, I'm sorry, but I don't come and work here to be yelled at by your wife.'

'I know—'

'I care about you and her, and I like working here, but I just don't need this. If I end up in this sort of situation again, I'll have to go. I'm sorry.'

'I understand.'

'Paul, I think perhaps... some women struggle after having a baby. She seems really distressed. Perhaps it would be an idea for her to speak to her doctor.'

Sally watched Paul's face. She thought he might argue with her, but he just nodded. 'You're probably right,' he said. 'I've taken my eye off the ball with this. I should have paid more attention to what was going on.'

'Okay, well, I'll get out of your hair and let you talk to her.'

'Sally, I know this is probably the last thing you want to do, but could you possibly look after Madeline in the house for half an hour or so while I talk to Tamsin in her studio? I won't be able to talk to her properly if she has the baby with her.'

Sally frowned and was about to say no, when the door burst open and Tamsin appeared, holding Madeline. 'What is going on here?' she asked. She moved her finger back and forth, pointing at the two of them. 'You're talking about me, aren't you?'

'I'm asking Sally if she can take care of the baby so that we can talk.'

'Why?' Tamsin said. 'Don't you trust me with her?'

Tamsin walked over to Sally and thrust the baby into her arms. 'Fine,' she said, 'Madeline hates me anyway. I'm sure she'll be glad to be with Sally for a while.'

Thirty-Two

Tamsin immediately felt soothed as she stepped back inside the quiet space. She loved her little studio. It was north-facing to give the best quality of light for her paintings, and there was a cosy two-seater sofa in the corner with a brightly coloured throw, a small bookcase with a few old paperbacks on it and an electric heater which kept the space lovely and snug in the winter. When she was in there, she could forget everything. And she had to admit in her heart that she was glad to be away from Madeline – she felt like the baby was sucking all the life out of her, and every time she looked at her face she thought about the scene the previous night with the blanket.

When Paul came in, he handed her a plate with a slice of toast and honey on it, and a glass with some sort of amber liquid at the bottom. 'What is this?' she asked, holding it up to her nose.

'Brandy.'

'It's not even eleven o'clock.'

'It's only a little bit,' he said. He sat down on the sofa and she plonked down beside him. 'Drink it,' he told her, 'it'll help.'

She did as he asked, and took a couple of bites of toast, but she felt sick.

'I didn't put the blanket over Madeline's face,' she said. 'And when I was in here the monitor was on. Didn't you see it when you came to say goodbye to me before you went out? It was on. I checked carefully, I check everything so carefully—'

Paul took her hand. 'I didn't look at the monitor when I came in here. I'm sorry.'

'Maybe it was Sally. Maybe she turned it off.'

'She came in here when Madeline was already crying. If the monitor was on you would have heard Madeline before Sally came in.'

Tamsin shot him a look. 'Maybe it was *you,* then – maybe you did it before you left.'

'Tam, you know no one would do these things. Why would I do it? Why would Sally do it?'

Abruptly, she threw the glass across the room and it smashed against the wall. 'I did *not* try to suffocate my baby!' she said. 'I didn't touch that blanket! I just tucked her in like I always do and then I went to bed—'

Paul put his arms around her and she tried to fight him, but he didn't let go, so instead she went limp.

'Sshh,' Paul said. 'It's all right, it's all right.'

He let go of her and Tamsin picked up the toast and ate the rest of it. She couldn't feel any emotions now. She'd pushed them all aside and made her mind go blank, cut herself off from it all. Over the years she'd grown very good at doing it, at somehow splitting her consciousness off so that things could happen to her yet at the same time not even touch her.

'Listen,' Paul said, 'you're under a lot of strain. You heard from Star that Michael was trying to find you right around the time you gave birth to Madeline. The last thing you needed was to start thinking about all that when you were a new mum. And Tam, let's face it, your memory can be a bit unreliable. It's not your fault, but you must know what I mean...'

Tamsin was only vaguely listening. She just let the words wash over her.

'...I think perhaps it's possible that you do things and then forget,' Paul continued. 'Perhaps you felt overwhelmed by Madeline and did the thing with the blanket but then—'

'Then what? I *forgot*?' she asked incredulously.

'Yes. People can get a sort of amnesia when something happens that is too distressing for them. They just block it out.'

'Really?'

'I think so, yes.'

Tamsin frowned. She screwed her eyes tight shut and tried to remember the previous night, but she had to admit she couldn't remember *any* of it that well. Not details, anyway. But nobody remembers precise details of exactly what they did at exactly what time, do they? She couldn't remember what she'd done in Madeline's room, but she went in there each night to check on her and tuck the blankets round her, and surely that's what she'd have done the night before. She pressed her fingers against her forehead. She *did* get confused, though. Reality seemed harder and harder to keep hold of, and she didn't always trust her own mind.

'You think I'm mad?' she said. 'That's what you mean, isn't it?'

Paul stroked her cheek. 'No, actually, I don't think that. I think you're overwhelmed. I think having a baby is a lot for you to cope with.'

'It's always a lot to cope with, isn't it? For anybody?'

'Yes,' he said, 'but you're not anybody. I think perhaps it's even harder for you. But I don't think you can always see it.'

'Are you going to start talking about adoption again?'

'You know what happened to your sister, Star?'

'Mm.'

'She went into care.'

'I know.'

'Okay, well, put it this way. If you keep doing things like you did last night, sooner or later it might be out of your hands—'

'I didn't do anything last night!'

'Tamsin...'

'I mean it, Paul.'

Paul looked down at the floor and didn't speak. The silence went on so long that she nudged him with her knee, and he turned on her, suddenly full of anger.

'Why can't you face facts?' he shouted. 'What do you suppose happened? That Madeline managed to pull the blanket up and place it neatly over her own face?'

'No!' Tamsin yelled back, 'but maybe you did!'

For a second Paul's face was white with anger, but she didn't feel afraid. 'You don't want her. So you're trying to make my life so hellish that either I give her up or she gets taken away.'

She fixed her eyes on his, daring him to disagree with her, but the anger left him, and when he spoke his voice was subdued. 'Tamsin, you know my first wife? I was never faithful to her. I mean, you know that – I was married to her when I met you, but even before that I cheated on her mercilessly–'

'What the hell has that got to do with anything?' she demanded.

He stroked her cheek, and she moved away. 'I have never had any trouble staying faithful to you,' he said.

'But you hate our daughter.'

'Tamsin, listen to me. I love you so much. You're the love of my life, and that you'd suggest I'd try to trick you like that...'

'Paul—'

'I don't think you've ever done anything that's hurt me so much. Even the times you've cheated on me didn't hurt like this does because I knew it didn't mean anything. I knew you still loved and trusted me, but now I wonder how you can feel anything for me at all when you're accusing me of *plotting* against you.'

Tamsin looked away from him. 'You don't want Madeline,' she said. 'You've said you don't want her.'

'And you can see why, now, can't you?' he spat. 'You have lost the plot since you've had her! For Christ's sake, I'm your husband, why are you accusing me?'

She threw up her hands. 'All right, all right,' she said, 'you've made your point. Stop with the histrionics, will you?'

He watched her for a second, and then to her surprise he pressed his lips against hers, and brought his hand up between her legs, pushing it hard against her body through the fabric of her jeans. She shoved him away. 'Get off me,' she said.

He let go of her and she made a show of looking away from him out of the window into the garden.

'Sally says you should see a doctor,' he said.

She stared at him. 'So *she* thinks I'm mad?'

'Can you blame her?'

'That interfering old cow,' Tamsin said, and she suddenly felt guilty. 'Look, Paul, I'm sorry I shouted at her. And I'm sorry I accused you. I don't know what happened, but I don't want to see a doctor. Don't make me see a doctor. I'm really not ill. I'm not.'

'I won't make you,' he said. 'We'll keep this between us. But you have to trust me, do you understand? I can't help with anything if you don't trust me.'

He kissed her gently and she rested her head on his shoulder. 'Thank you, Paul,' she said. 'I really am sorry.'

'I know,' he said, 'I know.'

...

As time went on, Tamsin tried to keep things together but felt herself slipping further and further away from her daughter. Nothing so dramatic happened as the night of the blanket, but everything seemed hard, her memory bad, her thoughts foggy and confused. Her emotions became dulled and she felt listless. Paul never commented on it, but she knew he saw, and she relied increasingly on him or Sally to help her with the baby while she retreated to her bedroom or her studio. She felt trapped, and she began to think that perhaps she *had* tried to hurt Madeline. The more she thought about it, the more she could almost remember having moved the blanket. To stop herself doing it again she avoided going into Madeline's room when the little girl was in her cot.

When the summer was drawing to a close, Tamsin sat one morning in the garden, and read the information Paul had given her about adoption. She resolved to tell Paul later that night that she'd made her decision, but around noon she got a phone call, and was surprised to see it was Michael.

Thirty-Three

Despite his conviction that it would be better to leave Tamsin alone, as time went by Michael found his thoughts increasingly turning to her. He still wondered why she'd come to the shop to see him, whether there was more she wanted to tell him, whether she was okay or whether something was wrong.

It was after he and Sadie spent an afternoon with Emily and Andy, who'd just had their baby boy, that his thoughts about her became almost constant, as seeing the couple again had reminded Michael of the visit where he'd found out about Rae's baby. On the drive home, he found himself voicing his thoughts, and Sadie gave him a look of frustration.

'You're worrying about Tamsin?' she said. 'I thought we talked about this.'

'I know,' he said. 'I just can't help wondering—'

'It's lovely that you care,' Sadie said. 'It is. But you shouldn't worry about her. She's happily married. She's got a baby, she's got her own life. And so have you. It's not that long now until our baby's due. Let's focus on that.'

Michael tried, but the next day at work he found he couldn't concentrate and in the end he picked up his phone. What harm could come of him just asking how she was? That's all he wanted to know; then he'd leave the whole thing alone again.

It took a while for her to answer, and when she did her voice was crisp and businesslike. 'Michael,' she said, 'what a surprise.'

'I just wanted to see how you are,' he said. He waited, but she didn't answer. 'Tamsin?' he said.

'Hm?'

'I asked you how you are.'

'I thought you wanted us to have nothing to do with each other?'

'I guess I didn't like how our last meeting ended,' he said, 'and I wanted to see if you're okay.'

'Oh,' she said, 'well, I'm fine, Michael, just fine. How are *you?*'

'I'm good. Busy getting ready for the baby.'

'What?'

'The baby... Sadie's pregnant. Sorry, I thought I told you when we met before—'

'Oh, yes,' she said. 'Babies, babies, babies.'

'How's Madeline?'

Her voice suddenly became guarded. 'Who've you been talking to?'

'What?'

'Why are you interested in my daughter?'

Michael shook his head in bewilderment. 'Tamsin,' he said slowly, 'sorry if I caught you at a bad time...'

'It's not a bad time. It's not like I'm shagging Paul or anything.'

'Ah, okay. Well, if you're all right... I just wanted to check, that's all—'

'You wanted to check up on me?'

'That was the wrong word.'

'No such thing. People say what they mean the first time round. Then they correct it to something less offensive. You think I need checking up on.'

'Of course I don't.'

'You're not the first person to think that way. I'm a big *problem*, you know? Everyone's problem.'

Michael began to feel really uncomfortable. What on earth was Tamsin talking about? 'I'd better go,' he said, 'I'm at work.'

'Let's meet up.'

'I'm not sure...'

'This afternoon,' she said, 'I'll text you where.'

'Tamsin—'

''Bye then.'

...

Tamsin sent him the address of a café in a small village that was about halfway between her house and his. He considered telling her he couldn't make it, but in the end he took the afternoon off work, and he arrived just as she was getting out of her car and putting Madeline in her pushchair.

'Michael,' she said as he made his way over to her. 'You look a little cross.'

Michael bent down to say hello to Madeline, but he wasn't used to babies and he felt a bit silly trying to talk to her. He stood up again and looked at Tamsin. She was immaculately put together – her make-up subtle apart from a warm red on her lips, a floral silk scarf around her neck contrasting with a simple black t-shirt and dark jeans. In her ears he spotted small earrings glittering. He knew it was a stereotype but he could just imagine Paul handing her a credit card and telling her to go out and spend whatever she wanted. The earrings must have been a gift from him.

'Michael?' she said. 'Are you cross with me?'

'No, of course I'm not, but I was at work. I can't just drop everything.'

'Well, you're here now.'

Tamsin said very little while they sat in the café, and Michael began to think the whole thing was a bad idea. She had to give Madeline her lunch while they were there, but she seemed uninterested in doing it, and when Madeline made a grab for one of their teacups on the table, Tamsin barely seemed to notice. Michael had to quickly push it out of the way.

Michael found himself watching the little girl in her high chair, how she kept staring at Tamsin, and how Tamsin was determinedly ignoring her, thrusting a spoonful from a jar of pureed vegetables in her direction from time to time and showing no reaction when Madeline ate the food happily.

'She enjoys her food then?' Michael said.

Tamsin turned and fixed her eyes on him. 'Have you ever been sure you did or didn't do something,' she said, 'but someone else is telling you the opposite?'

Michael was about to say he didn't understand what she was talking about, but decided he'd just take the question at face value and answer it.

'Yeah,' he said, 'sometimes.'

'How did you react?'

'What kind of thing are you talking about?' he asked. 'Forgetting to lock the door, or leaving the iron on or something?'

Tamsin scraped the last bit of food from the bottom of the jar and fed it to Madeline, who spat most of it down her chin. 'Kind of,' she said. 'What do you do, when something like that happens?'

'Well, I guess it depends. If it's clear it must have been me who did or didn't do it, then I was obviously mistaken. It's not a big deal.'

'Even if you felt completely sure.'

'Tamsin, I'm not really sure what you're getting at. Everyone forgets things sometimes.'

'Do you think somebody could do something bad and then forget?'

Michael looked at her closely. 'What sort of thing are you talking about—'

'Oh, forget it,' Tamsin said, as she wiped Madeline's face a little roughly with a baby wipe, 'you obviously don't understand.'

Thirty-Four

Once they'd finished their drinks, Tamsin suggested they go for a walk, so Michael followed her through the winding streets until they reached a narrow path along a river, where at times they had to walk single file.

'Does Sadie know you're here?' she asked him eventually.

'No,' he said, 'but I'll tell her.'

'Will you?'

'Why wouldn't I?'

'I suppose you could see it,' she said, changing the subject.

'See what?'

'That I'm not very good at looking after Madeline.'

'You seem fine to me.'

She gave him a look. 'You're lying,' she said.

'I guess you seem a bit withdrawn.'

'Well, I've made up my mind,' she said, 'and I guess withdrawn is a good word for describing how I feel, because I'm going to have her adopted.'

...

They talked for a long while. Michael tried to draw out of her what the problem was, but all she would say was that Madeline hated her, and that the two of them would be better off without each other.

'She even likes *Sally* better than me,' Tamsin said.

'Who's Sally?'

'Our housekeeper. Imagine that. *I'm* the one who tries to do everything with her, and she prefers someone who's not even family.'

'I guess Sally is sort of part of your family though, isn't she? If she's there a lot, I mean—'

'She's just some old woman we pay to clean our house and cook for us!' Tamsin said. 'She judges me, you know. They both do, her and Paul. They think there's something wrong with me.'

They'd reached some picnic benches in a little grassy area that opened up by the side of the river and they sat down together. 'Tamsin,' Michael said, 'I'm sure no one's judging you.'

'They are,' she said, 'they're always talking. Always *whispering* about me. I used to like Sally. But I don't trust her now.' She stretched her legs out. 'It doesn't matter any more,' she said, 'they've won. Madeline will leave, and then everything can go back how it was.'

Michael thought about it. 'Well, what does Paul say? You must have talked to him about it.'

Tamsin was silent for a long time, then abruptly she laughed. Her manner seemed different all of a sudden, like she was taking part in a different conversation. But she answered what he'd asked her. 'Paul?' she said, 'why should he care? He isn't even Madeline's real dad.'

Thirty-Five

Michael was too taken aback to speak for a second, then he said, 'who—'

'One of Paul's friends,' she said. 'He met up with some old school mates. They came to our house, and a couple of them stayed with us. I sat on my own in the living room watching TV all evening while they talked and got drunk. I'd been looking forward to them coming. I get fed up sometimes, not seeing anyone, but they didn't seem to want me there.'

Michael looked round at her. She was talking animatedly, like she had when she told him how she'd met Paul. He listened, but he wasn't quite sure what he was listening to. Her emotions were all wrong for the words she was saying, her body language was wrong, the way her gaze was so intent yet strangely unfocused.

'When they were all pretty hammered, Paul came to get me,' she said, 'and he sort of brought me into the kitchen like he was showing me off. It's not like him to do things like that. I thought it was strange.'

She fell silent, so Michael prompted her. 'What happened then?' he asked.

'Like I said, they were drunk,' she told him. 'There were no chairs left, and one of them said I could sit on his lap. I wanted Paul and the rest of them to have fun, so I did it. I thought it was just a bit of messing around. They all laughed when I did it. But then Paul's friend started putting his hand up my skirt. I didn't make a big deal out of it, I just said something flippant. But Paul said, "Why don't you let him, Kitten?"'

Michael frowned. Kitten? Her old name?

'The others were all just laughing. He said something about how that's what I liked to be called. He was saying perhaps I should have sex with one of them, since I was acting so frisky. He got up and took some cocktail sticks from the kitchen drawer, and he snapped one of them in half and held them all in his hand, so they could pick which one...' She trailed off again.

'*Paul* did that? To you?'

'Of course it ended up being the guy whose lap I'd sat on,' she said, her voice brisk again. 'If it'd been one of the others, they might not have gone through with it. Most of them were married. In fact, he was married too. Well, separated, I think. I had sex with him in one of the bedrooms upstairs, and it turned out he gave me a baby.' She turned and smiled at him. 'How about that?'

...

After her announcement, Tamsin was keen to leave. She felt exhausted, and her head was beginning to throb. Michael was saying kind things to her as they made their way back along the river, but it was like she couldn't hear him and it was just white noise. When they reached their cars, she was surprised when Michael put his arm around her.

'What you did with our baby, with Scarlett, all those years ago, was very brave,' he told her. 'You did what you thought was the best for her, and for you. You can make the right choice about what's best for Madeline, but make sure you give yourself enough time to really think. And forget about Paul,' he said angrily, 'and the man from that night. You're better off without either of them.'

'You didn't like it when I cut you out of our baby's life,' she said.

Michael sighed. 'All right,' he said, 'well, maybe you should tell this other man. But you've dealt with so much on your own. You can do more than you think you can.'

She stepped closer to him, and then closer again, until her lips were near enough to his that she could feel him breathing. She closed her eyes, but instead of feeling his lips she felt his hands on her shoulders, and he gently moved her away.

'No,' he said softly.

'It's all right,' she said. She reached down to his left hand and touched his wedding ring. 'Take it off if it helps,' she said.

Michael pulled his hand away. 'Tamsin, listen,' he said, 'this isn't what I want.'

Tamsin stared at him. She felt like something inside her was beginning to break.

'Tamsin,' he said, 'I'm sorry.'

She gave him a shove. 'Well, fuck you!' she shouted, and she ran away down the path, leaving him with Madeline.

He called after her but she ignored him, and she ran back the way they had come, her hair streaming out behind her in the breeze.

For a moment she thought about simply continuing to run and run, leaving Madeline behind, but she was surprised to feel a funny tugging sensation, as though she and her daughter were attached by an invisible elastic band, and the further she ran the greater the tension. She slowed from a run to a walk. Then, as if her feet were moving of their own accord, she found herself turning back.

...

That evening at home, she sat down with Paul. What she'd told Michael about Paul not being Madeline's dad was nonsense. She wasn't even sure where the story had come from, but she shrugged it off. Sometimes when she opened her mouth she was as surprised as anyone by what came out. But she was glad she'd said it because somehow it had helped her feel more resolved in her mind, and she made sure she expressed herself with as much clarity as she suddenly felt.

'I'm going to keep Madeline,' she told Paul. 'I looked at the adoption stuff earlier. I had pretty much made up my mind that she'd be better off elsewhere, but I was with Michael today and he helped me see it differently. I can do it, Paul. I really think I can—'

'What?'

'I'm saying I can—'

'You were with *Michael?*'

'He called me earlier. Asked how I was. I met him at that café, Mayfield's, by the river – the one we go to sometimes. He talked to me, he said how I made a brave choice with his baby, having her adopted—'

'You didn't *have* her adopted!'

'I know, but, he still had a good point. Paul, don't get distracted with Michael. He's not important. Just listen to what I'm saying. I left Madeline with Michael for a few minutes – I walked off because I couldn't handle it. But then it started to hurt. Being separated from her hurt me, and that's love, isn't it? That's wanting to be with somebody.'

'So your mind's made up, is it?'

'I think so. Paul, I know you don't want to be a dad, but perhaps it won't be so bad, if I get better. Because I was thinking that perhaps I *should* talk to the doctor, because I do feel a bit weird sometimes, like... not really myself, and if it means I can look after Madeline better I'm prepared to get some help. That would be best for us all, surely.'

Paul didn't reply straight away, but then he held her tight and kissed her hair. 'If that's really what you want, Tamsin,' he said, 'I'd rather you didn't go to the doctor though, because I don't think it's necessary. But you know I'll support you, whatever you choose.'

She closed her eyes and let him hold her, even though she could feel his body was rigid with anger.

Thirty-Six

The next day Tamsin felt so energised by her decision that she decided she would take Madeline swimming in the afternoon – something she'd all but given up on doing because she usually felt so drained. Paul was out most of the day, but by the time she got home in the late afternoon he was back, and Sally was there too, dropping off a lasagne for them to eat for dinner. Tamsin left Madeline asleep in her car seat in the hall, and took the bag of towels and swimsuits into the utility room to put them in the wash straight away. She collected a few of Madeline's other dirty clothes from upstairs, and she met Sally on her way back down.

'I can do that,' Sally said.

'It's all right,' Tamsin said, 'I'll do it.'

Sally smiled and nodded towards Madeline who was still fast asleep. 'I think you've worn her out,' she said.

...

Tamsin had little reason to think of the afternoon again until a couple of days later, when she undressed Madeline to give her a bath, and found that her back and tummy were covered in an angry red rash.

'Paul!' she called out, 'Paul! Come and look, come and look at this—'

She heard him running up the stairs and she tried to calm down, but the sight of the rash was making her panic. She felt Madeline's forehead to see if she had a temperature, but she felt cool, and aside from the rash she seemed well.

'What is it?' Paul asked as he came in, then his eyes fell to the baby.

'What's wrong with her?' Tamsin asked, but then she remembered. It had happened once before when Madeline was tiny, and they'd washed her clothes with biological washing powder.

Paul knelt down and looked at Madeline. 'Did you use the non-bio powder when you washed her clothes the other day?' he asked.

She frowned at him. 'I don't do the washing,' she said.

'You did. After you went swimming, remember? Weren't these clothes in with that wash? I remember seeing them hanging up to dry.'

Tamsin picked up the little skirt and top that Madeline had

been dressed in. 'I always make sure I'm using the right stuff—'

'But you hardly ever do it,' Paul said. 'You just said so yourself. So perhaps you picked up the wrong box of powder by mistake.' He scooped Madeline up in his arms. 'There, there,' he said to her. 'Ssh, ssh.'

He looked at Tamsin. 'Madeline's okay,' he said. 'It doesn't seem to be upsetting her much. It was just an accident. Don't feel bad, these things happen.'

Tamsin stared at him. Then all of a sudden she was sure she saw something in his face. Like he was pleased. 'This was *you*,' she said, jabbing her finger at him. 'You did this!'

'Tamsin,' he said, 'Calm down. We've talked about this—'

She stood up. 'No! I won't let you try to talk me round again! It was you! It was you, or it was Sally, or… it was the two of you working together! I should never have started to trust you again!'

'Tamsin,' he said gently, 'be reasonable—'

'No!' she screamed, 'I used the right powder! I swear I did! I've been feeling better, Paul, I was concentrating—'

'Stop it,' he said, 'just stop it! I'm sick to death of this, you making these crazy accusations. Do you really think that Sally and I go messing around with washing powder? What the hell for?'

'I don't know!' she said, her mind racing. 'Maybe you're having an affair with her!'

Paul put Madeline down on the changing mat and he stood up and put his hands on Tamsin's shoulders. 'Calm down,' he said.

'No! I was doing better. I was doing better and you didn't like it! The two of you, you're always *whispering.* Are you trying to get rid of me? Me and the baby, are we in your way—'

'Tamsin, for God's sake, I'm not having an affair with *Sally.*' He let go of her shoulders, and Tamsin looked down at Madeline, who had rolled onto her tummy and was trying tentatively to push up onto her hands and knees, but kept slipping back down onto her front again and letting out a funny little noise of frustration each time.

'I did not use the wrong washing powder,' she said, her voice brittle.

'All right,' Paul said, 'fine. Whatever Tamsin. I guess me and Sally went and tampered with it. Right after we'd finished screwing each other.'

Tamsin stared at him furiously. She was beginning to feel ridiculous, but she knew that was what Paul wanted. 'I hate you!' she shouted. 'I don't know why you're doing this to me!'

She looked at him one moment longer, and then she ran out of the house to her studio, pausing only to grab her phone. Then, without giving herself any time to gather her thoughts, she called Michael.

Thirty-Seven

When Michael answered the phone, he was in the middle of cooking dinner, while Sadie was upstairs relaxing in the bath. He sighed when he saw it was Tamsin, but he turned the hob off and sat down to listen to what she had to say.

'Slow down,' he said, as he struggled to keep up. 'You think Paul did *what*? To *what*?'

He listened in bewilderment as she started another long tirade about washing powder.

'Tamsin, I'm sure you just made a mistake,' he said when she finally paused for breath. 'It's easily done—'

'I did *not* make a mistake!' she exploded.

He waited a long time before speaking again, and Tamsin had fallen into silence too. 'Tamsin—' he said at last.

'I can look after my daughter,' she said. '*You* told me I can. I told Paul I wanted to keep her, and then *this* happened.'

'Tamsin, maybe you're tired—'

She let out a cry of frustration, and then she hung up.

Michael wanted to forget the conversation, but what Tamsin had said was too unusual, and too worrying for him to set it aside, so in the end he went upstairs to talk to Sadie.

She smiled at him when he came into the bathroom, but then she took a closer look at his face. 'Oh, God, Michael, what now?'

She listened quietly while he explained, and he hated how heartbroken she looked about the fact he was in touch with Tamsin.

'Michael,' she said at last, 'do you know what tomorrow is?'

'Tomorrow?'

'It's my last day at work before I go on maternity leave.'

'Oh,' he said, 'I—'

'You'd forgotten,' she said. She sat up awkwardly in the bath and put her hand on her bump. Some bubbles clung to her hair, and Michael thought she looked very tired. 'You know, when the baby is here our lives will change forever. And for me, it's huge. But I look at you, and it's like you don't really care. Your real priority is her.'

'It's not like that.'

'It's how it feels,' she said, 'and it *hurts*. You're really hurting me. I understand why you care about her, but right now *I* need you. Can't you see that?'

He stared at her. She always seemed so able and confident

that he found it surprising to hear her say something like that. 'It's just that the things she was saying about the washing powder—'

Sadie's brow furrowed, but she didn't speak.

'You're thinking what I'm thinking, aren't you?' Michael said, 'I mean, that's not a normal thing for someone to think, is it? That people are deliberately doing things to hurt your baby.'

Sadie didn't meet his eye, but eventually she shook her head.

'Do you think I should be worried?'

'What *exactly* did she say?'

Michael went through it again – how Tamsin had insisted that Paul or Sally had either added the wrong powder to the wash in addition to what she'd already put in, or that they'd added a layer of biological powder to the top of the non-bio box so that that was what she'd scooped out and put into the machine, or that they'd swapped the contents of the boxes around completely.

'Well,' Sadie said, 'it's not likely that her husband or her housekeeper would do that, is it? Not at all likely.'

'No,' Michael agreed, 'it seems more likely that she's...'

'...not very well,' Sadie finished his sentence.

They carried on talking about it over dinner, and although Sadie's initial thought was that Michael should try to speak to Paul, in the end they decided that perhaps it would be worth him visiting Tamsin and asking her about the call face to face, to see how she responded. Michael was impressed by how amenable Sadie was being to the idea of him seeing Tamsin again but she simply said, 'hopefully we've got this all wrong. But if Tamsin really does believe her husband is doing things like that, it could be...' She struggled for the right word. 'Perhaps we're overreacting,' she said, 'but it could be really bad for her, and the baby. And if you're the one she trusts with her fears, perhaps you're the only one she'll talk to about it.'

Thirty-Eight

As Michael arrived at Tamsin's house the next morning, he was praying for Paul not to be there, and when he saw only one car on the drive he was relieved to recognise it as Tamsin's. He had to wait a while before she answered the door, and when she did she said, 'You. What do you want?'

She let him inside, despite the fact she seemed angry. The house felt cool, and she was dressed in a crisp, pale blue dress with her hair tied back loosely. Her feet were bare, and her toenails were painted a pearly grey colour.

'How's Madeline?' he asked her.

Tamsin's eyes glittered dangerously. 'What do you mean?' she said.

'I was just making conversation...'

'She's in the kitchen,' she said, her voice a little softer. 'She's practising crawling but she can't do it yet, so she just stays wherever you put her. It's quite useful, actually.'

Michael followed her through to the kitchen, where sure enough he saw Madeline lying on her tummy on a soft blanket, surrounded by toys. 'So you see, she's fine,' she said, 'and I'm fine. You've had a wasted trip.'

'You know why I'm here,' he said.

'I don't, actually,' she said. 'And if you keep coming round, Paul will think we're having an affair. And he'll kill you.'

She pulled herself up onto the worktop and sat watching him, occasionally kicking her legs against the cupboard. He plonked himself down on a wooden stool by the kitchen island. He decided to try not to antagonise her by asking her straight out about her call, but found himself asking about Paul instead. 'Does he get jealous?'

Tamsin was gazing absent-mindedly across the kitchen towards her daughter, but at his words she turned to him. 'You're putting words in my mouth,' she said.

'Tamsin, you can talk to me, you know, if you want to—'

'Ever since I had her,' she said, 'things keep going wrong. Little things. I go out and don't have what I need with me. I make mistakes. I start feeling depressed and frustrated and Madeline picks up on it. Half the time she cries when I come in the room. People keep telling me it's normal to forget things and make mistakes, but I am double- and triple-checking. I am not making mistakes. I'm not being careless. Something is going on.'

'Uh, okay...' Michael said.

'I began to think I was going mad,' she said. 'That's what you think, isn't it?'

'I don't—'

'Yes, you do. But I've been thinking about it. I've been thinking about it very carefully. Paul denies it, but I know. These aren't isolated events. It's a *campaign*. Somebody is doing this and if it's not him, then it's Sally. But I think it's him.'

'But *why*—'

'*That* is what I have to work out,' she said.

He didn't get a chance to reply before he heard the sound of the front door opening.

'Tamsin, it's only me,' a cheery voice called out. A short, neat woman in her late fifties came into the kitchen and smiled at Michael. 'I saw you had a visitor,' she said to Tamsin. Michael waited, expecting Tamsin to introduce him, but instead she slid down from the kitchen counter. 'I'm going upstairs,' she said. 'Why don't you talk amongst yourselves. *Talking* about me seems to be what everyone likes doing best.'

Thirty-Nine

Sally smiled uncertainly as Michael introduced himself. She wasn't sure what they'd just been talking about, or what she should say.

'I'd better go,' he said, after she gave her own name. 'Tamsin obviously doesn't want to talk to me.'

'She finds it hard,' Sally said, on the spur of the moment, 'to remember about her babies.'

Michael frowned at her. 'Her babies? What do you mean? Do you mean the adoption?'

Sally's skin began to prickle. Why had she said anything?

'What?' Michael said, immediately noticing her expression. 'What is it?'

'Nothing,' she said. 'Nothing.' She pulled out one of the dining chairs and sat down on it.

Michael hesitated a while, then he sat opposite her. 'How long have you worked here for?' he asked.

'Oh, seven... eight years,' Sally said. 'Something like that.'

Michael got up and pushed the kitchen door completely closed. 'Listen,' he said as he sat down again. 'I'm sorry to spring all this on you, but I'm here because Tamsin called me last night. She sounded really upset. She was accusing Paul, or you, of tampering with Madeline's washing powder—'

Sally sighed, then she looked sympathetically at Michael. He seemed like a kind man. She noticed a wedding ring on his finger, and he smelt of something pleasant – a warm scent. Citrusy.

'The thing with Tamsin...' She took a deep breath and when she carried on her voice was steadier. 'The thing with Tamsin, she's had a difficult time of it. She gets upset, and God knows she has enough things in her past to get upset about, but some of the things she says, you have to, you know, take them with a pinch of salt.'

'You mean you think she was *lying* when she called me?' Michael asked in surprise.

'No,' she said, 'no, of course not. I'm sure she was saying what she felt at the time.'

Michael's eyes searched her face. He pulled at his shirt a bit. 'I've got my own baby on the way,' he said, 'and my wife needs me. I don't know why I came here.' He stood up. 'Thank you, Sally. Tell Tamsin... could you just tell Tamsin I needed to go?'

125

He started towards the hall, but Sally stood up to stop him. 'Maybe it might be worth trying to talk to her again before you leave,' she said. 'Let me go and find her.'

'I don't know.'

'It'll only take a second.' She hesitated. She wasn't sure how much she should say, but she couldn't help but trust him. 'She doesn't mean it,' she said.

'What?'

'When she says things that aren't true. When I started here, she told me all sorts of stories about her life, about her and Paul. Some of it sounded a bit fantastical, but I believed her. You do, you know? But then her stories started to contradict themselves, or I'd be talking to Paul and mention something she'd said, and he wouldn't know what I was talking about. It felt a bit like she was making fun of me, but then I realised, it's just her way. You have to read between the lines.'

'What are you trying to tell me?' Michael asked. 'I know she's lied in the past; she lied about her family and who she really was. But do you mean she still does it now?' Sally saw his face change as something occurred to him. 'Has she made things up about my baby—'

'I'll go and see where she is,' Sally said quickly. 'Could you keep an eye on Madeline, for a second?'

Sally made her way up the stairs while Michael waited in the kitchen. She found Tamsin sitting on the window seat on the landing, leaning against the wall with her eyes closed.

'You finished your chat, then?' she said.

'Michael is concerned about you, that's all.'

Tamsin sprang up from the window seat like a cat. Sally wouldn't have been surprised if she'd actually started hissing. 'What did you tell him?' Tamsin asked. 'Did you say I'm crazy?'

'Of course I didn't.'

Tamsin made her way towards one of the bedrooms, one with a little wooden heart on the door. She usually went to hide there when she was upset, knowing that Sally never came in unless she had to.

'Tamsin,' Sally said, 'why don't you talk to Michael? He's waiting downstairs with Madeline.'

'Don't tell me what to do!'

'Tam—'

'I said no!'

...

In the kitchen, Michael knelt down beside Madeline. He could hear voices upstairs, and assumed that any second Tamsin would come back down. He watched Madeline as she rolled from her front onto her back, then she fixed her wide blue eyes on him. 'Da?' she said.

He smiled awkwardly. He wasn't sure if the word really meant anything to her or if she was just making noises. He thought it was the latter, but found himself saying, 'Da? Your da isn't here.'

'Da?' she said again, 'ba-ba.'

'Ba-ba,' he repeated back to her.

Madeline waved her arms and legs. 'Bah!' she said loudly.

At that moment, Michael heard Tamsin's voice raised some-where upstairs. He wasn't sure if he should leave the room, but it seemed like Madeline would be okay for a minute or two, so he made his way out into the hall. Upstairs, Tamsin was yelling – more conspiracies about Paul, and Sally, and he could hear Sally trying to reason with her. He made his way up the steps slowly and saw Tamsin beginning to open the door to one of the bedrooms – one she hadn't shown him when she'd given him a tour of the house. As he reached the top of the stairs he froze in shock as the door swung open revealing two beds, one against each wall, a girl's name spelt out in pink wooden letters on the wall above each. The names were Bella, and Scarlett.

Forty

Michael's mind raced as he drove home. He expected the house to be empty, but to his surprise he found Sadie in the living room curled up on the sofa. On the coffee table were a few presents; a teddy, some flowers, a little t-shirt that said "I love my mummy". He remembered it had been her last day at work, but he wasn't sure why she was home so early.

'How did it go?' she asked, sitting up. 'I felt a bit funny, so I came home after a couple of hours—' His face stopped her in her tracks. 'Michael, what happened with Tamsin? Are you okay?'

He sat down next to her, so angry he was shaking. When Tamsin had realised he'd seen the room, she'd done nothing except smile silently, as if it was a joke to her. When he'd asked her what it all meant, she'd said it was nothing to do with him, until eventually Sally had encouraged him to go home. 'Does my daughter live here?' he'd asked Sally. 'Did Tamsin *keep* her?' But Sally had said nothing.

'Michael?' Sadie said softly. 'Michael, please?'

'She lied to me about the baby!' Michael exploded suddenly. 'There was a child's bedroom upstairs. With two beds in for two little girls. She lied to me. She *lied* to me—'

'Slow down,' Sadie said, 'and calm down. Are you sure about what you saw?'

'She's got my daughter there,' he muttered, 'my daughter lives there and she's trying to keep me away from her!' By the end of the sentence his voice had grown loud again, and he could hear roaring in his ears.

'So, hold on,' Sadie said. 'You said there were two beds. So you're telling me that Tamsin has *two* daughters, well, three including Madeline?'

Michael put his head in his hands. 'I don't know,' he said, 'God, I don't know. Maybe...' He sat bolt upright. 'Maybe she had twins—'

'Michael, you're getting way, way ahead of yourself. What did Tamsin say?'

'Nothing. She said it was nothing to do with me.'

'Then maybe it isn't,' Sadie said. 'Perhaps the girls are Paul's daughters.'

'But why are they never there? She's trying to hide them from me. She's a *bitch*. A lying bitch.'

'Michael,' Sadie said gently, 'don't call her that. You're being paranoid. There could be hundreds of reasons why you've never seen the girls. Perhaps they go to boarding school. Maybe they spend a lot of time at a friend's house. For all you know they might not be there because they are ill, or even… perhaps… perhaps they died.'

Michael stared at her. All of a sudden he realised how rash he'd been. 'Oh, God,' he said, 'I've made such a mess of this, haven't I?'

'Did you get angry while you were with her? Or did you manage to keep yourself together until you got back home?'

'I…' He thought back but it all seemed like a bit of a blur. 'I think I might have raised my voice a bit, but I thought she had my daughter there! I mean, if they are Paul's daughters, why not say that? Why can't she just say what's going on instead of everything being a bloody riddle!'

'So you yelled at her?'

'Wouldn't you have done?'

'Probably,' she said. 'But if you did you've probably blown your chances of finding anything out – she'll just clam up more than ever now.'

'What do you think I should do?'

'I don't know. It's a really confusing situation and I have no idea what to make of it either. Maybe if you give her some space she'll tell you what's going on when she's ready. Pushing her will probably make things worse.'

After dinner they were about to go straight to bed – neither of them really felt tired, but they couldn't concentrate on anything and didn't know what else to do – but then there was the sound of the doorbell, followed by loud banging on the door.

'What on earth—' Sadie said.

'I'll get it,' Michael told her. 'You stay back here.' He made his way cautiously out into the hall. He had an uncomfortable feeling that whoever was there had something to do with his confrontation with Tamsin earlier and he was afraid it might be Paul.

Sure enough, as soon as he unlocked the door it was shoved open and Paul was inside the house.

'Paul,' Michael said, 'look, if this is about—'

Paul grabbed him and pushed him up against the wall. 'You know exactly what this is about! What did you think you were doing? Coming into my house, upsetting Tamsin—' Paul pulled him forward and then slammed him back again. Sadie cried out, and Michael wanted to retaliate but instead his body filled with fear as Paul's actions brought back the memory of how he'd been brutally attacked ten years ago. 'You've got no right to talk to her!' Paul continued. 'I told you to stay away, so stay away! Do you understand me?'

Suddenly, Michael's anger overcame his fear and he pushed Paul away. 'If she's hiding my daughter from me, I've got every right to know!' he shouted. 'She can't pretend it never happened—'

'Tamsin had an abortion,' Paul said, stopping Michael in his tracks. 'There is no child. Okay? There is nothing for you.'

'I don't believe you!' Michael said. 'Why wouldn't she just tell me—'

All the heat suddenly went out of Paul's face, leaving a man who looked so world-weary that Michael wondered how he could have felt threatened by him moments earlier. 'Because she likes to pretend. That's the truth of it.'

'I don't trust you,' Michael said. 'Tamsin told me about you. About who Madeline's dad really is. One of your friends—'

Paul's face showed an expression of such utter bewilderment that Michael realised the truth in an instant. Sally had been right, he really had to take what Tamsin said with a pinch of salt.

Forty-One

'Look,' Paul said, 'maybe we should sit down.'

Michael eyed him suspiciously. However, he felt at this moment like maybe he could trust Paul more than he could trust Tamsin.

He showed Paul through to the living room, where he sat down on one sofa while Michael and Sadie took the other.

'I'm sorry I showed up like this,' Paul said. 'I spend a lot of time worrying about Tamsin, trying to make sure she's okay. She's really struggled since having Madeline and it's tricky trying to hold things together.'

'She thinks you or Sally are interfering with Madeline's things,' Michael said. 'Something about washing powder...'

Paul nodded sadly, and Michael felt a surprising rush of sympathy for him. He could see concern for Tamsin written all over Paul's face. 'She has these bouts of paranoia,' he said. 'It's worse now she's had Madeline.'

Michael wasn't sure what to say, so he turned the conversation back to his baby. 'So she never had my child... Scarlett?'

'No. She didn't even know it was a girl, she just *invented* her. She didn't lie to you maliciously – when she told you about the adoption, she probably believed it herself. Sometimes she says she can see Scarlett in her mind as clearly as if she was standing in front of her.'

'What about the other girl, Bella?'

Paul sighed. 'She got pregnant when she was thirteen, and she didn't keep that baby either. I mean, how could she have done? She was so young. Far too young.' He paused for a while. 'I don't know much about it, only what I've managed to piece together over the years, but the whole thing was very disturbing for her. Her family situation as well, I don't know what you know about it...'

'I met her sister, Star. And I found out that Tamsin was called Kitten before she changed her name to Rae—'

'Yes,' he said, 'she was so determined to get herself out of the life she had. Her mother neglected her. She was an alcoholic and I think there may have been other things going on too. Drugs, possibly. Crime. I mean, you get the picture. It was a very difficult place for a child to grow up in. So she made up an entirely new persona in Rae – she tried to change everything about herself. She worked so hard to get into university, she just didn't give up.'

Michael felt a surge of admiration for her. 'That,' he said, trying to put his thoughts into words, 'that's—'

'But becoming pregnant again when she was with you brought it all back to her; all the stuff with Bella and how tough things were for her back then, and in the end she decided that she couldn't have your baby either.'

'She didn't lie to me because she thought I'd judge her about the abortion, did she?' Michael asked.

'Like I said, Michael. The truth is very fluid to her. And I think there's only so many times a person can try to reinvent themselves before the make believe catches up with them. That's the best way I can describe it. I guess you might call it compulsive lying. But I prefer not to think of it that way.'

Michael suddenly remembered something. 'She gave me a photo of the baby…'

Paul nodded. 'She found some photos in the back of one of the old books in my study. I knew she had them, but they seemed to make her happy so I turned a blind eye. I probably should have said something, but I don't really know how to handle it.'

'You must have realised she was making that bedroom in your house,' Michael said, 'putting beds in it for children she never had. It can't be healthy—'

'She did it when I was away with work for a week, so when I came home it was all there. It wasn't long after we got married and everything that happened with you was very raw to her. I guess it's like she's grieving. I don't really understand it but I can't stop her because she'll think I'm against her and she'll stop trusting me.'

Michael didn't know what to say, and his mind turned again to the picture of "Scarlett". 'So the photo is just some random baby.'

'I'm sorry, Michael. I really am,' Paul said. 'But half the time Tamsin doesn't know what she's saying. She keeps getting worse. I'm not sure she knows fact from fiction any more.' He stood up unsteadily. 'I'd better get back to her. But Michael, please, I understand you're worried about her, but having you around is only making it worse. Please try to understand.'

Reluctantly, Michael nodded.

…

After Paul left they went upstairs and Sadie sat on the bed and started to cry. 'I hate this,' she said. 'It's all so *horrible.*'

'What do you think of him? Of what he said?'

Sadie shook her head. 'I think Tamsin is putting a huge amount of pressure on him. It must be so hard trying to be there for someone who accuses you of things and who makes things up—'

Suddenly, she gasped and her hand flew to her stomach.

'What is it?' Michael said, 'what's wrong? Are you—'

She gasped again and Michael noticed a large wet patch spreading out across the duvet under her body. She followed his gaze and cried out. 'No!' she said, 'no, not right now! The baby, it can't come now! It's supposed to be another few weeks yet, I'm not ready... Michael...'

Michael put his arms around her, though he was scared too. 'Don't worry,' he said, 'don't worry about any of it, Sadie. I'm here.'

PART THREE

Forty-Two

Tamsin waited anxiously for Paul to get home from Michael and Sadie's house and by the time he did it was late. She jumped at the sound of the car outside. When he came into the sitting room, she searched his face but she couldn't read his expression.

'Well,' he said, 'I've told him the truth.'

Tamsin nodded. She didn't feel anything, just numb. 'About Bella too?' she asked, her voice almost a whisper.

Paul sat down beside her. 'I had to,' he said. 'He asked who she was.'

'What did he say?'

'Not very much.'

She fell silent, and Paul took her hand. 'This is what happens,' he said. 'It would be so much simpler if you'd told him the truth.'

Suddenly, she did feel some emotion. It was sharp, dangerous. 'Why don't I tell him the truth about *everything,* Paul? You complain about the lies, but sometimes they suit you just fine. Like me lying about how I met you. *That* certainly suits you, doesn't it?'

Paul gave her hand a squeeze. 'You're confused,' he said, 'Tam, listen to me. About Madeline—'

'Madeline, Madeline,' she said, 'what are you going to say now? Are you going to have another go at me? Tell me again that I'm imagining things?'

He gave her a long look. 'No,' he said, 'I'm not going to say anything. There's no point, is there?'

'You obviously want to. Why don't you just spit it out?'

'No,' he said. 'I don't think you really hear me any more.'

The next morning Madeline slept late and Tamsin woke when Paul brought her a tray of breakfast and coffee which he placed on the bed in front of her.

'What have I done to deserve this?' she asked as she pulled the tray onto her lap.

Paul got back into bed. 'Nothing,' he said. 'I just want you to be okay. I—' To her astonishment his voice cracked, and she stared at him. 'Paul?'

'I don't...' he said.

'Paul, what is it?' she asked, 'what's wrong with you?'

'I don't want you to be ill!'

Tamsin frowned down at the food in front of her. She picked up a croissant and took a bite out of it, while at her side Paul let out a couple more sobs and then seemed to get control of himself.

'I'm not ill,' she said. She pointed the croissant at him. 'I know my own mind.'

'You were okay. Before we had the baby.'

'Or,' she said, '*or,* perhaps now I've had the baby I'm seeing more clearly. And perhaps you don't like it.' She peered at him closely. 'Anyway, if you really thought I was sick, you'd make me see a doctor. Yet you seem very reluctant for me to go.'

'I don't want to put you through that.'

'But you want to drag me through adoption proceedings?'

'I'm trying to do what's best for our family.'

'Are you?' Tamsin said quietly. She pulled off a piece of croissant and popped it in her mouth. 'I wonder,' she said. '*I* think you're very selective about who you want me to talk to. *I* think you're worried that if I get sat down in front of somebody who decides to scratch beneath the surface, all sorts of secrets are going to come tumbling out.'

'What?' he said, 'what secrets?'

Tamsin blinked, and suddenly felt very confused. What had she been talking about? 'I...' she said, 'I don't know, Paul...'

He kissed her gently. 'Just eat your breakfast, Tam. And get some rest. We can talk about this again another time.'

He got out of bed, and left her on her own. She had a strange feeling inside her body – it was uncomfortable, like she'd been put together all wrong, and reality seemed to fade out until it seemed as though she was in a bubble and nothing happening around her could be trusted. She shook herself and the feeling dropped away. Then she stuffed the last of the croissant into her mouth.

Forty-Three

It was a couple of days after Paul's visit that Michael heard from Tamsin again. He was in hospital with Sadie, and, with their baby girl Rose not even a day old and fast asleep in her cot, he rejected the call as soon as he saw Tamsin's name. It was obvious that Tamsin had had her struggles over the years and he had some sympathy for her, but he couldn't face any more of her half-truths right now.

'Who was it?' Sadie asked sleepily. 'Was it your parents?'

'No.' Michael stroked Sadie's hair. 'It's nothing. You just rest.'

She narrowed her eyes. 'It's not *her,* is it?' She must have seen the look on his face, because she sat up in bed and said, 'Michael, no. Not now.'

He put his phone away. 'I don't want to talk to her,' he said, 'I'm sick of it all. I really am.'

Throughout the day she phoned a few more times, until finally in the late afternoon when Sadie and Rose were both sleeping soundly he slipped out into the corridor and answered her call.

'What?' he said, his voice sharp. 'What do you want?'

'Michael,' she said. He thought her voice was unusually reserved. 'Don't be angry. Paul said he told you about Scarlett.'

'I'm not angry,' he said. 'I'm just not in the mood for talking right now.'

'I just wanted…'

'Tamsin, I'm not sure I want to hear it.' He looked through a window into the ward, and he could just about see Rose in her cot next to Sadie through a gap in the curtains around her bed. He thought back to the photograph Tamsin had given him of a stranger's newborn baby, and felt a pain in his chest. 'I really *felt* something,' he told her. 'Thinking there was some little girl out there who was my flesh and blood. Even if I never met her, I felt *different*, in myself, knowing that. Having that weird room in your house is one thing. By lying to *me* about *my* child—'

'I didn't… I wasn't…'

'Don't,' he said, 'just don't.' She didn't reply, so he said, 'Do you know where I am today?'

'No,' she said. 'I guess somewhere you don't like, since you're in such a bad mood.'

'I'm at the hospital,' he said. He turned away from the window, and stood back against the wall to allow some people to walk past. 'Mine and Sadie's daughter was born yesterday,' he told her. 'So now I have a *real* daughter, and my own life.'

'Great,' she said, '*congratulations.*'

He didn't reply.

'You're not even going to let me explain?' she said.

'I just told you where I am. I'm with my wife and newborn baby. I don't want to talk to you right now. In fact...' he took a deep breath. 'I'm not trying to be unkind, but I think you should focus on your own family—'

'Instead of bothering you, you mean?'

'Well, yeah.'

'Okay,' she said, 'okay, Michael. Fine. You don't want any answers, I won't give you any answers—'

'Goodbye, Tamsin,' he said firmly, cutting her off. She'd just begun to speak again, but he ended the call. He turned around to go back inside the ward and was startled when he saw Sadie standing in the doorway. He could see from her face she'd heard what he'd said and she gave him a small nod and a little smile. 'You've done the right thing,' she said. 'Let's hope that's the end of it now.'

'The lies,' he said, 'I just can't get over it. How can someone *lie* like that?'

'Well,' Sadie said, 'maybe it's like Paul said – she just does it without thinking, without even being aware that she's lying.'

'You know the worst thing?'

'What's that?'

'I'm still worrying about her. Even now.'

A brief flash of irritation crossed Sadie's face, and he put his arm around her. 'I'm still worried,' he said, 'but it's not important. Her crap isn't important to me any more. You and Rose, you're the only ones who matter now.'

...

For the next week, he really did forget about Tamsin as all his attention was focused on Sadie and Rose. It seemed like their every waking moment was dominated by the new baby and he barely had time to gather his thoughts, let alone dwell on anything Tamsin had said or done. But when he went back to work he found that his mind kept wandering back to Tamsin again and to the couple of years they were together. Had *everything* been a lie? If she was prepared to lie about the baby, to make up an entire new persona in Rae Carrington, perhaps nothing she had ever said to him had been true. He found himself thinking of the picture of the young girl, Kitten, that he'd seen at the youth centre, and of the words Pattie had said when she remembered her – how she'd said that the other kids found Kitten odd, that they said she always *made things up.* And he thought about what Tamsin had said about how she met Paul. And about the story of her having sex with one of Paul's friends – such an unpleasant story that he couldn't think why she'd want to fill her head with made-up tales about things like that.

He rubbed his face with his hands and tried to refocus on something else. He wanted to forget about all of it – why was he unable to? In the end he managed to resist calling her while he was at work, but late in the evening when Sadie and Rose were both asleep he crept downstairs and phoned her.

She answered surprisingly quickly, but Michael felt so awkward he couldn't speak to begin with, and when he finally managed to open his mouth he ended up starting the conversation by saying, 'Are you alone?'

Tamsin laughed. 'Am I alone?' she said. 'What sort of question is that? What are you going to ask next, what I'm wearing?'

'No! Sorry, I just meant—'

'We can have that kind of conversation if you want to, Michael,' she said lightly. 'I'm quite good at it actually. When Paul goes away—'

'I just meant is Paul with you?'

'No,' she said, 'I'm in my studio in the garden.'

'In the dark?'

'What is this?' she asked. 'It has lights, Michael.'

'Yes,' Michael said, 'no, I mean... this is coming out all wrong.'

'I would say so. I certainly have no idea what you're talking about.'

Michael took a deep breath. He wasn't even sure what he was trying to say.

'So,' she said, 'you're not done with me then?'

'What?'

'You said you have a real daughter now, and you don't want to talk to me any more.'

'Sadie had just given birth and I hadn't slept all night. I wasn't really thinking straight.'

There was a pause. 'You're an odd little man, you know, Michael.'

'Can I see you?' he found himself asking, 'I just want to

understand.'

'Talk about blowing hot and cold,' she said. 'One minute you want us to talk, the next you don't. You can't pick me up and drop me on a whim. Perhaps *I* am done with *you* now.'

'Are you?'

She laughed. 'What's the point in you talking to me? You say you want to understand, but surely you can't believe a word that comes out of my mouth now, can you? Paul's told you I'm a liar. And some sort of juvenile delinquent, getting pregnant so young.'

'Don't say that. It doesn't make me think any less of you. If anything...'

'What?'

'Well, if anything I think more of you,' he said. He felt a bit embarrassed, but it was true all the same.

'Why?' she said.

'Because I can't imagine how scary it must have been to find out you were pregnant when you were so young. But you got through it.'

'I don't get scared,' she said. 'And getting through stuff isn't brave. Getting through things is just taking all the shit that gets thrown at you and keeping your mouth shut.'

'Tamsin—'

'Fine,' she said. 'If you want to see me I'll come by the shop. When I feel like it.'

'No, let's—'

'See you then.'

Forty-Four

Michael was busy with a customer when Tamsin decided to visit the shop, and he watched as she sat down on one of the sofas with Madeline in her pushchair by her side. She looked as well dressed as ever, in tight grey jeans with a white blouse tucked into them and a floral silk scarf around her neck. He saw her check her appearance in a little silver mirror, but mostly she sat still and silent, with just the occasional word or two to Madeline.

Eventually he was free, and he went and sat beside her. 'I was about to nip out for some lunch,' he said. 'Come with me, if you want.'

She raised an eyebrow. 'Lunch,' she said sarcastically.

'Well, what did you want to do?'

She shifted her body on the sofa, so that she was sitting closer to him. Uncomfortably close.

'Tamsin, what are you doing? I just want to talk—'

'Really?' she said. 'Are you sure you don't just want to fuck? Because I'm not stupid. All this wanting to see me one minute then telling me to leave you alone the next. Getting cross with me, when really you're angry with yourself.'

She didn't lower her voice to say any of it, and a couple who had just come through the door looked round at them. Tamsin laughed, and Michael glared at her.

'Oh, come on,' she said, 'lighten up.'

'I'm going to get something to eat,' he told her. 'Come with me if you want, or don't, but I don't have time to just sit here.'

She uncurled herself from the sofa and followed him out onto the street, pushing Madeline along in front of her in the push-chair.

'Sorry,' she said insincerely, when they'd been walking for a couple of minutes. 'I didn't mean to *embarrass* you.'

'I'm not embarrassed.'

'You were, though. You know, when I was first with Paul I had a job, for a little while. But then I got fired. They said that things I said and did were *inappropriately sexual.*' She said the last two words with relish. Michael ignored her and they went to the bakery he'd visited with her last time she'd turned up. He bought himself a sandwich, but Tamsin said she didn't want anything. When he looked at her more closely, he thought that perhaps his initial assessment of her had been wrong. She may be as smartly dressed as ever, but she didn't look quite herself. She looked tired and drawn. In fact, she didn't even look very well. Her eyes were dull, and slightly red around the edges, though she'd tried to disguise it with make-up.

'Tamsin,' he said, 'are you all right?'

'What?' she said. 'Yes. Of course I am.'

They found a bench in the middle of the busy high street, and sat down together. Tamsin put the pushchair in front of them, and Madeline turned her head and gave Michael a tentative smile. 'Hello,' he said to her, 'how are you today?'

'She's teething,' Tamsin said.

'Oh.'

He ate in silence for a while, then she said, 'So Sadie's had the baby now.'

'Yeah.'

'She's beaten me in every respect then.'

'What do you mean?'

'I mean you chose her. You think she's better than me. And now you know we don't even have a daughter together.'

'That's surely not why you told me we did have a baby – so that you could be equal with Sadie, or something.'

'No,' she said.

'Tamsin, why *did* you tell me she'd been adopted?'

'Because I'm a liar, aren't I?' she spat. 'A *compulsive* liar. I'm sure that's what Paul said to you.'

'And is he right?' he shot straight back at her.

She didn't reply straight away. And when she spoke, her words took him by surprise. 'Why do you think I turned myself into Rae Carrington?' she said. 'Do you think I did it on a whim? Do you think I said it on the spur of the moment because I just couldn't help myself?'

'I don't know. I don't know why you do anything. I thought I knew you, but all I knew was someone who didn't exist.' He looked at her but she wouldn't meet his eye. She didn't even seem to be listening. 'How can you do it?' he asked her. 'Making up other lives. Other personas. Don't you feel like nothing is real? Doesn't it get difficult to keep track of it—'

'When I was Kitten,' Tamsin said, cutting him off, 'I didn't have a future. I pretended I did, but I didn't.'

'Why not?' Michael asked gently. He was so surprised that she was willing to say anything about her past that the last thing he wanted to do was spook her and make her go silent again. He watched as she smiled a little, but then her voice was hard. 'When I was fifteen I sat down one day, and I made a list.'

She paused, and Michael waited patiently for her to carry on.

'I listed all my ways out. Everything. Right from suicide up to winning the lottery.'

Madeline coughed a couple of times and Tamsin rolled the pushchair back and forth to calm her. 'I had all sorts on there,' she continued. 'Running away. Marrying a rich man, selling my organs...' She laughed. 'Can you even really do that?'

'I don't know.'

'Well, anyway. Most of those options, they make no sense. I didn't want to die, because the way my life was was other people's fault, not mine. I wasn't about to punish myself for that. I couldn't rely on luck, like winning the lottery, because that was just another kind of helplessness.'

'So,' he said, 'what did you decide was the way out?'

'It was simple,' she said, 'I had to make myself successful. I had to get myself a career. Not a job. A career. I know that sounds idealistic. Silly. Naive, even.'

'No,' he said, 'it doesn't. But I don't understand why you couldn't do that as Kitten.'

'Because Kitten was just a little skank!' Tamsin exploded. 'All she did was go around begging for attention like a *dog*! She used to go to parties and end up... and end up...'

Michael watched as her face changed. It was like she'd forgotten what she was talking about. 'Tamsin?'

She shook her head. 'It wasn't that hard for me to start doing well. I found I could soak up information. I asked teachers for extra help. I stopped thinking of myself as Kitten, and started thinking of myself as Rae.'

'Tamsin, it's incredible you managed to have that much clarity and willpower, at that age.'

'You think so?'

'When I was a teenager I had no motivation to do anything until I was nagged to.'

She shrugged. 'I'd always remembered the Carringtons, from when I was at the youth club and I met them. I thought their life seemed perfect. They told me about their sons. I've always fancied having a brother.' She was distant again for a second. 'I did a bit more research on them,' she continued. 'Before I started university I had to be completely convincing. I wanted to change everything about who I was. I wanted a completely new back story, a new family, a new everything.'

'I just don't understand why you did it,' he said. 'A name change is one thing, but why try to rewrite the past? It makes me feel like none of it was genuine – you and me. I really loved you. But not... *you*. Rae. I really loved Rae.'

'Rae was real,' she said. 'I *was* Rae. It wasn't a game to me.'

She fell into silence, and then reached forward and fussed with Madeline's clothes, checking whether she was too warm or too cool. Michael found himself thinking over what Paul had said about her home life when she was growing up, but he didn't know how to ask anything about that, so he didn't. Instead he said, 'Who – if you don't mind me asking – who was the baby's dad? When you were thirteen, I mean. Was it a boy from your school—'

Tamsin whipped round to face him. 'That's all anyone ever wants to know!' she shouted.

'I'm sorry—'

'Why do you feel you have to ask? What interest could it possibly be to you?'

'I just... it's none of my business,' he said finally. 'I'm sorry, I shouldn't have asked.'

All of a sudden her mood changed completely. She smiled at him. 'Good,' she said. She tapped the side of her nose. 'Because it's a *secret.*'

Forty-Five

The next day Sally arrived at the house to discover Tamsin sat on the landing wrapped in a towel, her wet hair hanging over her shoulders, apparently deep in thought.

'Oh,' Sally said, 'sorry, Tamsin, I didn't realise you were up here.'

'Why would a man not want his own baby?' Tamsin said.

Sally frowned. 'Are you talking about Michael?'

'Michael?'

'Sorry... who are you talking about?'

'Paul.'

Sally sat down on the window seat. She wished Tamsin was dressed, but it wasn't that unusual for her to be wandering around in underwear or nightwear or to have just got out of the shower, and Sally tried to be as unembarrassed about it as Tamsin apparently was.

'Paul loves that little girl,' Sally said, 'he loves you both very much.'

'He never even wanted her.'

Sally watched as Tamsin pulled the towel more closely around herself. She tried to think what to say.

'I'm right in thinking Madeline wasn't planned?' she said.

'No,' Tamsin said quietly.

'Change is difficult for anybody at any time in their life,' Sally said, 'and changes don't come much bigger than a baby.'

Tamsin was looking down at the floor, but Sally was sure she was listening so she carried on. 'The thing with Paul, I suppose he's got very used to being able to do things the way he wants to.'

'Wouldn't it be nice to do something different?'

'It might just take him some time to get used to it. But I can see how much he cares about you. *And* Madeline, even if he's finding it a tough adjustment.'

In the nursery down the hall Sally heard Madeline start to cry, but Tamsin didn't react. 'No,' Tamsin said, 'it's not just that. He says all these reasons. He says it's because he doesn't like our life being ruled by a baby, that he doesn't want our life to be like this, but I don't believe him. There's something else.'

'I'm sorry, Tamsin, I'm afraid I don't really know what you're talking about.'

'Paul! He's trying to get me away from her.' She stood up and pointed her finger at Sally. 'He's trying to separate me from my daughter and I've got to figure out why, but I'm too *stupid* to think of it—' Tamsin clenched her fists and made a noise of frustration. 'Why are you on his side?' she said. 'Has he told you to try to reason with me?'

'Of course not,' Sally said. 'Look, I'll make you some coffee while you see what Madeline wants.'

'She wants a mum who can keep her safe!' Tamsin said. 'Because she's in danger. I know I'm missing something. She's not safe here. Paul won't let her be safe here.'

Sally started towards the stairs. She'd rarely seen Tamsin this agitated, and instead of continuing to talk to her, she decided she'd slip quietly into the kitchen and phone Paul.

...

When he arrived home, Tamsin still hadn't got dressed. She was clutching Madeline in her arms and the little girl was screaming but Tamsin didn't seem to know what to do.

'Don't take her!' she shouted when Paul and Sally approached her.

'Give me Madeline, please,' Paul said. He held his arms out for her and Tamsin drew back.

'It's not me,' she said, 'you're trying to make me think it was me... all these things that have happened, but it's not. I'm going to work it out. I *will* work it out!'

Tamsin looked between the two of them with her eyes wide and wild. Then she deposited the baby in Sally's arms and disappeared into the room with the little wooden heart on the door.

As Sally carried Madeline downstairs she turned to Paul, who was following her quietly. 'Has she seen a doctor yet?' she asked. 'I'm worried about her.'

'She's just having a difficult day.'

'Paul, that's not...' Sally lowered her voice right down, 'it's not *normal*—'

'Tamsin's never been normal.'

In the kitchen, Paul heated up a jar of baby food for Madeline while Sally sat her in her high chair. She didn't want to overstep the mark, but she'd found Tamsin's behaviour disturbing enough that she felt she couldn't leave it.

'You're not alone,' she said. 'My daughter-in-law knew of someone who had—'

148

'Who had *what?*' Paul snapped before she could finish.

'She thought people were trying to hurt her baby and she wouldn't let anyone else near him. I think she's okay now, though. A lot better than she was, anyway.'

'There's nothing wrong with Tamsin,' Paul said, 'apart from the fact she's trying to look after a baby when she's like a child herself. You've been here long enough that you know what I'm talking about.'

'She thinks you're trying to hurt Madeline. She says that Madeline is in danger and she can't keep her safe.'

Sally watched as Paul spooned the warmed baby food into a bowl. His back was rigid, but then to her astonishment his shoulders started to shake.

She rushed over to him, and put her hand on his back. 'Paul, there's a lot of help out there nowadays for mums like Tamsin, the two of you don't have to struggle like this—'

Paul wiped his eyes with his hand and seemed instantly composed again. 'Sally,' he said, 'you've been a huge help to Tamsin and me, you know that. And the things you've put up with from her over the years...'

Sally knew what was coming before he said it.

'I'll pay you for the full month,' he said, 'but I don't think we need a housekeeper any more. I'm sorry. Today is your last day.'

Forty-Six

'You *sacked* Sally?' Tamsin said in amazement.

Paul sat down beside her on the bed that said "Bella" above it. He was holding Madeline against him, and Tamsin reached out for the baby but he didn't hand her over.

'I had no choice,' he said.

Tamsin frowned as a memory flitted through her mind but before she could grasp it, it had slipped away. Nevertheless she found herself saying, 'You don't like people asking questions.'

'I don't like people asking *you* questions.'

'Why not?'

He looked at her like she was stupid. 'Because I never know what the fuck you're going to say, do I? You told Michael you had his baby! You told him I'm not Madeline's dad. You say all this ridiculous nonsense about Madeline—' he stopped himself. 'But I don't want to get into all that.'

Tamsin eyed him suspiciously. 'They'd ask me questions if we said we wanted her adopted. Lots of questions.'

'I'd figure something out.'

She reached out for Madeline again. 'Give her to me, Paul.'

'No.'

'Give her to me!'

'Fine,' he said as he thrust the baby into her arms. 'In fact, you'd better get used to having a whole lot of her.'

'What are you talking about?'

'I'm going to be spending less time here.'

Cold dread started to spread through Tamsin's body. 'What are you talking about?'

'I'm not happy, Tamsin. I've tried, but I don't see why I should try any more. I told you I didn't want children, and you got pregnant—'

'By accident! I got confused with my pills—'

'But you went through with the pregnancy, when I couldn't have made it any clearer how much I didn't want you to. And now you won't consider adoption, and I don't want to be miserable the rest of my life.'

'So you're leaving me?' Tamsin said. She stood up. 'You're just fucking off, are you?'

He didn't answer.

'Well, go on then!' she shouted. 'If you want to go then go. Don't let me keep you!'

150

Paul still didn't move or speak, and she began to feel silly. She sat down on the other bed, opposite him.

'Tamsin, I've loved you from the second I laid eyes on you. Every day since we met my whole life has been about you. The last thing in the world that I want is for us to be apart.'

'Then why can't you stay? I don't understand why we can't be a family.'

'We just can't.'

'But why? She's only a baby—'

'No,' he said. 'She's like a cancer. I cannot be around her.'

'But why not? Paul, I don't understand! Why do you hate her? What's wrong with her?'

He looked guarded all of a sudden, and she latched on to it. 'Paul?' she said, 'is she ill? Is something not right with her? No, I would have known. I would have realised.'

'Tamsin, I don't *hate* Madeline. And there's nothing wrong with her. But for the sake of our marriage, and our happiness, and for Madeline's sake too, please, *please* do as I ask. Have her adopted.'

'And if I don't then you'll leave?'

He looked straight at her. 'Yes,' he said, 'eventually. For the moment I'm just going to reduce the amount of time I spend here. By at least half.'

He got up to go and Tamsin rushed after him. 'No!' she said. She found herself consumed with blind panic. 'I don't like being on my own! Paul, stop, stop it!' She held Madeline to her with one arm and with the other she grabbed Paul. 'You can't do this to me. If you do this I....' Some words suddenly popped into her head. 'I'll tell!' she said.

He looked her up and down. 'You'll tell what?' he said.

As quickly as the words had appeared in her mind, it was as though a curtain fell and she no longer knew what she had been talking about. 'I... I don't know...'

'Goodbye, Tamsin.'

Forty-Seven

Once he'd had a bit of time to mull over his conversations with Tamsin, Michael found himself becoming more worried rather than less, and he kept wondering what he should do. He considered talking to Sadie about it, but when he was at home with her they were both busy looking after Rose and he felt she had enough on her plate. Eventually he hit upon an idea: that instead of trying to talk to Tamsin again, which never got him very far, he could go to Frinchford-on-Sea and attempt to get more information from Star, or Pattie.

He knew the trip would take him at least one whole day and possibly overnight too, and he didn't want to tell Sadie where he was going and worry her, so he came up with a convenient story.

'A funeral?' she said.

Michael nodded, though his insides twisted with guilt. They'd gone out for the afternoon, and Rose was fast asleep in her pram while they sat together on a bench, shaded from the early autumn sun by a huge horse-chestnut tree.

'Yeah, it's an old school friend—'

'Not Tim, or Chris…' she said, her face filling with horror.

'No,' he said, 'it's not someone you've met. We weren't very close, or anything. But I feel like I should be there.'

'Do you want me to come?' she asked.

'No. You stay here with Rose. I'll be fine.'

'I'm sure I can ask my mum to look after Rose. Funerals are difficult, and they must be especially troubling when it's someone your own age. I'm happy to support you.'

He smiled at her and he started to feel sick. She was so kind, and he hated lying, but he knew she wouldn't understand about Tamsin.

'Really,' he said, 'it's fine. It's a long drive – I'll try to leave first thing in the morning and come back the same day, but it might be late when I get home. There's no point in dragging you along as well; I'd rather think of you at home with Rose.' He put his arm around her and she rested her head on his shoulder.

'It makes you think, doesn't it,' she said.

He looked down at her and saw her eyes were closed.

'Hm?' he said.

'For someone to die so young. Do you know what he died from?'

'Oh…' Michael said, quickly grabbing for an answer, 'no.

Not precisely. He'd been ill for a few years, I think.'

Sadie snuggled closer to him. 'I don't ever want to lose you, Michael,' she said.

...

A couple of days later, Michael set off. He wasn't sure what Star or Pattie would be able to tell him, but since he stood little chance of getting straight answers out of Tamsin, he felt he had no choice but to try.

He arrived at Star's house not long after midday, and she took so long to answer the door that he thought she wasn't home. When it eventually opened, she was dressed in a furry purple dressing-gown, her hair wrapped in a towel, and he felt that the fact he'd disturbed her in the middle of a bath or a shower was a bad start to what was already likely to be a difficult meeting.

'I don't believe this,' she said when she saw him. 'I told you to leave me alone! Are you soft in the head or something?'

'I'm sorry to come and disturb you again, I just—'

'You just what? You've spoken to Kitten now, haven't you? Because I *did* pass your messages on.' She narrowed her eyes. 'Against my better judgement.'

'Could we talk inside?' he asked.

She recoiled slightly, as if the question had shocked her. '*No,*' she said. 'I'm not even dressed.'

'It's just not the sort of conversation I want to have in the street,' he said. 'It's about Tamsin... Kitten—'

'Well, who else would it be about?'

'Um... yeah, I mean, it's about her past...'

'Her past, huh?'

'Yeah.'

'And it's not a conversation we should have in the street?'

'Not really.'

'Maybe it's not the sort of conversation we should be having at all then,' she said. She started to close the door, and in his desperation Michael put his foot in the way.

'Move,' she said. 'Move, or I'll call the police.'

'Please!' Michael said. 'Why are you so desperate not to talk to me? I'm not a bad person! I'm worried sick about Tamsin... uh... Kitten. She comes out with all this stuff and I can't make any sense of it...'

Star stopped trying to close the door and smiled. 'Kitten's famous lies. She was known for it. Especially when she was a teenager—'

'Around the time she got pregnant?'

'Oh, so you know about that, do you?'

'She's acting very shifty about it.'

'What's that got to do with anything now? It was getting on for twenty years ago.'

'I don't know. Probably nothing. But I was wondering about Paul, too. You were at their wedding, weren't you?'

Star sighed. 'All right. I'll tell you what, *Michael,* I'm going to go and get dressed. You can wait out here. Then we can talk, but God knows what good you think it will do you.'

Forty-Eight

Michael thought that once she went back inside Star possibly wouldn't open the door to him again, so he was relieved when five minutes later she returned, dressed in trousers and a pale blue polo shirt that had "Pebbles Leisure Centre" embroidered on it.

'I've got work in an hour,' she said, 'so I don't have long.'

She showed him through to a small living room with lots of kids' toys scattered around. He moved a well-worn teddy bear out of the way and sat down on the sofa.

'So, what do you want to know?' Star said.

Michael wondered where to start. 'Well,' he said, 'Tamsin seems to think that someone's trying to make her give up her baby, Madeline. Or to stop her loving her, or something.'

Star didn't reply, just watched him in silence.

'She's said some odd things to me,' Michael continued. 'She told me she had *my* baby adopted, when really—'

'—she got rid,' Star said, 'like she did when she was thirteen.'

'Do you know if that's really what she wanted? When she was thirteen. Nobody *pushed* her to get rid of her baby?'

'What makes you ask that?'

'She...' Michael paused, not sure whether Tamsin would appreciate him talking about the room. 'She has a room in her house for the two children. Mine, and the one from when she was a teenager.'

He expected some reaction, but Star didn't seem at all shocked.

'You don't think that's odd?'

Star shrugged. 'Nothing Kitten does surprises me,' she said. 'And in answer to your question, I don't know if anyone pushed her because I didn't live with her then. But I can't imagine anyone pushing Kitten to do anything she doesn't want to.'

'So, you don't know—'

'Michael, there's nothing I can tell you. When she got pregnant I had no contact with her. I lived with her and my mum again when I was sixteen, so it was a year or so after all the stuff with the pregnancy. It was non-stop with her. Drama, drama, drama. She'd get so drunk she'd end up in hospital, then she'd get in a fight, or she'd have another pregnancy scare. She was *always* the centre of attention. And if nothing had actually happened, then she'd make something up.'

'She told me that she decided to change all of that and focus

155

on her exams…'

'I was gone again by then.'

'When I asked her who the baby's dad was, she just said it was "a secret."'

Star got up from the sofa and started to tidy some of the toys away into a corner. 'It's true that no one ever got a name out of her,' she said. She turned to look at Michael. 'I asked her myself, and she just said it was "a boy". That's all she ever said to anyone, as far as I can tell. Well, apart from you. But she probably told you it was a secret to wind you up.'

…

Michael watched as Star finished tidying the toys away, then she sat back on the sofa. His mouth felt dry and he wished she would offer him a drink, but that wasn't very likely. He wasn't getting anywhere with asking about Tamsin's past, so he decided to try another topic.

'What about Paul?' he asked. 'Do you know anything about him?'

'I know he has a big house, a flash car, and plenty of cash,' Star said, 'because Kitten fell over herself to tell me about it.'

'What about their wedding? Was it a big day?'

'Small. Weird, I thought. But I guess it's his second marriage and he's old enough to be her dad… her *grandad,* even, so—'

'Weird how?' Michael asked, cutting her off.

'It just seemed kind of sad. There were a couple of other men Paul's age there – friends of his, I guess, or people he knew from his work – whatever it is he does. Then there was me and Jamie. Kitten did have a couple of guests – colleagues from the fancy department store where she worked. She was being really over-friendly with them. They seemed like they wanted to leave. But that's how Kitten is.'

'What do you mean?'

'You dated her, so you should know.'

'Know what?'

'That she's an attention whore.'

She looked at his face and laughed. 'Don't pretend you don't know what I'm talking about. Loud. Dramatic. Over-the-top, always flirting, pretending to be *posh,* exaggerating, talking about sex every five minutes like she's the only one who ever gets any. She even did it at her wedding, making these jokes about what her and Paul got up to, getting so drunk he had to scoop her up off the floor by the end of the night. I don't like him much but I felt sorry for him having Kitten make such a show of herself like that. But I guess the benefits he gets from their marriage make it worth it for him. It's certainly worth it for her. Kitten always lands on her feet. I'm not sure she's ever *really* worked a day in her life, not the kind of work you do standing up, anyway.'

Michael felt a rush of anger. 'She's your sister!'

'Do you want me to be honest with you?'

'I'm not sure.'

'My guess is that Kitten is deliberately worrying you, while she sits back and gets a big kick out of watching you squirm.'

'No,' Michael said, though he felt uncertain. 'She wouldn't...'

'She would.' She nodded at his hand. 'You're married,' she said. 'I bet Kitten doesn't like that. If I know anything about it she'll make you run round after her, fluttering her eyelashes one minute and then dropping hints about some terrible secret the next, until your marriage has gone down the drain and then she'll turn round and spit you back out again.'

Michael stared down at the ring around his finger. What *was* he doing here? Was Star right, was he just running around chasing scraps Tamsin was throwing to him for no reason other than her own amusement? She'd never really *asked* him for help, after all.

'I think I'd better go,' he said. 'Thanks for talking to me, Star.'

'Just do me a favour and don't come back here again, yeah? Talking about Kitten gives me a migraine.'

Forty-Nine

Michael sat in his car for a while, thinking over the conversation he'd just had with Star. Then he started the engine and drove to the youth club. He wasn't sure any more what he was trying to achieve, but since he had driven all this way he thought he may as well see Pattie.

When he arrived, the building was all closed up, so he turned the radio on and sat with his eyes closed in his car until he heard someone pull up beside him. He quickly opened his eyes, and when he looked round he saw Pattie eyeing him curiously from the parking space beside his.

When they'd both got out of their cars, she frowned at him as though she was trying to remember where she'd seen him before.

'I'm Michael,' he said. 'I came here with my wife, months ago now. I—'

'I remember,' she said, 'you were asking about your ex-girlfriend.' She opened the boot of her car and took out a couple of shopping bags. Michael noticed that her hair – which had been dark purple the first time he'd met her – was now bright red and short and spiky.

'Let me help you with the bags,' he said, when he saw there were a few more in the car. She looked like she was about to refuse, but then she shrugged. 'Sure.'

He followed her into the building and as they placed the bags in the kitchen she said, 'Did you find her? Your ex-girlfriend?'

'Yes.'

'Good,' she said, 'that's good.' At that moment he heard someone else come into the building and a voice called out, 'Hi, Pattie.'

'That's one of our volunteers,' she said. 'Give me a minute.'

Michael waited awkwardly in the kitchen while Pattie went into the hall and he heard their muffled voices. Then Pattie popped her head round the door. 'Michael, I don't have very long,' she said, 'but we can talk in the office for a minute if you want. I'm not sure there's much more I can tell you, though, if that was what you were hoping for.'

...

To begin with Michael thought she was right. Pattie was talkative but their conversation didn't go anywhere useful until he said,

'Did you know that Kitten got pregnant when she was thirteen?'

A shadow fell over Pattie's face. 'No,' she said, 'I didn't know that.' She thought for a moment, then shook her head. 'It must have happened just after she stopped coming here. Poor little thing. It must have scared the living daylights out of her when she realised.'

'No one seems to know who the baby's dad was.'

She gave him a funny look. 'Michael, do you mind if I ask why you and Kitten... Tamsin... broke up?'

'Rae,' Michael said, 'she was called Rae then.'

'Rae. Why did you and Rae—'

'I cheated on her.'

Pattie nodded and sat back in her chair. 'That's an honest answer,' she said.

'Why do you ask?'

'Because I'm wondering why you're trying to find out all of this.'

'I'm really worried about her, she says all these things—'

'Did you find out what happened to your baby?'

'Yes,' he said, 'eventually.'

'Why "eventually?"'

'She wasn't honest with me at first.'

'Michael, do you want my advice?'

'I... yes,' he said, finding that he really did.

'I think you really loved her, didn't you?'

'Yes.'

'And you feel guilty about what you did, even worse once you found out she was pregnant, and now you don't know whether you're coming or going because you can't get any straight answers out of her.'

'That pretty much sums it up.'

'I didn't remember much about Kitten when you first came here. But since then I've thought about it and I do recall that trying to have a sensible conversation with her was like trying to catch water in a sieve. A lot of kids lie to get themselves out of trouble, but the way she lied was like she didn't know she was doing it. It wasn't deliberate, or calculated. It was just who she was.'

'I've heard someone else say something very similar.'

'Who was that?'

'Her husband and her housekeeper.'

Pattie raised an eyebrow.

'Her husband. He's wealthy.'

159

'Michael, does your wife know you're here talking to me about your ex-girlfriend?'

'No.'

'Where does she think you are?'

If it was anyone else, Michael probably wouldn't have answered, but somehow he felt very comfortable with Pattie and he said, 'At a funeral.'

He didn't want to see her expression so he put his face in his hands. 'God, I don't know what I'm doing here.'

'I think you know what you should do, then.'

'I just have this feeling. Like she's trying to tell me something.'

'Perhaps she is,' Pattie said. 'Only you can decide whether to carry on trying to find out. But it strikes me that she's playing with you, a bit? Getting a little revenge on you for cheating, maybe?'

'I've told her how sorry I am. If I'd known she was pregnant I would *never*... I'm not that sort of person.'

'What sort of person? Human? You can't dwell on it. As far as I'm concerned, wasting years of your life feeling miserable about something you can't change is much worse than making a mistake in the first place.'

'Yes,' he said, 'yes, you're right.'

'Go home, Michael. And leave the past in the past.'

Fifty

Tamsin was napping in her studio when her phone rang, and she was surprised to see it was Star.

'What do you want?' she asked, still half asleep.

'Hello to you too,' Star said.

'I was asleep.'

'I had your ex-boyfriend round here again,' Star said, 'poking his nose into your business.'

'What?' Tamsin sat up. It was late afternoon, and she felt hot and thirsty and still a little disoriented from being asleep. Since Paul's ultimatum and his dismissal of Sally, she was restless at night and spent increasing amounts of time in her studio whenever she could.

'You need to call him off, Tamsin.'

Tamsin rubbed her eyes. 'Call him off?' she said. 'He's not a dog.'

'I'm serious,' Star said. 'I did my best to discourage him. I made sure he knows what a little liar you are, that you're doing all this for attention. Just like you always have done.'

'Well,' Tamsin said, 'it's not hard for me to get attention from men.'

There was a short silence, then Star said, 'And what's this about you telling him Paul is trying to make you give up Madeline?'

'He is.'

'Then perhaps you should do what he wants.'

'I don't want to give up my baby.'

'No? Because you didn't think twice about getting rid of the first two, did you? *You* as a *mother!* It's ridiculous, Kitten—'

'Don't call me that.'

Star's voice became hot and angry. 'Do you know how lucky you are to have Paul? Someone supporting you like that, no matter what kind of shit you get yourself involved in? Yet instead of being grateful you start bad-mouthing him, just like you always bad-mouthed mum. You didn't even go to her funeral! You're a selfish little bitch.'

'I'm glad that mum's dead! I would have gone and spat on her grave except she'd been cremated. Paul would have done too.'

Tamsin waited for Star to reply, but there was just silence. Tamsin yawned hugely. She still felt sleepy.

'I wish it was you who was dead,' Star said matter-of-factly.

'You should have gone. Not mum.'

'She didn't even feed me,' Tamsin said, 'hardly ever. I thought I was going to die, once or twice.'

'Don't be so fucking childish! Of course mum *fed* you. You're being ridiculous.'

'You don't know. You weren't there.'

'I'm not listening to this. Just get Michael to stay the hell away from me. I'm sick of getting dragged into your shit. Just stop it. Just *grow up.*'

Tamsin put her phone in her pocket and wandered back towards the house. Madeline was napping in her cot, so Tamsin went into the kitchen and took a half-full bottle of white wine from the fridge. She had no idea whether Paul would come home that day, or the next day, or the next. The days were growing hazy in her mind, with her and Madeline cloistered inside the house without so much as a visitor, while her head filled with vague memories and questions that didn't have answers.

...

Once Madeline was asleep for the night, she sat down on the floor of the studio with the baby monitor by her side and pulled some paper and a pencil towards her. In the middle of the sheet she wrote: "why would he not want his baby?" She drew a big circle around it, and then lines coming out from it with ideas. "He thinks the baby is someone else's?", "he just really doesn't want a baby", "he thinks I can't look after her", "he thinks there's something wrong with her." She circled the last option and wrote, "but what?" Then she sat for a long time staring at what she'd written. *Was* she just being paranoid?

"I'm too stupid to look after a baby," she wrote on the paper. "Stupid. Stupid. Stupid."

She started to cross the words out again and then found that she couldn't stop herself and she scribbled all over the whole sheet. It was useless. Perhaps the most logical explanation really was that she was mad. Maybe even the conversations she thought she'd been having with Paul were a figment of her imagination.

She took out her phone and realised it was late – much later than she thought. She must have sat for a huge amount of time just staring at the paper and thinking, even though it had felt like only a few minutes. When she called Michael he answered quickly, his voice hushed, and she assumed he must be at home with Sadie and the baby.

'He's insisting I have her adopted,' she said straight away.

Michael didn't answer immediately, then he said, 'Tamsin—'

'I'm writing down all the possible reasons.'

Again, there was silence.

'You went to see Star earlier.'

'How do you know?' he asked in surprise.

'She called me and said you've been sniffing around again. She's getting fed up of it.'

'I was worried. But I'm sorry I went behind your back talking about you like that.'

'I don't mind,' she said. 'But Star is biased. You shouldn't believe everything she says.'

'I don't know what to think. I'm not sure I know you at all. I'm not sure I ever did—' He stopped talking suddenly.

'What's wrong?'

'Nothing. I thought I heard...'

'Oh,' she said, 'you thought *Sadie* might have overheard you talking to me.'

'Don't say it like that.'

'Why is Paul so determined to get Madeline out of the house?' she asked him. 'I've been trying to write a list of reasons. He says he just doesn't want a baby, but I don't believe that's all there is to it. He seems...' She tried to think what emotion it was that she saw in him. 'He seems *scared.* He's always seemed scared,' she said, and memories suddenly flooded back. 'Right from the start he was horrified when he found out I was pregnant, and when we went for scans his face was *white.* I'd forgotten about it. Paul isn't someone who gets scared. Why would a baby scare him? It's like he thinks there's something wrong with her. Like she's *evil* or something...'

'You think Paul is trying to get rid of your baby because she's evil?' Michael said.

'No,' she said, her mind racing. 'No. Paul isn't superstitious. He's rational. Logical. Calculated. That's why he does so well in business – he takes calculated risks, he understands... he understands about...' she trailed off as an idea began to form. But it was crazy. *Impossible.* 'Blood,' she muttered to herself. 'I said to him something about how could he not want her. How could he not want her when she's his blood...'

'Tamsin, I don't understand.'

'It seemed to make him angry. He said, who gives a fuck about *blood*? Who gives a fuck about *blood*...' She dropped the phone as something occurred to her and it clattered to the ground.

She could still hear Michael saying, 'Tamsin? Tamsin, what's wrong? Tamsin?'

"WHO GIVES A FUCK ABOUT BLOOD?" she wrote on the back of the sheet of paper. She drew several circles around it, and with each circle, it was as if she became more sure that the idea that had sprung into her mind was correct. She ended the call to Michael, and tore up the sheet of paper into little pieces. Her hands were shaking, and her skin felt ice cold. But for once, this wasn't just speculation – some wild idea that she'd never be able to convince anyone of. If this was about Paul's relationship to Madeline, it could be proved one way or the other. She looked down at her trembling hands. It was all about blood, she realised. *Everything* was about blood.

Fifty-One

Feeling shaken from his conversation with Tamsin, Michael went downstairs and found Sadie curled up on the sofa in a pair of leggings and a baggy t-shirt, her hair tied back in a scruffy ponytail. She was watching the TV on mute, and when she heard him come in she whispered, 'Ssh, don't disturb her.' He looked closer and saw that Rose was nestled against her, wrapped up in a blanket that made her almost blend in to Sadie's t-shirt. He knelt down beside them both and smiled at Sadie. She smiled back and he felt a rush of relief – they looked very settled, and he was sure it couldn't have been them that he'd heard on the stairs.

'I missed you two today,' he said. He'd only been back about five minutes when Tamsin phoned. He hadn't even had a chance to say hello to Sadie and Rose, and now he felt exhausted.

'How was it?' Sadie asked. 'Was it...' She tried to find the right word. 'I don't know what you say about funerals. Was it a nice service?'

'Yes, I suppose.'

'Were many people from your school there?'

'Quite a few.'

She nodded. 'Rose smiled today,' she said. 'Her first smile. It was a bit of an odd one, but I'm sure that's what it was.'

'I wish I'd been here to see it.'

'Yes,' she said, 'so do I.'

She snuggled closer to Rose, and stroked her hair. 'Emily and Andy have invited us round for lunch on Saturday. Can you come, or will you be too busy at the shop?'

'I can probably come for an hour or so,' he said. 'As long as... I don't really want to get into all the stuff about Rae and the baby—'

'I've already told Emily about it, so I'm sure she'll have told Andy.'

'Right.'

'That's the main thing you're thinking about, is it? Whether you'll have to talk about Rae. You're not interested in seeing their baby, or anything?'

'Of course I am,' he said, though in truth he hadn't really thought about it. 'That goes without saying.'

'It would be nice if you did say it.'

'I've just been to a funeral,' he said, and his insides twisted with shame.

She looked at him, then smiled sympathetically. 'Yeah,' she said, 'yes, I know. I'm sorry, Michael. I'm really tired.'

'Go to bed then. I'll stay with Rose if she's not properly asleep yet.'

'I think she is sleepy,' Sadie said, 'but she cries when I stop cuddling her.'

'I'm sure I can handle it. You go on up.'

'Are you sure?'

'Yes, go.'

Once she'd left, Michael bundled Rose up close to him and kissed her plump round cheek. 'I feel like I'm losing my mind,' he said to her. 'What do you think, baby girl?'

He looked down at her, and to his surprise she managed to move one corner of her mouth upwards into a lopsided little smile.

...

The lunch date with Emily and Andy didn't get off to a particularly great start. Michael was held up at the shop with a customer and arrived late, to find the others already eating. He slipped into the free chair at the table, but he felt as though there was an atmosphere, and he wished he could leave again. Once they'd eaten, Emily wanted to show Sadie something in the nursery upstairs and they disappeared off with the babies in their arms. Michael was left sitting with Andy, like the time almost a year ago when he'd found out Rae had been pregnant.

'I heard about Rae,' Andy said.

Michael nodded.

'At least you know what happened now...'

Michael found he couldn't bear it, so he muttered that he needed to use the bathroom and began to make his way upstairs. He could hear Emily and Sadie's voices, and he walked more quietly, pausing at the top of the stairs.

'So, you haven't *asked* him about it?' Emily said.

'No. I guess I'm scared what he'll say...' To his shock Sadie's voice cracked, and he realised she was crying. 'I felt so *awful* this morning... calling up one of his school friends to ask whether he was really at a funeral earlier this week. God knows what he thought of me.' He heard a sob.

'I can't believe he lied about being at a *funeral*! I never had him down as—'

'And then even when he got back that day,' Sadie continued

166

without waiting for her to finish, 'he was talking to *her* on the phone. Within five minutes of getting in the door! He didn't even say hello to us first, not until he'd made sure *she* was okay.'

Her words were cut off as Rose also began to cry. 'Oh for God's sake!' Sadie said.

Michael quickly scurried towards the bathroom, and once inside he closed the door and leant against it, making an effort to pull himself together. He realised how much he'd allowed himself to get drawn back in to Tamsin's world again. He thought it hadn't been obvious, but Sadie had seen it. He needed to get his head straight. It had been hard not to get caught up in the drama, but he had enough drama going on at home. Now wasn't the time to go asking for any more.

Fifty-Two

'I heard you talking to Emily,' Michael said when they were both back at home in the evening. Sadie was rinsing out some of Rose's clothes in the kitchen sink while Michael emptied the dishwasher. 'I know that you overheard me talking to Tamsin on the phone the other night,' he continued, 'and that you know I wasn't at a funeral.'

Sadie threw down the little dress she was holding and he thought she'd start yelling at him, but then she picked it up again and calmly finished rinsing the stains on it, before putting it into the washing machine.

'Sadie?' he said.

'I don't want to talk about it,' she told him quietly.

'You don't want to talk about it?'

'No.'

'You don't even want me to explain—'

'No!' she said, her voice almost a scream all of a sudden. She took a deep breath and regained some control. Then she said, 'If he's done it once, he'll do it again.'

'I don't understand.'

Sadie pulled off the pink rubber gloves she'd been wearing and sat down at the kitchen table. 'When I was fourteen,' she said, 'there was this boy at school. I liked him, but he was already going out with someone. I mean, none of this was very serious, they'd probably been together a couple of weeks, or something.'

'What are you talking about?'

'Just listen,' she said. 'So, one day, I got talking to him, and he kissed me. I told my mum about it later that evening, I asked her whether I should go out with him, and that's what she said to me. She said, if he's done it once, he'll do it again.'

'Sadie, what are you getting at?'

'Do I need to spell it out? You were with Rae when you had sex with me. So why should I be surprised, now that you're with me, that you would cheat on me with her. It's my own fault.'

'I am *not* cheating on you with her.'

'If you're saying you haven't had sex with her, then fine. I believe you. But actually, perhaps it would be better if you were just screwing her, rather than...' A tear dropped onto her cheek and she wiped it away angrily.

'Rather than what?' he asked softly.

'You're never really with me,' she said. 'When you're here,

you think about her. We've got a baby together and it's like half the time you don't even see her. Or me. All your thoughts, all your energy, it's with Tamsin. And I really, *really* could do with your attention being on me!' She started to cry properly and he touched her arm but she shook him away.

'No,' she said, 'no. I don't care. Just leave me alone.'

'I'm not going to leave you alone.'

'Why wouldn't you want her, after all? I get it. She's glamorous and exciting. And I'm certainly not, am I?'

'You really think... Sadie, don't be ridiculous—'

'So now I'm ridiculous too?' She slammed her hand on the table. 'Why does it always have to be about *your* feelings? Why do you make me feel bad just for wanting you to pay attention to me?'

'All right,' he said, 'all right. Will you listen?'

'I don't want to hear excuses.'

'I don't need to make excuses. I haven't done anything wrong—'

'You haven't done anything wrong?' she exploded. 'You—'

'Stop,' he said, 'stop. Please listen. Obviously I have done things wrong, but it's not as bad as you think. I wanted to talk about it with you, but I thought it would make you worried. I know I've ended up worrying you even more by lying, I can see that now and I'm sorry. I'll explain what's been happening, but first, I swear on Rose's life, I haven't slept with Tamsin. I haven't so much as touched her, not in that way. She did try to kiss me once—'

Sadie's face turned thunderous and Michael quickly said, 'I made it absolutely clear it wasn't what I wanted. And it really, really isn't. Sadie, it isn't. You just had my baby, for God's sake. I love you and Rose more than anything.'

'Then why are you so interested in her?' Sadie said. 'Why don't you just stop?'

'I don't know. I guess I just want to understand. All these name changes. All these weird lies...'

'She's a nutcase! Why can't you see it? She lies, cheats, manipulates. She is a nasty, *nasty* piece of work.'

'Maybe,' Michael said. 'I don't think she's *nasty,* but I'm beginning to think that the lies are just... they go too deep. When I try to get to the bottom of one lie, there are hundreds more...' He trailed off and sighed. 'When I said I was at the funeral, I was really in Frinchford-on-Sea. I spoke to Star and Pattie again and they both said the same – that all this is probably a game to her. I think I'm starting to believe that now.'

'So, what are you going to do?'

'I don't know. I guess I need to tell her once and for all that I can't have anything to do with her any more.'

'Haven't you done that already?'

'I'll mean it this time.'

Sadie gave him a long hard look. 'You're really not in love with her?'

'No.'

'Honestly?'

'I can't help but care about her. But it's not love. It... maybe it's old love—'

'*Old love*?'

'Sadie, I don't want to lie to you. But if you're asking me if I love her like I love you, or if I want to be with her, then the answer is definitely no.'

'I don't like this, Michael.'

'Please believe me. I just wanted to know that she was okay. And I wanted to understand why she made up Rae Carrington, because Rae was such a big part of my life for a few years, and if she was a lie, then it feels like part of my own life is a lie. But I don't think I'll ever reach a point where I can trust what she's saying, so now I'm going to let it go and focus on what really matters to me. Rae is just my past. You and Rose are my future. I should have realised that from the start, but I swear Sadie, I realise it now.'

Despite their talk, Sadie said she was too upset for him to sleep in the same bed as her, so Michael went into the spare room while she stayed in the master bedroom with Rose. He struggled for ages to sleep, until in the small hours of the morning he heard his door open, and Sadie crept inside. She put Rose down in her carrycot at the foot of the bed and then she lifted the duvet and got in beside him.

'I still think you're a bastard,' she told him, 'but I couldn't sleep on my own.'

'Okay,' he said, 'well, I'll take that.'

'I... I do love you,' she said. 'I hate you right now, but I know the love is under there somewhere.'

'I'll tell her,' he said, 'I'll tell her I'm going to stay out of her life and that I want her to stay out of mine. I won't call her again and if she calls me I won't answer. If she turns up out of the blue at the shop, I'll ignore her. It's over, I promise. I'll make sure she understands.'

'Good,' Sadie said. 'The sooner the better.'

Fifty-Three

The next day Michael phoned Tamsin to arrange to see her, and she sounded distracted and agitated. He managed to get out of her that Paul was away, so he said he would visit after he finished in the shop for the day. Just before he hung up she said, 'Michael, it's awful. It's so awful. I'm going to go to hell.'

'What?' he said, but she'd already gone.

When he arrived, the house was dark. He stepped out of the car and made his way towards the front door but when he reached out to knock he realised it wasn't completely closed. 'Tamsin?' he called softly into the house. 'Tamsin? It's Michael.'

He didn't want to yell loudly and wake up Madeline, so he pushed the door open and called out softly again. He took a step inside and realised he could hear muffled sounds coming from the living room. He made his way across the hall and knocked gently on the door but he received no response, so he pushed it open and then took a step backwards in surprise at the sight that greeted him. Two bodies on the sofa, Tamsin with her dress pushed up around her waist and her bare legs looking luminous in the dim light, while the man she was on top of leant back against the sofa cushions with his eyes fixed on her as she moved, his hands planted firmly on her thighs. 'Oh,' Michael said stupidly, and the two faces turned towards his. Tamsin's mouth twisted into a smile, while the man said, 'Shit,' and started pushing her away from him. 'You said he wouldn't be back,' he shouted at Tamsin. 'What the fuck is wrong with you?'

Tamsin smoothed her dress down with mock seriousness and said, 'I told you my *husband* isn't around. Michael isn't my husband.'

The man finished sorting his own clothes out and gave Tamsin another shove before starting towards the door. Michael stepped into his path.

'Don't push her,' he said. 'Apologise to her. Now.'

The man – who was maybe a few years older than Michael, but shorter and with his face bleary from drinking – stopped and looked back at Tamsin. 'She is a fucking mess,' he said. 'You're welcome to her.'

Michael glanced over at Tamsin, who had picked up a nearly empty vodka bottle from the coffee table. Reluctantly he stepped out of the man's way to let him leave so he could rush over to her.

'I think you've had enough,' he said. He tried to take the bottle but she clung on to it until he ended up trying to wrestle it from her hands and it slipped away from both of them, smashing against the coffee table and showering the carpet with shards of glass. Tamsin sank down next to it and accidentally put her palm on top of some of the glass. 'Ah!' she said, and she held up her hand in front of her, looking at the tiny fragments sticking out. Michael turned on the ceiling light and sat down beside her. 'Here,' he said, 'I'll get those out.' He managed to carefully extract them between his nails, and Tamsin looked at the little spots of blood. 'I think you'll live,' he told her.

Tamsin carried on looking at her hand.

'Who was that man?' Michael asked.

She shrugged her shoulders.

'He shouldn't have treated you like that.'

'I don't care.'

'Well, *I* do.' He looked at her. In the bright light her face looked nearly white apart from areas made colourful or dark by make-up, and there were knots in her hair. When he glanced across to where she and the man had been having sex, he noticed some black lacy underwear under the sofa. He reached across and picked them up carefully between his thumb and finger. 'Your... um... do you need these?' he said awkwardly.

'Maybe,' she slurred. She grabbed his hand and pushed it against the inside of her thigh. 'Why don't you have a feel and find out whether I'm wearing any.'

Michael moved his hand away. 'You're drunk,' he said. 'You don't know what you're saying.'

'Don't I?' she shouted at him, her face suddenly twisting into an expression of hatred and anger. 'Why don't you want me, Michael? Am I not *good* enough for you any more?'

'Stop,' he said. 'Don't do this.'

'Was I really that bad of a fuck that *Sadie* is better than me?'

Michael stood up. 'Where's Madeline?' he said. 'Is she upstairs?'

'What do you care?' She got unsteadily to her feet and took a step towards him. 'Michael, listen, no one's going to find out if you have sex with me. I probably won't even remember, so it can be your little secret.'

'No,' Michael said when she reached out her hands towards him. 'I don't want to.'

'Why? Am I not attractive now you know who I really am? What is it you find most disgusting? That I was poor, that my mum didn't look after me properly, or that I started fucking when I was so young?'

'None of it!' he said. 'None of those things have anything to do with how attractive you are! And I don't think of you as better or worse than Sadie – Sadie is who she is, and you are who you are, and I care about you *and* her. I don't like seeing you like this. Look, I'll be honest, I came here tonight to tell you that I want us to stop seeing each other. But I'm not going anywhere until you tell me where Madeline and Paul are and I'm happy that you're safe.'

'Safe? I don't think I've ever been safe!' she said.

'What do you mean?'

A shadow fell across her face and she shook her head. 'Get out,' she said.

'Tamsin—'

'You think I'd want to have anything to do with you anyway? You were crap, Michael! It's ridiculous how much better Paul is at sex than you. Even that guy just then…' She ran over to the window. 'In fact, has he gone? Since you're not up to it, perhaps I can get him to come back—'

'I'll go upstairs and check for myself if Madeline is okay,' Michael said. 'Then I'll make you some tea.'

'Tea,' she said, 'yeah, that'll help! Paul has *left* me, Michael. Because he hates Madeline so much. He thinks she's going to destroy our lives. He says nothing good can come of her being here.'

'Paul has *left* you?'

'He wants me to fall apart and agree to have Madeline adopted. Then he'll come back.'

Michael stared at her. Was she telling the truth? It didn't sound like it could be true. 'Tamsin, I spoke to Paul when he came to my house. He was worried sick about you. Are you sure he's not just away with work? I can call him for you, if you like? I won't tell him about that man…'

'It's not the first time I've shagged other guys since we've been married.'

'Uh… right. Just wait here for a minute and I'll be right back. Is Madeline upstairs?'

She nodded, and then she said, 'Paul will lie.'

'What?'

'If you phone him, he'll lie.'

Michael watched her in confusion, but she just lay down on the sofa and closed her eyes.

'I'll be back in a second,' he reassured her.

...

Michael ran upstairs, and found Madeline sleeping soundly in her cot. Feeling a rush of relief, he made his way back down to the kitchen, where he put the kettle on to make Tamsin some of her green tea. There was a landline phone on the dresser, so instead of disturbing Tamsin to get Paul's number he found an entry in its address book that said "Paul Mobile", and he dialled it.

Fifty-Four

Tamsin lay in silence, listening to Michael moving around the house and then shutting himself in the kitchen to do whatever he was doing. She began to feel uncomfortable without any underwear on, but she tried to ignore it because her knickers were the other side of the room where Michael had left them. She'd always felt very uncomfortable without underwear. Even in bed she'd wear it under her nightclothes, and she'd struggle to get to sleep if she didn't.

After what felt like a long time, Michael came back in and set down a mug of tea on the floor beside her.

'I suppose you want to call Paul.'

'I have done. I used your phone in the kitchen.'

'I can guess what he said to you.'

'Tamsin, I know I said I wouldn't, but I did tell him about the man who was here. He was very understanding. He said he's not far away and I can wait with you until he gets here.'

'I don't want to see him.'

'Look, Tamsin, the thing is I have my own family, and as much as I care, Paul is the one who can really be here for you.'

'I don't trust him. And soon I'll get proof of who he is.'

'I don't understand. Who is he?'

Tamsin let out a little breath of air, and with it came the words, 'The devil.'

When Paul arrived, Tamsin watched through the window as Michael spoke to him on the drive. The two men were acting as though they were best friends. She made her way to the front door, wrapping a coat around her body before she stepped out.

'Tamsin,' Paul said when he saw her. 'Michael's told me everything.' He walked over and put his arm around her. 'It's all right,' he said, 'I'm here now.'

'Until you go again!' she shouted. She pushed him away. 'Leave me alone!' she said. 'I know what you're doing. I know what you are!' She saw Michael looking sympathetic, and with a stab of anger she realised his sympathy was not for her, but for Paul.

'Go,' Paul told him. 'I appreciate you staying with her, but she'll be all right now.'

Tamsin watched as Michael made his way across the drive and she broke away from Paul's embrace to run inside the house. She quickly scribbled down some details on a scrap of paper and dashed back out towards Michael's car.

'Wait!' she cried out, 'wait!'

He stopped and she thrust the note into his hand, speaking quietly. 'These are Sally's details,' she said. 'Go and see her. Paul sacked her when she started asking too many questions. You should ask her why he fired her. She'll tell you it was weird. It must have been weird. Perhaps she knows something. Perhaps she found something out—'

'Tamsin...'

'Please, Michael. I'm not crazy. I'm not—'

Michael quickly got into his car, reversed into the centre of the driveway, and with a small spray of gravel he drove away from her house. Slowly, she made her way towards Paul.

'Have you changed your mind about Madeline?' he whispered to her.

'No,' she said.

'Then you're on your own.'

He held her face in his hands. 'I love you, Tamsin. I don't care about the other man. I don't even care that Michael was here. We have to be together, but we can't do that with Madeline. You know we can't, sweetheart.'

'She's my daughter.'

'Yes. Well let's hope she hasn't inherited as much from you as you did from *your* mother.'

'What?'

'You. Getting wasted and fucking some stranger while your innocent daughter sleeps in her room upstairs.'

'I'm allowed to have fun.'

'Were you having fun, though? Were you keeping her safe? What if you passed out, and that man was alone in the house with her?'

'She's a baby, what on earth do you think he'd want with a baby—'

'I don't know. And neither do you. You can't keep her safe.'

'I can.'

'Believe what you want. You'll realise soon enough what you need to do.' His expression softened. 'Tamsin, I don't like to see you in this downward spiral. But if getting to rock bottom is what it takes for you to see sense, then rock bottom is where you're going to go.'

Fifty-Five

When Michael got home, the contrast between his life with Sadie and Rose and the evening he had had with Tamsin struck him forcefully. While being with Tamsin had been disturbing and upsetting, his house felt warm and welcoming. The sight of Sadie on the sofa drinking hot chocolate filled him with a sense of belonging and relief, and he wanted to tell her how he felt but didn't know how to explain it.

'Michael,' Sadie said when she looked up at him. 'You look terrible.'

She carried on watching as he sat down beside her. 'Talk to me,' she said. 'What's wrong? What did Tamsin say? Did it go badly?'

'It went very badly.'

Sadie put her drink down. 'What exactly happened?' she asked.

Michael shook his head. 'She was drunk,' he said. 'Some other man was there, and after he left she said some weird stuff to me. She doesn't seem to trust Paul at all. She says he's leaving her, but when he turned up he was perfectly kind to her.'

'Well,' she said after she'd digested it, 'although I didn't like the way Paul barged in here that time, he does seem like a good man. It's obvious he loves Tamsin.'

'She said he's the devil.'

Sadie put her arm around him. 'I can only imagine how upsetting it must have been to see her so disturbed.'

Michael took out the piece of paper on which Tamsin had scribbled down Sally's details. 'She gave me this. She said Paul sacked Sally because she asked too many questions.'

Sadie took the paper and put it inside a drawer in the living room sideboard. 'I'm going to bed,' she said. 'You should come too.' She stopped and smiled at him sympathetically. 'Michael, don't worry so much. Paul will look after her.'

Once Sadie had gone upstairs, Michael checked his phone for messages from Tamsin and found an email with Sally's details and the words: *Talk to Sally. She must have said something Paul didn't like for him to fire her.*

Michael stared at the words for a while and then closed the message with a heavy feeling settling in his stomach. When he got into bed with Sadie, he tried to put it from his mind as they curled up together and held each other close.

Fifty-Six

Sally woke with a start. She felt anxious – more so than normal, anyway, as she'd felt uneasy every day since Paul had told her that her services were no longer required. She tried to shake it off but the feeling only became more intense, until she decided that once she'd had breakfast she would visit Tamsin and put her mind at ease.

There was a chill in the air and a blustery wind as she made her way out to her car. Autumn seemed to have come on suddenly and determinedly, and great drifts of dead leaves had appeared overnight. She sighed as she got into the car. None of it was her problem – her husband told her that at least once a week – but she felt like it was, nonetheless. In truth, she had always been worried about Tamsin. From the first day she had gone to the house and spoken to her and Paul, she'd felt unsettled by them, but as she'd grown used to them her misgivings had been pushed aside. Paul, of course, was ordinary enough. Perhaps a little overprotective of Tamsin, but then he had every reason to be because the girl was like a piece of fragile china – beautiful and serene, almost cold, one minute – then she shattered into a thousand sharp little fragments with just the tiniest knock.

When Sally arrived at the house, she met the postman, who was just starting up the drive with a couple of letters. Sally smiled at him. 'I can take those,' she said, and he handed them over with a nod of thanks. She knew he recognised her after all the years she'd been working at the house.

She knocked on the front door, but it was a while before Tamsin answered, and were it not for the fact she could hear Madeline crying inside the house she would have assumed Tamsin had gone out. When the door finally opened, Sally was taken aback by Tamsin's appearance.

'Sally,' Tamsin said desperately, 'please. Please help me with Madeline.'

She held the baby out and Sally took her, but her eyes were on Tamsin, who was dressed in an old t-shirt with stains down it that looked like they were from several hours ago or perhaps the day before. Her hair was all ruffled up as if she hadn't brushed it for days and her eyes were wide and staring, with a glint in them that made Sally think of a trapped animal.

Sally tried to shrug away the feeling of fear that was spreading through her body. 'I came to see how you are,' she said cheerfully.

Tamsin's eyes fell to the post in Sally's hand. 'What's that?' she said. 'Give me those!'

She snatched the letters and ran back inside the house and into the kitchen. Sally followed her and watched as she began to tear one of the letters open.

'You expecting something important?' she asked casually, but Tamsin seemed unaware that she was even there. Sally watched as Tamsin pulled a piece of paper from the envelope and unfolded it.

'Madeline's grown,' Sally said, trying to make conversation. 'Is she still enjoying her food?'

Suddenly, to Sally's shock, Tamsin screamed. Sally's heart raced and she almost dropped Madeline. 'What is it? What's the matter?'

Tamsin was just staring at the letter, and Sally had no idea what to do. 'Tamsin,' she said, 'Tamsin, are you all right?' Sally began to feel truly frightened. She had never seen a look on anybody like the one on Tamsin's face.

'I...' Tamsin said, then she dropped the letter onto the table and ran over to the sink to be sick.

Sally stood silently, trying to see what the letter was, but at the same time not wanting to invade Tamsin's privacy. She couldn't really see it very well – there were a couple of columns with something written in them, and some lines of text at the bottom. In her arms Madeline started to squirm, so she pulled some funny faces for her and Madeline tried to grab at her nose and chin.

'Tamsin,' Sally said eventually, 'what's wrong?'

Tamsin spun round. 'Get out,' she said.

'Let me make you some tea—'

'I said get out!' Tamsin yelled. She picked up a wine glass from beside the sink and threw it across the room at Sally. 'Get out, get out!'

More glasses began to fly, and Sally quickly darted out of the way. She put Madeline down in her pink bouncy chair on the floor, and ran out of the room and out of the house, the sound of Tamsin screaming and smashing things following her right the way to her car door.

...

Tamsin sank down to the floor, and put her face in her hands. She could hear the sound of Sally driving away, and Madeline was cooing and babbling away in her chair. For a second, she thought she would be able to calm down. She'd suspected what the result of the DNA test would be and had her next move planned out. But then the horror of what she'd discovered hit her all over again, and she pressed her palms more firmly against her face, and screamed.

PART FOUR

Fifty-Seven

A few days after his final meeting with Tamsin, Michael woke in the early hours of the morning. He looked around, feeling disoriented, and then realised Sadie was awake too.

'I can hear crying,' Sadie said, 'a baby crying.'

Michael sat up in bed and looked at Rose in her carrycot.

'It's not Rose,' Sadie said without looking. 'Rose's cry isn't like that.'

'It must be coming from next door,' he said.

'Next door don't have a baby.'

Michael watched as Sadie got out of bed and pulled on a dressing-gown. 'I'm going to see if I can figure out where it's coming from.'

Michael considered going back to sleep but the baby's cries were too distracting, so he got up and followed Sadie. 'It's so loud,' she said. 'I don't understand where it's coming from. It sounds like it's downstairs.'

She began to make her way down the steps and Michael continued to follow. The cries grew louder and Sadie began looking around. 'Am I imagining things?' she said. 'You can hear it too, can't you?'

'Yes, I can hear it.' He made his way down the hall towards the front door. The sound was getting louder and louder. Sadie followed close behind him and when he opened the door, she gasped in shock.

A baby, strapped into a car seat and covered with a pink blanket, was on the doorstep. Next to her was a bag, which Michael picked up. He looked inside and saw a jumble of clothes, feeding bottles, a tin of powdered baby formula, some jars of baby food and a couple of toys.

'Oh my God,' Sadie was saying, 'oh my God. What is happening? What is *happening?* Why is there a *baby*—'

'It's Madeline.'

'What?' Sadie said. She was beginning to reach down for the baby, but hesitantly, as if she couldn't make up her mind whether to touch her.

'Madeline,' he said. 'It's Tamsin and Paul's baby.'

Sadie stared at him. 'What?' she repeated quietly.

'It's Tamsin's baby.'

'I heard you!' she shouted. 'Michael, why the *fuck* is Tamsin's baby outside our house?'

'I don't know,' he said, 'I don't know. Let me think…'

He picked up the car seat and put it inside the hall where Madeline would be warmer, and Sadie reached down to scoop the baby up into her arms. Her eyes had filled with tears. 'She's just a baby,' she said, 'why would she leave her *baby?*' She began to carry the little girl inside the house when Michael noticed something.

'Wait,' he said, 'wait a second.' Sadie stopped and he reached for the piece of notepaper that was folded in half and attached to Madeline's blanket with a safety pin. He tore it off and opened it. The message inside was scrawled in huge capital letters.

DO NOT LET PAUL HAVE HER.

'Sadie,' he said, 'Sadie, look at this.'

He showed it to her and she read it quickly. 'What does this mean?' she asked. 'Why has she done this?'

Michael looked at Madeline, who was still crying intermittently. He didn't know how to answer.

'We need to call the police,' Sadie said. 'Or social services. She needs help—'

Her words were cut off as Michael quickly ran outside and started looking up and down the street.

'Michael, where are you going? Michael…'

'Get my phone,' he called to her. 'While I see if Tamsin is still outside.'

He looked around again but there was no sign of her car, and when he went back inside Sadie was holding out his phone to him.

'I already tried her number,' she said. 'Her phone's off.'

Michael tried again himself and found that she was right.

'Okay,' he said, trying get his head together. 'Okay. I'm going after her. I'll take Madeline with me. It can't be that long ago that she did this. If I hurry, perhaps…'

Sadie hugged Madeline close to her. 'Perhaps what? You don't know where she's going. If she's left the baby here perhaps she's running away. She could be anywhere.'

Michael didn't reply. Sadie thought for a second, and then she had a change of heart and held the baby out to him. 'Perhaps you're right,' she said. 'Go after her. See if she's gone back to her house and I'll stay here and call the police. Even if you can't find Tamsin hopefully Paul will be around. Madeline should be with her family, no matter what Tamsin thinks right now.'

Fifty-Eight

Michael drove as fast as he could towards Tamsin's house. In the back of the car Madeline was screaming, and the sound pierced through him and made him feel like his head was going to burst.

'Be quiet!' he told her, 'please, be quiet.'

In the end he pulled over and searched desperately through the bag Tamsin had left. He gave Madeline one of her toys but it didn't help, so he took her out of her seat and walked around with her until she calmed down. After another ten minutes of driving, he was overwhelmed with relief when she fell soundly asleep.

It was dawn when Michael reached Tamsin's house. He had been wondering whether Paul would be there but the only car was Tamsin's. He was relieved to see evidence that she had driven back to her house, but she didn't answer the door and when he called through the letterbox there was no response. He left Madeline in the car while he tried the kitchen door and the French doors at the back of the house, but they were all locked and there wasn't so much as an open window. A feeling of foreboding took hold of him. 'Oh God,' he said to himself, 'oh God, please say she hasn't… she hasn't…'

He ran to the front door again and called desperately through the letterbox. When she still didn't answer, he stepped away and stared uselessly at the door. 'What do I do?' he said out loud to himself. 'I don't know what to do, I don't know what to do.' He forced himself to stay calm. Then an idea struck him. Sally. Tamsin had emailed him her phone number, and if she lived nearby and knew some way to get into the house, it would probably be quicker than calling 999.

Sally sounded groggy, but to his relief she managed to tell him that there was a spare key to the house, hidden in the garden.

When Michael stepped inside, it was still and silent, the emptiness making his palms sweat and his skin prickle. He called out Tamsin's name and when she still didn't reply he quickly made his way through the downstairs rooms. There was no sign of her. Upstairs, he checked a few bedrooms which were empty, until he reached the bathroom door and somehow felt he knew what he was going to see even before he did.

'No!' he cried out when he saw her. 'No, oh God, no!'

He rushed over to her but he couldn't think what to do and found himself staring stupidly at all the blood in the water, the kitchen knife on the floor and her closed eyes. In desperation he shook her, and her eyes fluttered open briefly. 'You're alive,' he said, 'you're alive!' He rushed across the room and grabbed a couple of towels, thinking he could wrap them around her wrists and try to stop her bleeding.

'Michael?' she said in a whisper.

He looked at her face and saw her eyes were half open again. 'Michael,' she said, 'go... go away.'

'I'll call an ambulance,' he told her as he wound the towels around her wrists. 'Everything is going to be okay, Tamsin, I promise. Let me help you.'

She closed her eyes again and said weakly, 'Do what you want. It makes no difference.'

'You're going to be all right.'

'I told you. Leave me alone.'

He sat down on the floor beside her and held her hand while he called 999, but she didn't open her eyes again, and he began to think he was too late.

ONE WEEK LATER

Fifty-Nine

Michael woke abruptly, sweating and shaking, and it took him several seconds to realise where he was – that he wasn't in the bathroom in Tamsin's house any more, that he was safe at home. He dreamt about finding her over and over again, every night since it had happened. He started to cry and Sadie snuggled in close to him. 'You dreamt about it again, didn't you?' she said.

He nodded and she stroked his cheek. 'You will start to forget it,' she said, 'I mean, not *forget* it, but you'll get over the shock. Right now it's very raw, and it's going to take a while for your mind to process it all.'

'It was... the *blood*... I really thought she was dead.'

'I know,' Sadie whispered, 'I know, Michael. But she's in the best possible place. You found her in time. You saved her life. I'm so proud of you. You should be proud of you too.'

'I didn't do anything,' he said, 'not really.'

'You did enough. You got her help, you stayed with her until the ambulance came, you told them the things she's been saying recently, how disturbed she's been. What more could you have done than that?'

'I should have seen it coming.'

Sadie snuggled even closer against him. 'No one could have seen it coming,' she said.

'Why hasn't she contacted me? Why can't she just tell me she's okay?'

'She's in hospital. She's safe, that's what's important. All these things she thought about Paul hurting the baby... when she gets help, she'll realise it's not true and she'll be able to be with him and Madeline again. It's out of your hands now. You did everything you could possibly do.'

Michael nodded but he didn't feel very reassured, and he lay awake for a long time in the darkness.

The next morning he was surprised when the doorbell rang and he found Sally standing outside, looking distraught.

'Sally,' Michael said, 'what's happened? Is there news, is she...'

She held her hand up. 'She's okay,' she said, 'well, not okay. She made another attempt last night, but she's all right.'

'Oh God.'

Sadie suddenly appeared in the hallway behind him. 'I really didn't think she was ill,' Sadie said to Sally, and a tear rolled down her cheek. 'I just thought she was trying to have an affair with Michael—'

'Nobody realised she felt this way,' Sally said gently. 'I've known her for almost ten years and I've never been able to predict a single thing she's done. I knew she was having problems, we all did, but this…'

She was silent for a moment, and Michael realised she was still just standing on the doorstep. 'Come inside,' he said.

'I hope you don't mind me turning up like this,' she said as she stepped into the house. 'I found your address in Tamsin's handbag when I was helping Paul collect some things for her.'

'How is Paul?'

Sally shook her head.

'Bad?'

'Strange. Very upset, of course, but he also doesn't want anyone anywhere near her. He keeps trying to get them to discharge her. He says she needs to be at home with him and that being in hospital is going to make her worse.'

'Where's Madeline?'

'She went into emergency foster care. Paul refused to take her and from pretty much the second she woke up all Tamsin would say was, "Don't let Paul have her."'

'But surely it's just because she's not well that she's worried about him being with Madeline? I mean, all of what she was saying about Paul messing with washing powder and things…' he trailed off as he saw the look on Sally's face.

'I've never seen him do anything,' she said quickly, 'of course I haven't, but he has acted very oddly about the whole thing. This has been going on for months, but he's never wanted her to see a doctor or talk to anyone to get support, and when I tried to talk to him about it he, well—'

'He sacked you.'

'Tamsin told you?'

Michael nodded.

'Well, when it first happened, when Tamsin went into hospital, I mean, I was the first person he called. But now that it's been a few days, he's not so keen to have me help with anything any more. He's told me not to go and see her – and I haven't, but I'd like to because God knows that girl could do with some friendly faces. In the whole time I worked at their house, I think the first time I ever saw her with a friend was when she was with you. Her sister came two or three times, years back, but they always argued. It was around the time their mum died. It was all a nasty business.' She looked at Michael very directly. 'But that's not why I'm here. Michael, I went to see Tamsin. The day before she... the day before you found her in the bath. I didn't realise Paul was away on business or I would never have just left her in that state.'

'What do you mean? She was upset?'

'She got a letter. I don't know what it was. But Michael, whatever was in that letter is the reason why she's done this. I haven't been able to get it out of my mind—'

'I'm sure it wasn't the reason—'

'No, you don't understand. When she read it she *screamed*. It made her sick. I've never seen anyone react to something like that, not ever.'

'A letter.' Michael said, 'just a letter.'

'Yes.'

'Do you know where it is now?'

'I can guess,' she said. 'And, Michael, I'm the last person to want to go prying into people's business, believe me. But I think on this occasion interfering might be the right thing to do. Tamsin obviously wanted to take whatever was in the letter to her grave. If we don't find out what it is, and she doesn't want to tell anybody, how can anyone help her?'

'I don't know,' Michael said, 'I don't feel like my getting involved has helped her so far.'

'Paul is at the hospital,' Sally said. 'I'm sure he'll be there all day. I have a good idea where Tamsin will have hidden that letter. What room it's in, at least.'

'You want to break into their house?'

'I've got the spare key because I've been picking up supplies for her. I don't expect Paul's thought anything of me having it, with everything that's been going on, or I'm sure he would have asked for it back. I expect he will soon, so we need to do it as soon as possible.'

'I don't know...'

'Go,' Sadie said quietly, taking him by surprise as he'd almost forgotten she was there.

He turned to her. 'Are you sure?'

She nodded. 'Tamsin needs your help, Michael. Please go with Sally. I'm okay here, honestly.'

Sixty

All was silent at the house. Paul's car was nowhere to be seen and although Michael felt ripples of anxiety as he remembered what he had discovered the last time he'd been there, he took a few deep breaths and the memories faded.

'Where do you think the letter is?' he asked Sally.

She'd been making her way across the hall towards the stairs, but she stopped when he spoke and turned to look at him. 'She may have got rid of it. If it's something she doesn't want found, she may have just put it through the shredder in Paul's study.'

'But you don't think she's done that?'

Sally rested her hand on the banister. She looked worn out. 'No, I don't think so,' she said. 'I think it's in that bedroom. You know... the one she didn't want you to see.'

'You mean Bella and Scarlett's...'

'Yes.'

Michael followed her up the stairs. She walked quickly, and though she hesitated briefly on the landing, she then made her way resolutely across to the door with the wooden heart on it. Once inside, they both started to look around. It turned out that there was very little in there aside from what Michael had originally glimpsed through the door: two beds, and the wooden letters on the wall above each one. Opposite the beds was a chest of drawers – the only other thing in the room – and Sally began to carefully search through it, leaving Michael to investigate the beds. He felt a combination of guilt and sadness as he pulled back the duvet on the first bed, which he assumed had never been slept in. He checked under the sheet and inside the pillowcase and even under the mattress, but there was nothing. Sally had finished the chest of drawers and she came to help him with the second bed.

'Maybe it's not here,' she said. 'I might not know her as well as I thought. I mean, I don't really know her at all.'

As she spoke she was feeling around in the narrow gap between the bottom of the bed and the carpet, and all of a sudden she said, 'Wait, there's something here. I can't... I can't quite...'

'Let me try,' Michael said. He knelt down beside the bed and slid his arm underneath, managing to grab at the paper he found taped to the bottom of the bed frame and pull it free.

'Well, here it is,' he said, showing the envelope to Sally. 'Does this look like the letter she had?'

'Yes, I think so.'

They sat down on the bed and Michael took the letter out from inside the envelope. Sally was fidgeting at his side and he also felt nervous at the thought of reading whatever might have led Tamsin to try to end her life.

'You really think we have to see this?' he asked Sally.

'I do,' she said, 'I don't really *want* to see it either. But she's suffered enough. I think all her life she's been trying to hide – maybe from this, maybe from something else, but it needs to stop.'

Michael nodded, and opened the letter.

Sixty-One

They both stared at it for a while, in silence.

Michael spoke first. 'It's a paternity test,' he said.

'Yes, I can see.'

Michael turned the letter over to check the back, then he read it all again, but nothing became clearer.

'What do you think it means?' he asked her. 'There are no names on it. It says the child and "alleged father" are a match, but this could just mean that Madeline is Paul's. We don't know whose sample this is.'

'But it shows she had doubts,' Sally said, 'and perhaps she got a sample from the other man if she had an affair.'

Michael sighed, and then he remembered what Tamsin had told him about Paul's friends visiting. 'She told me once that the baby wasn't Paul's,' he said, 'but it seemed like it wasn't true. It was horrible, how she said it happened.'

'That must be what it is! That's why she was so horrified, but, you'd think she would have expected the result, if she had her suspicions. You should have seen how she reacted—'

Suddenly there was a knock on the front door and they both jumped. 'Who's that?' Sally said.

'Stay there,' Michael told her and he made his way out onto the landing and across to a window that looked out over the drive. He saw a delivery van, and rushed back to Sally. 'It's just someone trying to deliver a parcel,' he said. 'But once he's gone we should go too.'

'What will you do with the letter?' she asked him.

'I don't know. Tamsin and Paul's marriage isn't really any of my business—'

'But perhaps Paul knows,' she said. 'What if all the things she's been saying about him and Madeline are true? I mean, I'm sure Paul loves Tamsin, but he doesn't strike me as someone who'd take kindly to bringing up another man's child. Not if she's cheated on him.'

'If it happened the way she said it did, it definitely couldn't be described as cheating.'

'Jealousy does weird things to people. And I could see Paul going to huge lengths to get revenge. If she was in love with someone else—'

'But none of it makes sense. The man she told me about – she was repulsed by him. And it was all Paul's fault anyway. She's never said anything about being in love with anyone else. I suppose it's possible, but would Paul try to make her think she was a bad mother to get her to give up her baby? Would he make her and the world think she was *ill* to get revenge on her for having another man's child?'

Sally shook her head. 'I don't know, Michael. I really don't know.'

Once the delivery van was gone, Michael and Sally double-checked that they'd put the bedroom back exactly how it was, apart from the letter, which Michael took with him. They'd driven to the house in separate cars, but as he got into his, Sally stayed hovering next to him. 'Don't go yet,' she said. 'I think I should tell you a couple more things. But not here. We can talk at my house.'

...

A few minutes later they were sitting at the kitchen table, each with a mug of coffee. Michael felt tired and his head ached, but something about Sally and her warm, pleasant home made him feel looked after. 'What was it you wanted to tell me?' Michael asked.

'I don't know where to start really,' Sally said. 'But... she said something once about her mum. It's probably got nothing to do with anything—'

'Her mum?' Michael said. 'Not anything about Madeline then? Or her and Paul...'

'No,' Sally said, 'I think you know as much as I do about all that. No, this was years and years ago, she said something to me. She... she basically said that her mum didn't feed her.'

'Didn't *feed* her?'

'She said she sometimes ate food out of the bin.'

Michael stared at her, then he remembered Paul telling him about Tamsin's childhood and he nodded.

'You knew?' she asked.

'I knew things were difficult for her.'

'It's always stayed with me,' Sally said, 'partly just because it's horrible, but it had a ring of truth to it. A lot of what she says doesn't. But that did.'

Michael swirled his coffee round in the mug. His headache intensified.

'Then there's her sister,' Sally said. 'Star.'

'What about her?'

'Around the time their mum died, many years ago now, I overheard them arguing. Tamsin wasn't planning on going to her mum's funeral – that was the first argument, Star trying to persuade her. Then a few months later Star came again, yelling at Tamsin. But it wasn't like siblings having a bit of a spat, it was *nasty*. Star was really laying into Tamsin – except she didn't call her Tamsin, she called her Kitten. She even called Tamsin a prostitute.'

Michael frowned, but he didn't interrupt.

'They would yell and scream at each other for a bit, then they'd go almost silent, but they were still arguing. They were whispering. Because they knew I was in the house.'

'What do you think they were arguing about? Something besides Tamsin not going to her mum's funeral?'

'I don't know. But there always seemed to be something very odd between them. The whole thing – her mum, her sister, even *Paul* looks like someone's walked over his grave when Tamsin's past comes up in conversation.'

'You don't know anything about Tamsin's dad, then?'

'No. But neither does Tamsin. She never knew him.'

Michael rubbed his face with his hands. 'I don't know what to do, Sally,' he said. 'I appreciate you telling me this, but having me start raking up things I don't really understand isn't going to help, surely?'

'I know,' Sally said, 'you're right. But she left Madeline with you. She trusts you. More than she trusts Paul right now.'

'So you think I should go to see her?'

'I don't know. But I have the details of the hospital. You might as well take them, have a think about it.'

She took a leaflet from her handbag and placed it in front of him. 'This is it,' she said, 'the visiting hours and the address are all in there.'

Michael looked down at the leaflet, which said "Greenfields Hospital: Information for Families & Friends."

'How long do you think she'll be there for? Can she leave if she chooses to?'

'I don't know exactly,' Sally said, 'but, no, I don't think they would let her leave right now. She's still in a bad way.'

Sixty-Two

Michael got home to find Sadie sitting in the kitchen with Rose on her lap. He stood in the doorway and watched them for a second, then Sadie looked round at him. 'Did you find the letter?' she asked.

He took it from his pocket and handed it to her.

'A paternity test?' she said. 'So she wasn't sure who Madeline's father is?'

'It seems not.'

'What's that?' she said, pointing at the leaflet Sally had given him.

'It's the details of the hospital where she's staying.'

Sadie nodded. She looked uncomfortable and distressed, and as if to distract herself she tickled Rose's feet. 'I'm sure I managed to get a giggle out of her earlier, doing this,' she said. 'I'm looking forward to when she can do a bit more. All she can do at the moment is look at things, and she doesn't even do much of that.'

Michael stroked Rose's downy baby hair. 'Madeline is only five or so months older than Rose,' he said, 'and she can do all sorts, so it won't be too long.'

'I feel so awful for Tamsin,' Sadie said. 'Couldn't they have kept her and Madeline together in hospital?'

'I don't know. I don't really know anything about it. She may not have wanted that, or perhaps they think Madeline is better off somewhere else right now.'

'Do you think finding out the truth about Madeline's dad was what made her do this?'

'It seems likely.'

'It's all so sad.'

'It gets worse,' Michael said. He sat down beside her. 'I was talking to Sally. She said some things about Tamsin's mum and Star. It seems like... I don't know. Like no one has ever really looked after Tamsin properly.'

'Well, that's what Paul said too, wasn't it?' She hugged Rose close to her. 'I hope Tamsin's okay,' she said. 'I honestly do, I'd never wish this on anyone.'

'I know.'

'So, are you going to go and see her?' Sadie asked. 'You can go today, if you want to. I don't mind.'

'I can't go unless I know Paul isn't going to be there,' he said.

'I really don't think he'd like me interfering. I'll ask Sally to let me know when he's at the house. But I can't take any more of this today anyway. I just want to be with you and Rose.'

...

It turned out there was an opportunity for Michael to see Tamsin the next day. He contacted Sally in the morning and she told him that Paul had a business meeting in the afternoon that he had to travel a few hours to get to, so he definitely wouldn't be at the hospital until late evening, or possibly not until the next day.

On the way Michael stopped at a supermarket and bought Tamsin a box of posh milk chocolates that he remembered her liking when they'd been together. He thought about flowers, too, but he didn't want to be over-the-top. He felt nervous as he drove – he wasn't sure what it would be like at Greenfields and he didn't really know what to say to Tamsin. She was still the same person, he reminded himself, despite what she'd tried to do, though he had to conclude he wasn't too sure what sort of person that was.

It was early evening when he arrived at the hospital. He waited uneasily at reception after giving his name and Tamsin's, wishing he could be back at home with his family. It seemed like a while before they let him in, and as he was led inside he gripped the box of chocolates tightly in his hand, trying to think what sort of things he would talk to Tamsin about. But then all his ideas went out of his head when he was confronted with her much sooner than he expected. He'd thought she'd be inside her room, but she was waiting just the other side of the door for him, dressed in a simple dark grey dress, her lips a warm coral colour that made her look reassuringly herself again.

'Hello, Michael,' she said crisply. 'I wondered if you'd show up.'

He tried to smile at her, but it was difficult because an image of how he'd found her in the bath flashed through his mind.

'I wasn't sure whether to see you,' she told him. 'I'm very angry with you.'

'I'm sorry.'

'Are those for me?' she said, pointing at the chocolates.

'Yes.' He held them out to her and she took them. 'I'm not eating,' she said. 'I feel sick most of the time.'

Before he could answer she turned and started walking off down one of the corridors. She didn't tell him to come with her but he followed until they reached a room right at the end of the hall. It was fairly large, and plainly decorated with wooden furniture and dark red curtains. She held the door open for him and once he was inside she sat down on her bed. There was an armchair by the window and Michael pulled it over and sat beside her. The room was on the ground floor and outside he could see grass and a low hedge, with the car park and some other hospital buildings beyond. Tamsin crossed her legs and looked at him. 'I wanted you to leave me in the bath,' she said. 'I told you to go away.'

'I wasn't going to leave you,' he said. His eyes fell on her bandaged wrists, and she folded her arms.

'Tamsin, I'm sorry I haven't... that I didn't listen to you, and that I said I didn't want to see you—'

'You don't think *that's* why I did it, do you?' she said. 'Believe me, Michael, I can live without you in my life.'

'Yes, of course. Sorry, I didn't mean—'

'Why are you here?' she demanded.

'To see how you are. Is it all right here? How are you finding it?'

'They keep checking through the door to see whether I'm dead.'

'Sally said you tried again?'

'She's turned into a regular little gossip.'

Michael was silent for a moment, then he said, 'Have they said anything? About why you're here?'

'You mean what's wrong with me?'

'Yeah, I guess so.'

'They said it's complex and there are lots of different things going on.'

'So, they haven't said anything specific?'

'They mentioned personality disorders. And another thing, too, that I didn't really understand.' She paused, thinking. 'Dissociation. Dissociative disorder... something like that. I couldn't take it all in. I don't really listen to them much. Neither does Paul. I told them I don't care why I'm here or how they can help me. It's all irrelevant. I don't care about being well, or getting better. I just need to sort things out. I told them this morning that I'm not going to try to kill myself again, and I told them I want Madeline to be adopted, but they won't take me seriously.'

'It's a big decision.'

'Not for me. When she's gone, things will be okay again.'

Michael watched her for a while. She wasn't making eye contact with him when she spoke; she was looking past him at the wall – staring very intently at it.

'Did you tell them that you think Paul has been doing things? That you think he wants Madeline away from him?'

'No. Because they'll think I'm delusional and I know that I'm not. I've found out why he's doing it. It all makes sense.'

They fell into silence. Tamsin continued staring, and Michael shuffled his feet and cleared his throat. 'Sally told me something else,' he said. 'About a letter.' He took it from his pocket and unfolded it, then he passed it to her. 'I know this is private, but we—'

Tamsin picked the letter up, and when she realised what it was, her face was filled with so much anger that he shrank away from her.

'How dare you?' she said.

'I'm sorry—'

She threw the letter at him. 'Get out,' she said.

'We did it because we care!'

Tamsin leapt up, grabbed hold of him and tried to physically pull him from the chair, so he stood up. 'I really am sorry—'

'No you're not! If you thought it was so wrong, why did you do it?'

'Because I'm worried about you—'

'Why are you doing this *now*?' she shouted, letting go of his arm. 'When I really needed you, all those years ago, you were fucking Sadie!'

He stared at her. And he realised she wasn't over it at all.

'I thought you didn't love me,' he tried to explain. 'You wouldn't let me get close to you. Why didn't you tell me the truth about who you were? Surely that would have been better—'

'I want you to go. Now.' She snatched the letter up and stuffed it into a drawer by her bed. 'This is nothing to do with you. Nothing.'

'Was it true what you told me? That it was one of Paul's friends who got you pregnant? Sally thinks you may have been right all along, that perhaps Paul does want Madeline away from him, if she isn't his—'

'*I* want Madeline away from me. And him.'

'But you love her. I can see that you do.'

'And that is why I'm doing this. I know what is best for my own daughter, and once I prove to these bloody people that I can make decisions for myself I will move ahead with the adoption. I don't care what you or anyone else thinks about it, because I know what is right.'

'Okay,' Michael said, realising he wasn't getting anywhere. 'But you can call me, any time…'

'I thought you wanted me to leave you alone.'

'I told you I was wrong to say that.'

'Well, now I'm telling *you*, Michael. Leave me alone.'

'I really am sorry.'

She threw the box of chocolates at him. 'And take *these* with you. They're not my favourites any more. They're sweet and sickly and I don't like them at all.'

Michael accepted it was useless. He made his way out of the door, and as he left he looked back and saw that she had curled up on her side on the bed, eyes still open. Just staring.

Sixty-Three

It was only about nine o' clock when Michael got home but he found Sadie was already in bed. He lay down beside her and she put her arms around him sleepily. 'How was it?' she asked.

'She didn't really want to talk. She screamed at me to leave her alone.'

'I'm not entirely surprised,' she said. 'It might take some time for her to come round. She probably thinks the whole world is against her right now.'

'She's really not okay,' he said. 'I don't think she's over me cheating on her—'

'Don't beat yourself up about that. That's not why she's where she is. Perhaps you shouldn't have gone and looked for that letter, but nobody can dispute that your heart is in the right place. I'm sure she'll see that, and she'll see she has a friend in you.'

'I hope you're right.'

Sadie rested her head on his chest. 'Just try to sleep,' she said. 'Try to put it out of your mind.'

Michael closed his eyes, but he didn't think he'd manage to sleep very much.

A couple of days later, he got a text from Tamsin while he was at work.

Please come and see me again michael I want to talk to you. Paul is at a meeting all afternoon, but he'll be here with me by the evening.

He called Sadie and told her what Tamsin had said.

'Go,' she told him.

'I can't keep leaving the shop—'

'I'll look after the shop. I'll bring Rose in. It'll be fine, I'm more than capable.'

...

Michael reached the hospital mid-afternoon, and as he got out of the car he noticed someone leaving and was surprised to see it was Star. She stopped in her tracks when she caught sight of him and then she carried on walking as he made his way towards her. 'Did you just see Tamsin?' he asked her.

'What else would I be doing here?' she snapped.

'How is she?'

Star shook her head impatiently. 'Oh, she's just fine,' she said, 'with everyone worrying about her, she's in her element.'

Michael tried to stay calm, but he couldn't help remembering what Sally had said about Star arguing with Tamsin, and found himself saying, 'She's not fine. She tried to kill herself.'

'For God's sake,' Star said, 'she did it for attention. And if you've got any sense you'll turn around and go home, because everyone rushing over here to see her is exactly what she wants.'

Star tried to walk past him but he stepped into her path. 'Get out of my way,' she said and she tried to push past, but he took her arm. 'Why do you do it?' he said, 'talking about her like that? How can you be so heartless? If you hate her so much, why did you even bother visiting her?'

'Heartless?' she said, shaking his hand from her arm. 'You think I'm heartless? She's got rid of two of her babies. She's happy to palm Madeline off to some stranger, while she sits in there being looked after like some little *princess.*'

'Then why did you visit her?' Michael shouted, unable to keep control of his anger. 'Why did you visit her if you think she's that bad?'

Star smiled nastily. 'To tell her what I think of her,' she said. 'I told her to take some responsibility. She's got a husband and a baby, and yet all she cares about is herself. She's a selfish little cow. Now get out of my way.'

Michael didn't move. 'Please tell me that's not really what you said to her. Did you *really* tell her she's selfish? Did you bring up her other pregnancies…?'

All of a sudden, Star lost it. She pointed towards the hospital and said, '*She* is a whore, Michael. A whore. If that's what you want to hang around with, fine, but—'

'Why do you keep calling her that? She's your sister!'

'We might share the same mother but I'm ashamed to have *anything* to do with her. You are completely blind if you think she cares about you, if you think she *ever* cared about you. Now let me get to my car.'

Michael still refused to budge. 'You can't say things like that and walk away,' he said. 'Tamsin and Paul's housekeeper told me she heard you calling Tamsin a prostitute. Tell me why you keep saying it. Is it because she married Paul and you think it's for his money?'

Star looked guarded, but she spat out an answer nonetheless.

'What is so hard to understand? It's because she used to have sex for money. It's not complicated.'

Michael stared at her. 'I don't believe you,' he said.

'Oh come on,' she said, 'how do you think she got the cash she threw about to back up her ridiculous story of being *Rae Carrington?* She got it because Paul paid her for sex. And, knowing her, he probably wasn't the only one. She has always been the same, as soon as she gets the slightest bit of *attention* from a man she just drops her knickers, let alone if she thinks she's going to get some cash out of it. I'm sorry if you don't see it. But I have known her for a lot longer than you have, and I know what she was like before she went to *university* and got all sorts of grand ideas about herself.'

Michael couldn't reply straight away, his mind reeling as he took in what she'd said. Surely it couldn't be true? And yet, how *had* she managed to back up her story of being Rae Carrington without getting into a mountain of debt? She'd always been splashing money around. He couldn't believe it had only just occurred to him to question it. 'I don't believe you,' he said defensively. 'She didn't even know Paul when she was at university, she only met him right at the end... she...' he gave up. He found he couldn't carry on fighting Tamsin's corner. He found he wasn't sure any more.

Star just smiled.

Sixty-Four

Michael was full of doubt as he made his way towards the hospital entrance. He wasn't sure what to say to Tamsin any more. He felt hurt and betrayed by what Star had told him, and no matter how much he hoped that Tamsin would clear the matter up and reassure him it wasn't true, he feared that instead she would just confirm it.

This time when he went inside she didn't meet him at the door. He was told she was in her room and he made his way tentatively down the corridor, and knocked softly on her door. He received no answer so he pushed it open gently and found her curled up in a ball on her bed. 'Tamsin?' he said. She didn't respond and he sat down on the armchair which was still by her bed from Star's visit.

'Tamsin, are you okay?'

She closed her eyes, and to his surprise a tear spilled out. He'd never seen her cry before. But no more tears followed. He reached out and touched her hand. 'I'm here,' he said. 'You said you wanted to talk to me.'

'You don't want to hear what I have to say,' she said.

'Yes I do.'

'I think you should go.'

'Is this because of Star? You don't have to listen to her.'

Tamsin didn't answer.

'She said some things to me…' he started to say. 'But it doesn't matter now.'

He waited for her to reply. Time slipped by. Seconds turned to minutes, and Tamsin stayed motionless and silent. She barely even blinked.

Eventually, she shifted a little. 'I'm going to go to hell, Michael,' she whispered.

He leant closer to her. 'Why would you think that?'

She wouldn't answer. More time went by, and Tamsin didn't move.

'Would you like me to get you a drink?' Michael asked. There was a small kitchen down the hall and Michael had seen other visitors in there making teas and coffees. She didn't reply and eventually he realised he would have to leave. 'I'll come back another day,' he told her. 'Message me when you'd like me to come.'

She gave no sign of having heard him and he left her alone,

pausing at reception to tell them how she had been acting, because he felt concerned. 'She wouldn't even move,' he said, 'she thinks she's going to go to hell.' The young woman he was talking to nodded. 'I'll go and have a chat with her,' she told him. 'Try not to worry.'

'Thank you,' Michael said. Everyone kept telling him not to worry, and yet worrying was all he seemed to do.

...

The next afternoon, while he was at work, he received a call from Sally.

'Michael,' she said. 'I'm glad I could get hold of you.'

'Why?' he said quickly, 'has something happened?'

'No, not exactly.'

He waited while she was quiet for a moment. 'The thing is, Tamsin is refusing to see Paul. He tried to go to the hospital this morning and she told them not to let him in. He tried again about an hour ago. That's when I found out, because he was so upset about it that he called me, and he asked me to go in and try to find out what's wrong.'

Michael remembered what Star had said about Tamsin's history with Paul, but he said nothing.

'I was about to go and see her, but then I thought I'd call you. Did anything happen yesterday? Did she say anything about Paul?'

'She barely said anything at all, she just lay on her bed in silence.'

'Oh.'

'Listen, Sally, I'm not sure I should see her when she hasn't asked me to.'

'I understand.'

Michael hesitated, trying to make up his mind. 'No,' he said, 'I will go. She messaged me yesterday asking me to come and talk to her, so perhaps she will be glad to see me.'

'Okay,' she said. 'I'll drop by the hospital this evening, if you're able to go now?'

Michael looked around his office. He supposed he'd have to get Sadie to help in the shop again. 'Yeah,' he said, 'I'll leave straight away.'

Sixty-Five

Michael arrived at the hospital to find Tamsin curled up on her side just like she had been the previous afternoon. The only thing that had changed was her clothes – she was wearing a pair of pyjama bottoms and a white t-shirt, and he thought she looked more like the Rae he used to know, rather than Tamsin.

He sat beside her again in the armchair and wondered what to say, but to his surprise, she spoke first.

'What did Star say to you yesterday?' she asked him. 'You said she told you something?'

'Yes,' he said uneasily, 'she did, but it doesn't matter now.'

Slowly, Tamsin sat up. 'It mattered to you enough that you mentioned it.'

'I'm not sure now is the time to talk about it.'

'I say it is.'

He looked at her carefully. She seemed like she'd be able to handle it. She certainly seemed better than she had the day before. 'Well,' he said slowly, 'she said something about you and Paul.'

'What?' she demanded. 'What did she say about me and Paul?'

'She said you had a...' He tried to think how to describe it. 'An *arrangement*.'

'An arrangement?'

'When you were at university, she said that he gave you money...'

A smile crossed Tamsin's face. 'Oh, that,' she said.

'Is it *true*?'

'Don't be so shocked.'

'It *is*?'

'When I was younger, my mum frequently did it for money. Or drugs. It was pretty normal. I quite often used to see her having sex with men who came to the house. She didn't try to hide it at all.'

'I...' Michael stared at her. 'I don't know what to say,' he said. 'You shouldn't have had to see that.'

'That's why it was easier to be Rae,' she said. 'You can't take it, Michael. It's too much for you to know what Kitten's life was. I didn't want you to find out.'

'What is *wrong* with you?' Michael said before he could stop himself. 'You could have told me the truth! Surely that would have been better than you letting Paul use you so you had the money to back up your story? Do you think that's what I would have wanted? You were my girlfriend! I loved you, and you were having sex with *him!*'

'Oh, for God's sake, calm down.'

'Why didn't you just talk to me? You didn't even have to tell me the whole truth – you could have just told me you'd made up the part about your family being so rich. Why did you even have to say that in the first place? Didn't you think it might be hard to find the money to support that story? I just… I don't understand. You should have just told me, you should—'

'Should, should, should!' she said. 'You sit there saying what I should and shouldn't have done like it's obvious. Do you ever think that perhaps it isn't obvious to me? Perhaps I didn't understand what I should do. Perhaps I didn't think through what would happen if I said I was rich. Perhaps I wanted to pretend that's who I was for *my* sake, not for yours!'

'I didn't think—'

'No, you didn't. Michael, you are so far away from ever understanding who I am. That's why in the end you got fed up with me and you decided that for once you wanted to shag someone normal.'

'It was nothing like that. It didn't happen like that…' he said, but he couldn't carry on, because he realised that perhaps there was a grain of truth in what she'd said.

She saw his hesitation and her mouth twisted into a smile. 'You see,' she said, 'it's true. You wanted to be with Sadie because, let's face it, being with me is too much like hard work.'

Michael stared at her. Then he reached out, and gently placed his hand against her cheek. She looked up at him in surprise. 'What are you doing?' she said.

He took his hand away again. 'I loved being with you,' he said. 'It wasn't hard work. It could be confusing at times, I'll admit, but it wasn't *work,* and I didn't want to walk away.'

'You're just saying that because I'm in hospital and you have to be nice to me.'

Michael thought for a moment. 'Star wasn't nice to you, was she?' he said. 'When she came to see you.'

'Star is different.'

'Why did you want to see me yesterday?' he asked. 'You wanted to talk to me, but she got to you first.'

'I can't,' she said. 'You're so hung up about the black and white truth. You get angry when you think I've lied. It's exhausting for me. I don't think you understand that my mind doesn't work like yours. When I do things, I don't see consequences. I don't think before I speak, and I can't always remember things. Sometimes I think things have happened and they haven't. Half the time I feel like I'm not even sure what is going on. All I've ever been told is that I'm mad and that I'm a liar. My mum, Star, even Paul, they all say it.'

'That doesn't mean they're right.'

'They want me to not remember,' she said suddenly, and her voice seemed different. 'And they want me to sound implausible. And I'm playing right into their hands.'

'Tamsin,' Michael said, his skin prickling, 'what are you talking about?'

'But I worked it out,' she said, 'and I have something nobody can argue with.'

'What's that?'

Slowly, she slid open the top drawer of the chest next to her bed. She took out the paternity test, which was folded in half, and handed it to him. 'I've already seen this,' he said. 'I don't know what it means.'

'Because there were no names,' she said. 'I've written the names on it now. The names of the people the samples came from.'

Michael frowned and then, with one swift movement, he unfolded the letter and looked down at it.

Sixty-Six

For a few seconds he just stared. The names were written in pencil and the paper was shaking a little in his hand, making the writing look blurry. 'What?' he said, 'no... I... no.'

He glanced up at her, but she was showing no emotion.

'This can't...' he said, 'this can't be. I don't understand what I'm looking at. What am I looking at?'

He stared down at the paper again, at the names written there.

ALLEGED FATHER *Paul Quinnell*

Then he looked again at the name written next to the word "child", willing it to say "Madeline" – to have read it wrong by mistake. But there was no mistake. In shaky, spidery letters was the name that made him feel sick with horror and revulsion. *Tamsin Quinnell.*

'I...' he said, having to force himself to speak, 'how could you not *know?*'

She shook her head.

'Does *he* know?'

She nodded. 'I'm sure of it.'

Suddenly, a thought struck him, and the implications almost made him cry out. 'But Madeline... Madeline *is* his daughter?'

'Yes,' Tamsin whispered, then she added, so quietly her voice was almost imperceptible, 'and his granddaughter.'

Quickly, Michael folded the letter back over again. He looked at Tamsin, but she didn't look back at him, and she lay down on the bed, and closed her eyes.

'I need some air...' he said, and with that he stood up and staggered out of her room.

Instead of leaving the hospital, Michael went into the little kitchen down the hall, which thankfully was empty. He placed his hands on the metal sink and took several deep breaths, fixing his eyes on the window. He tried to open it to get some air, but it would only move a couple of centimetres. He stood for a long time, thinking he was beginning to get his head together, and then the shock hit him again and he found he could do nothing but stand motionless, and try to get his breath.

After maybe five or ten minutes, he managed to take a step away from the sink. The word kept swirling around in his head. *Incest.* For a moment he wondered whether this could be one of

Tamsin's lies too, but he was sure that it wasn't. She'd seemed different when she said it. She'd seemed real.

He was trying to build up the courage to go back to her room, when he turned and found her in the doorway.

'Michael?' she said, 'I thought perhaps you'd left.'

She had her arms wrapped around her body, her hair falling in two thick curtains, making her look like a little girl.

'Paul,' he said quietly, 'Paul is your dad.'

She nodded and a tear rolled down her cheek.

'Let me make you something to drink,' he said. He took out two cups, and put a spoonful of instant coffee in each.

'I don't like the coffee here,' she said. 'I've got my green tea.'

Michael tipped the coffee granules away and put one of her tea bags in the cup instead. Tamsin didn't say a word while he fumbled about making the drinks, and back in her room she didn't speak straight away either.

'You're too disgusted to look at me,' she said.

'I can't really take it in.'

Tamsin held her hands in her lap, and he noticed her dig her fingernails into her skin as she spoke again. 'That's why he wanted Madeline to be adopted. He thought he would be found out if she stayed with us.'

The weight of it all made Michael feel he was being crushed. 'I should have listened to you,' he said. 'You tried to tell me something was wrong.'

'It doesn't matter now,' she said. 'The only thing that matters is that Madeline is safe from this. She can never know.'

'Is that why you left her with me and Sadie? And then tried to...'

'I wish I had died,' she said. 'And I'm not just saying that. I really do.'

'But you didn't know, it's not your fault—'

Tamsin swiped the air with her hand in annoyance. 'Oh, it makes no difference! I've been sharing a bed with him for almost ten years! I've made a baby with him.'

She went back to holding her hands in her lap, intermittently digging in her nails, or scratching mindlessly at her skin.

'That's why you told me you're going to hell.'

'I'm in hell already.'

Something occurred to Michael. 'Is Madeline... *okay*?' he asked, 'I mean, is she well? There's nothing wrong...'

'No,' she whispered, 'there's nothing wrong. She's okay. As far as I can tell.'

'It's not *certain* that she'll get a genetic disorder, is it?' he asked. 'It just makes it more likely—'

Tamsin looked intensely uncomfortable. 'I wish I could take her to a doctor,' she said, 'and ask them, and get some sort of peace of mind, but...' she paused, and then spoke again, her voice quiet. 'That's why Paul was so desperate for me to have an abortion. He got on his knees and *begged* me one time.' She rubbed her face and then let her hands drop again. 'During the scans he looked like he was going to be sick. I think I laughed about it at the time, at how nervous he was, but he was... I guess... I don't know. I guess he was trying to count how many *fingers* she had—'

'Tamsin—' Michael reached out his hand for hers and she moved away. 'I'm so stupid!' she said, 'stupid, and weak, and... and *blind*. It's so obvious now. Why he wanted the adoption so badly. Why he doesn't want any involvement with doctors, or hospitals. He wanted me to fail at looking after her and give her up, and he was doing the right thing. He's done more to try to keep her safe than I ever have!'

'He should never have got you pregnant! He can't even be married to you. It's against the law – the whole thing, it's... how can he be married to you?'

'Nobody knows he's my dad. Mum probably knew, I guess, but she obviously didn't care enough to even tell me about him.'

'But if she knew he was your dad... I mean, she wouldn't have let you marry your own father—'

'She probably never knew. Star may have told her I was getting married, but whether she would have said it was to Paul...'

'Does Star know who he really is?'

'No,' she said, 'I don't think so.'

'Is he *her* dad too—'

'No.'

'Tamsin—'

'It *has* to stay secret,' she said, fixing her eyes on his. 'It has to. If Madeline is adopted, if she has a new life, with new parents, then even if she gets a genetic disorder, maybe they'll never work out why. It can happen to any couple, it can just be terrible luck, not...' Tamsin reached out and grabbed his arm. 'Michael, imagine what could happen to her. Apart from knowing herself where she's come from, if other people find out she would never hear the end of it. Imagine if children at her school found out that her *granddad* is her *dad*. She can't... she can't know. She can't know!'

She was so distressed that Michael nodded. Then he remembered something she'd said to him. 'Tamsin, you told me that it was in their interest for you not to sound plausible. What were you talking about? If it's not about Paul being your dad, then what...?'

Instead of answering, Tamsin lay down on the bed again, and closed her eyes.

Sixty-Seven

Michael waited. He drank some of his coffee, though he had no appetite for it and it tasted like ashes in his mouth. He could see a line between Tamsin's eyebrows, and he gently touched her arm to let her know he was still there and still listening. When she started to speak again it was so quiet he didn't realise to begin with, and he moved closer to her, eventually getting up from the chair altogether and sitting on the floor beside her.

'I don't remember anything very well,' she said, her eyes still closed. 'I remember people. Strangers. It was always very out of control, but it didn't feel out of control to me, it just felt like my life.'

'You mean, when you were a child?'

'Mum had Star when she was sixteen,' she said. 'She went into care before I was born. Then she had me just before she was nineteen. Paul would have been in his twenties. I don't know where she met him. She never said anything about him, she never told me who my father was.'

Michael's stomach clenched uncomfortably as he thought about how vague Tamsin was about the father of her baby when she was thirteen.

'Some times were worse than others. I remember being hungry. Thirsty. Confused. It's like my memories are all just funny bits of images and feelings, they don't seem to link together. I can't remember what order things happened, and some of the finer details, I don't know whether they happened at all. I remember making up stories – that I was rich and spent all my days shopping and going to swanky parties, or I'd imagine I was on a desert island, or, when I was a little older I pretended my parents were the Carringtons.'

'You were trying to escape?' he said, 'imagine you were somewhere else?'

She didn't answer him directly. 'I never really had any friends. They didn't like me because I said strange things. I said things that were too childish one minute and then the next too adult. Sexual. I wasn't doing it deliberately. I just didn't know. I didn't know any different.'

'Did no one realise you were having such a difficult time? Star... I mean, if she was taken away from your mum, someone *somewhere* must have been aware of you...'

'I don't know. My mum was very clever. Very manipulative.

She knew what she was supposed to say to authorities. And there were some better times. She had a boyfriend not long after I started school. I liked him. I think things weren't so bad then. When he left it hit mum hard, and me too. But I think by then we must have fallen off of everyone's radar.'

She shifted a little on the bed. 'I'd been at secondary school a year or so when the money problems got really bad,' she continued. 'Mum always seemed to owe people, but never quite so bad as that. Men would turn up and she'd yell and scream at them. I tried to stay out of the house as much as I could. I started drinking – there was always alcohol around. Then one day there was Paul.'

'He came to see you?'

Tamsin screwed her face up. 'I don't... remember...' she said.

Michael leant forward and put his arms around her. 'Try,' he said into her hair. 'What happened when Paul came? Did he speak to you? Was he talking to your mum about how she was caring for you, or something?'

Tamsin shook her head, as if she was trying to force herself to think. 'I didn't know who he was,' she said. 'I guess I thought he was my mum's boyfriend. Or someone she owed money to.'

'Perhaps he was her boyfriend. If he'd had a relationship with her before...'

'He would talk to me,' she said, and he saw the corner of her mouth twitch in a little smile. 'He would talk to me, and buy me things. I think he even helped me with my homework...'

'He was trying to be your dad?'

'I don't know. Maybe that's what he wanted. I remember hoping that he would look after me. I asked him once if I could live with him and he said... he said...' she opened her eyes and spoke with sudden clarity, and he thought she must be repeating the exact words, or very close to them. '"I wish you could too, Kitten. But my wife would be jealous."'

'His wife would be *jealous*?'

Tamsin frowned again. 'It was a secret,' she said. 'It had to all be a secret.'

'What...' Michael pressed her, 'what did?'

She looked as though she was going to fall silent and Michael shook her shoulder. 'Tamsin, what had to be a secret? What did he do when he came to see you?'

She felt limp under his hand. 'Tamsin!' he said. 'Tell me this isn't what I think it is.'

'I can't remember.'

Michael lowered his voice. 'Did he try to have sex with you?'

He heard her breathe out. 'Did he, did he *actually* have sex with you, Tamsin? Just nod or shake your head. You don't have to say anything out loud—'

'Late at night,' she said, 'that's when they'd come.'

'*They?*'

All of a sudden her face changed. She stared at Michael and said, 'What was I talking about?'

Sixty-Eight

Michael held her hand and squeezed it. 'Tamsin,' he said, 'you said someone came and saw you in the night...'

'What?'

'When you were a child. You said, "Late at night, that's when they'd come."'

'Who would come and see me in the middle of the night?' she said. She looked out of the window. 'I wish I could walk outside,' she said. 'They might let me if you were with me. I've been out with one of *them* a couple of times. I guess they're worried that if I'm not supervised I'll jump in front of a bus, or something.'

Michael's mind was racing. How could he get her to talk about it again?

'Tamsin,' he said firmly. 'Tell me about Paul. Tell me what happened between you and Paul when you were a child.'

'I didn't know Paul when I was a child.' She laughed. 'That would be messed up, wouldn't it?'

In desperation Michael grabbed the paternity test and shoved it in front of her. Then he felt guilty for being heavy-handed, and he folded it up and put it on the chest of drawers next to her bed.

'Do you want me to ask if you can go outside with me?' he said gently. 'Perhaps a walk would be nice—'

'For God's sake,' she said, and her voice was different again, 'feed that girl properly and get her some decent clothes. Otherwise someone will start asking questions and we'll all end up in fucking prison. It's not like I don't give you enough cash...'

She fell silent and Michael stroked her hand. 'Who said that?' he asked her. 'Did Paul say that to your mum?'

'They used to tell me I was dreaming.'

'Who did?'

'The men.'

'The men who came at night?'

'They'd whisper. They never spoke out loud. I was supposed to think they were all Paul. Paul was my boyfriend.'

Michael felt tears prickle his eyes.

'He said it was okay for me and him to be together,' she said, 'but that other people wouldn't think so, so it had to be a secret. He said that he would get in a lot of trouble, but that *I* would be in the most trouble of all.'

Michael's whole body felt tense. He was rigid with anger over

217

what Paul had done, but he didn't want it to show. Tamsin had started to cling on to his hand and he thought that if his anger showed it would scare her into going silent again.

'How old were you?' he asked, and a lump formed in his throat.

'Thirteen,' she said.

Michael's heart was pounding. He struggled to bring himself to speak. 'And your mum knew about it?'

'He'd come to the flat,' she said, 'and she'd let him go in my bedroom with me while she played loud music and got drunk in the living room. He said he loved me. I loved him too.'

Michael wanted to be strong, but when she said the words, something in him seemed to crack. He began to cry and tried to do it silently so that Tamsin wouldn't notice, but he didn't succeed, and she looked at him in surprise. 'Why are you crying?' she said.

'I can't... I'm sorry,' he told her. The tears overcame him again and he couldn't even focus on her face. 'I don't understand how this could happen.' He took a deep breath, then another and another. Then a thought struck him. 'No...' he said, 'the baby, when you were thirteen... Bella...' he saw her flinch. 'He made you have an abortion?'

'I couldn't have looked after her,' she said after a short pause. 'I felt attached to her... to the baby... but he did the right thing to make me get rid of it. I couldn't have been a mum. I got asked lots of questions when I went to the clinic, because I was so young. I just kept saying it was a boy my own age. I said I didn't remember his name. Paul told me that's what I should say, and my mum went with me and backed up my story. It felt like it went on forever, all these different people asking me things. But Paul was there for me through all of it. He helped me to stay strong.'

'He did it to cover his own back,' Michael said, unable to contain himself. 'He didn't care about you, it was a business! He and your mum made money out of letting those men—' he forced himself to hold his tongue. She let go of his hand, and her eyes seemed to go cloudy.

'When they were with me, I'd imagine really hard that I was somewhere else. I had these little fantasy worlds I'd go to, so that even if my body was in the bed with them, *I* wasn't.'

Michael stroked her hair. 'It wasn't your fault,' he said. 'You know that, don't you?'

'You're wrong,' she said. 'I led Paul on. I liked the presents he bought me. I liked talking to him. I said I loved him and that I wanted to be with him, and I meant it.'

'That makes no difference.'

'It was hard for him too,' she said. 'He said he felt guilty. He told me he couldn't sleep sometimes for worrying about it—'

'It didn't stop him though, did it? And the others—'

'He said there were no others. He was determined for me to believe it was only him. But after the baby the others stopped coming. I knew it was him who'd refused to let them see me any more. My mum wouldn't have cared.'

'It was probably just because the risk was getting too high,' he said, and then he stopped himself. He could see he was hurting her. He got up from the floor and sat beside her on the bed. 'Listen to me,' he said softly. 'I know you say you loved Paul, and that he was your boyfriend, but you were far too young for him to be having sex with you. You do understand that, don't you?'

'I don't know,' she whispered.

'Tamsin, you were a child. He was an adult.'

'I knew what sex was.'

'So does every other thirteen-year-old! Knowing what it is doesn't mean you're ready to have it!'

'Perhaps it wasn't real. Or maybe I am just a liar. Or a little slut who was asking for it—'

'Tamsin—'

'Star got frightened,' she said suddenly, 'when she found out I was in here. She knows that she should have told someone what was happening to me. She was sixteen when she moved back to my mum's and she realised what had been going on, but she kept quiet. She was jealous of the attention I got, and she hated me because I stayed with mum while she was in care. But she's had years and years since then that she could have gone to the police. She thinks that if anyone finds out now, they'll start asking questions about why she stayed silent, and she worries her children might get taken away or something.'

'Maybe they should be!' Michael spat.

'I don't want her to lose her children.'

'Why are you showing any loyalty to her?'

'She used to tell me I was lucky. She said being in care was a hundred times worse than anything that happened to me while I was with mum. When I was young, I believed her. I felt guilty. I realise now that she was trying to make me feel bad, but she's still my sister.'

Michael took in a deep breath and let it out as a sigh. He knew what he had to say. 'Listen to me,' he said gently. 'Forget about Star. What I'm about to say is going to hurt but... but you know Paul might have done this to other girls, don't you?'

Tamsin didn't reply.

'Look, I won't say the word. But you know what he is, don't you?'

'He's my husband.'

'He's not your husband. He's your father, and what he did to you was wrong. Tamsin, I'm not trying to upset you, but adult men don't have thirteen-year-old girlfriends. It wasn't love, it was abuse. You must understand what I'm saying.'

'No.'

'Tamsin—'

'I said no!' she shouted. 'He's not sick! He's not... he's...' She started to cry. 'He's the only person... not the only man, the only *person,* until you, who ever said that they love me. So don't say it wasn't real. Don't you dare say his love wasn't real!'

She dissolved into tears, and Michael watched her helplessly.

Sixty-Nine

Michael sank back down onto the armchair and Tamsin watched him with her eyes glittering. 'I should never have told you,' she said. 'I knew I shouldn't have told you. You think you're something now, don't you? With your righteous anger, making judgements.'

'He should be in prison!' Michael said.

'That's not your decision to make.'

'Tamsin, please! I don't understand any of this. Why did you marry him after what he did? Why are you protecting him?'

'He helped me. When I decided I needed to get away from everything and try to change my life. Rae Carrington was real for me, Michael. Absolutely real. Star and my mum didn't like it. They thought it was ridiculous. But Paul didn't. He helped me with my school work. He encouraged me. He bought me a brand new laptop to take with me to university. He gave me money. After you and I broke up, he was there for me. He gave me a place to stay. He looked after me, and then he asked me to marry him, so that I'd have a home with him forever.'

'It doesn't change what he did.'

'Would you have me lose my husband?'

'Well, do you want to lose your daughter? Being with him would mean you'd have to give her up. If you were happy as Rae, change your name back again. Take your daughter back. When you're well and safe, she'll come out of foster care, won't she? You could start again with her.'

'I can't.'

'Why not?'

'I can't look after her.'

'You love that little girl. I know you do. You've done nothing to be ashamed of.'

'There...' she said quietly, 'there have been times, since we got married, that I've enjoyed it... with him.'

'And you think that means you're not fit to be a mother?'

'What would I do? If my marriage to Paul isn't even legal, I'll be left with nothing. I can't... last time I had a job I got fired. I wouldn't be able to look after Madeline, I can't even look after myself—'

'I'd give you a job. You could work at the shop. Tamsin, you're far more capable than you think.'

'No,' she said, 'it's too... I can't think right now. I can't

221

think...'

'I'm sorry,' he said, 'I'm rushing you. Don't worry about it yet.'

He reached out and stroked her hair again.

'I wish you'd told me,' he said. 'Years ago, I mean.'

'Told you what?' she said, 'all of it?'

'Yes, all of it. I was your boyfriend. You could have trusted me.'

'And when would you have had me tell you?' she said. 'On our first date? When we first kissed? When we first had sex?'

She watched him but he found he couldn't answer her. 'Exactly,' she said. 'You wouldn't have wanted to know. If I'd told you it would have ruined everything.'

'I wouldn't have let it,' he said, 'I would have done my best to help you—'

'Help me?' She sat up and shoved his hand away. 'Perhaps I didn't want or need that. Perhaps I didn't want you to think of me as someone you had to *help*. Perhaps I didn't want you to look at me like I was made of glass, or to think you were doing something wrong when you slept with me.'

Michael rubbed his eyes. 'Tamsin, I know I'm saying all the wrong things, but it's because I don't know what the right things are. If I knew, I would say them.'

'I didn't want you to have to think of the right things to say. I wanted you to treat me like any other girl.'

'I could have done that.'

She let out a strange, barking laugh. 'No you couldn't,' she said. 'You used to blush if we watched a film that had a sex scene in it! You'd only been with one girl before me and even that was only a handful of times. There's no way you could have got past it if I'd told you the truth – you would have found the whole thing...' She shook her head. 'You would never have looked at me the same again. You would have pretended it made no difference, but it would have poisoned everything. You'd have stayed with me out of pity and resented me for it.'

'How do you know what I'd have felt? Yes, I would have found it hard to hear, I'm finding it hard now. But it wouldn't have put me off you, if that's what you think. I wish you could have felt you trusted me.'

She didn't answer him directly. 'I was worried it would be a big shock for you, finding out I was pregnant,' she said. 'But it was kind of a relief to me when I discovered that I was. Because I knew what kind of person you were. I knew you would support me, I thought you would probably ask me to marry you—'

'I would have.'

'But I was too scared to tell you. You kept pushing me about why I wouldn't let you meet my family. I was getting confused. I started to lose the plot a bit... I...'

'And then I cheated on you.'

'I was... I wanted to die, Michael. Or for you to die. I was so angry. So *hurt*.'

'So you never told me about the baby.'

'Not just that.'

'What do you mean?'

'I called Paul and told him what had happened. What you'd done.'

Michael stared at her. 'It was him, wasn't it?' he said, as the pieces fell into place. 'It was him who beat me nearly to death?'

Tamsin nodded.

Seventy

Michael thought back to it – to what he could remember, which was very little except a woman's scream.

'He drove down straight away and I took him to the house where the party was. We waited around, out of sight, until you came out. We followed you.'

'Then you stood and watched Paul beat the living crap out of me,' Michael said.

'We went back to his car after,' she said, ignoring him. 'He was angry with me. He said, "Look what you've done, you stupid, *stupid* little girl." I begged him to take me home with him but he said he was washing his hands of me. He was always so angry with me since I met you. He had been giving me money to help me through uni, but when he found out about you, that's when he said I had to earn it if I wanted to keep my lie going. I resisted as long as I could, I ran up huge credit card debts. I got in such a mess...' She stopped and shook her head. 'I was so angry when you cheated,' she continued. 'But not just with you. With him. With everybody. I decided to change my name to Tamsin. I decided Tamsin was going to be the incarnation of me that wouldn't take any shit, so I went after him. I threatened to go to his wife, and when he called my bluff I really did go to his wife. All of that happened, I wasn't making it up. He took me to a hotel, like I told you, and he took care of me. He's taken care of me ever since, and I love him. He saved me. Kitten was on a dark path – after Bella, all I did was drink and get myself into situations. Bad situations. And then when Rae started losing control, then Tamsin, he has always been there to set me right again. He's not always kind. But I can't function without him, Michael. That's the truth of it. Me and him. We're one.'

Outside, the light was just beginning to fade. 'They'll want me to go and have dinner soon,' she said.

'Look,' Michael said to her. 'I didn't say the word before. But I'm going to say it now because you have to understand. Paul is a paedophile, Tamsin. He's a criminal. I know this is a really complicated situation. And the fact that he's your *dad*—'

'Nobody can know that.'

'People are going to have to know that.'

'Nobody has to know anything.'

'No!' he said, 'no. Tamsin, listen to me. Don't let him get away with it. How about if I go out there and I tell one of the doctors or nurses what you told me. I can say it for you so you won't have to say the words yourself. You'll have so much support. I will support you, I'm sure Sally will too, even Sadie. All the people here at the hospital. *Everyone* will be on your side.'

'No,' she said, 'Michael, no. I don't want to talk.'

'Tamsin, you have to.'

'I don't have to do anything!'

'Okay, well, not tonight. In the morning. I'll come back—'

'No, Michael.'

'You can't—'

'Stop!' she said, 'just stop. *Please.*'

He saw how desperate she was and he put his arms around her. 'I'm sorry,' he said. 'I'm being pushy again. I can't help it. I'm sorry. I'm so sorry this ever happened to you. I'm sorry. I'm sorry.'

'I don't want to talk to anyone.'

'I understand. Just take a bit of time. Concentrate on yourself. But we have to make them pay, Tamsin. All of them. We have to.'

He began to let go of her, but she pulled him towards her again. 'I don't want you to go!' she said. He was so surprised to hear her say it – to admit that she needed him – that he held her close again. 'I won't go,' he said, and he kissed her cheek. 'I won't go anywhere. I'll stay until they kick me out, I promise.'

Seventy-One

About half an hour later there was a knock on the door for dinner, but Tamsin said she wasn't hungry.

'You can go and eat,' Michael said. 'I'll get myself something and I'll come right back.'

Tamsin stared at him and he could see she was scared that given half a chance he'd either disappear, or that he'd talk to somebody.

'It's all right,' he said, 'you can trust me.'

Reluctantly she nodded and Michael got up from her bed and followed her down the corridor. He gave her hand a squeeze and reassured her again that he'd come back and then he headed towards a café he'd seen outside. He bought himself a sandwich, but he couldn't eat it, so he sat in his car for a few minutes before calling Sadie.

'Michael?' she said, 'will you be back soon? You've been a long time.'

Instead of answering, he began to cry.

'Michael!' Sadie said. 'Oh, God, Michael, what's happened?'

'I'm going to be back late,' he said. 'And I'll have to come here again first thing tomorrow morning.'

'Michael, you're frightening me…'

'I can't tell you why just now,' he said, 'but if you knew, you would understand.'

'Okay,' she said, 'okay, well, I trust you. Don't worry about me and Rose.'

'Thank you,' he said. 'I'll see you later tonight.'

'Do what you need to do,' she said. 'I really do trust you, Michael. You're a good man. I know you'll do what is right.'

…

As Michael started back towards the hospital he saw Sally.

'Oh, Michael,' she said, 'I thought you were coming earlier.'

'Sally… I…'

'My God,' she said, looking at his face, 'are you okay?'

'Yes. No. I've been here all afternoon. I'm going back in now. Sorry, I should have called you. I forgot you said you were coming this evening.'

'I'm happy to go and talk to her if you want to go home to your family.'

'Uh... Sally, the thing is, she's had a really tough afternoon. She wants me to stay with her. I don't think she'll be up to seeing anyone else—'

'It's fine,' Sally said lightly, 'I completely understand.'

She handed him a carrier bag. 'It's just some magazines that she likes, and a couple of other bits and bobs,' she said. 'Paul put it together for her. Oh, and he says he's really looking forward to her home visit, and that he understands if she needs some space for a day or two while she gets her head around it.'

'Her what?'

'Oh, didn't she say? I think the plan is for her to go home, just for an afternoon, with Paul. To see how it goes.'

Michael shook his head. 'That can't happen,' he said.

'Michael, what is it?'

'That can't happen.'

'I'm sure they won't let her home if they don't think she can cope with it.'

Michael stood for a while in silence while Sally watched him curiously.

'I... thank you Sally,' he said finally, 'for these magazines and things. I'm sure she'll appreciate them.'

'Are you sure you're okay, Michael?'

'I'm just a bit tired.'

'Yes,' she said, 'with a new baby it would be weird if you weren't.'

'I need to go back inside.'

'Okay,' she said, 'tell her I send my love.'

'I will. Thank you.'

He made his way back towards the hospital. He didn't like the sound of the home visit, but if Tamsin was refusing to let Paul into the hospital, she probably wouldn't go through with it. He was very aware of the handle of the carrier bag in his hand. Sally had said Paul had put it together for Tamsin. Paul. For a second Michael was so angry that his head rushed with blood and he had to lean against a tree and take deep breaths to calm down. Right now, he told himself, I just need to be there for Tamsin. That's all that matters.

Seventy-Two

All evening, Michael stayed right by Tamsin's side. He suggested they venture down to the TV room, and reluctantly she agreed. No one else was in there, and she rested her head against him while they watched a documentary that neither of them really listened to. He hugged her tightly before he left, and promised her he'd be back in the morning.

But when he arrived the next day, she wouldn't let him in.

He was so surprised that he wasn't sure what to do. Then he made his way out of the reception area and stood outside the building to call her. She took a long time to answer and when she did she said, 'I don't want to see you.'

A feeling of panic went through him. 'But we need to talk,' he said. 'About what you told me yesterday.'

'I didn't tell you anything yesterday.'

Michael closed his eyes. This couldn't be happening. 'Tamsin,' he said, 'you did. You know you did...'

'I made it all up.'

'No you didn't!' Michael said. 'Look, I know how frightening it is, but you managed to tell me and if you can tell me, you can tell other people too. I know it's going to be hellish. I know you don't want to talk about it—'

'Talk about what?'

'Don't do this. You can't shut me out.'

'I don't know what you're talking about. Anyway, it's not convenient for you to be here today. They're having a meeting about my care this morning and then in the afternoon Paul is coming in so we can talk things through with the psychiatrist, about what happens next.'

'What?' Michael said, 'Tamsin, no! I thought you were refusing to see Paul. He can't... you can't...'

'He's my husband.'

'Listen to me, you... Tamsin... please won't you let me come in to talk to you?'

'There's a class this morning about relaxation techniques. I thought I'd go to it.'

'Tamsin, you can't...'

'If Paul realises you keep coming here, he'll kill you for real,' she said.

Michael felt a rush of anger and he closed his eyes to try to steady himself. 'Tamsin, this is driving me crazy. I can't keep

228

silent about what you told me.'

'I don't know what you're talking about.'

'Tamsin, no! You told me that for your whole life this is what your mum, and Star, and Paul have wanted. For you to not sound plausible. For everyone to think you're a liar.'

'I am a liar.'

'No. You made things up to cope. And you got so used to doing it that you carried on, but that's not the same as being a liar.' He sighed. 'Please just let me in.'

To his surprise she said, 'Fine. You can come in. But I don't have anything else to say to you.'

'Thank you,' he said, 'thank you, Tamsin.'

When he stepped inside her room, it felt cool, and she seemed perfectly composed, dressed in smart jeans and a tight white t-shirt. He closed the door and sat beside her.

'Is this because you're trying to protect Madeline?' he said. 'Because you don't want her to ever find out about any of this?'

'What is this? Twenty questions?' She smiled at him. 'Even if you get it right, I won't tell you that you have.'

'This isn't a game.'

'No,' she said, 'because games are fun. And this is extremely tedious.'

'Do you really not remember what you told me? Or are you just trying to block me out?'

'Paul is my husband. I love him. Perhaps you're jealous of him, but that's not my problem.'

Michael lowered his voice. 'He's a *criminal,*' he said. 'He doesn't deserve your loyalty.'

She didn't reply, and he began to feel desperate.

'Tamsin, please,' he said. 'Drop this act! When you talked to me yesterday, it was the only time I've ever seen you talk like that. I'm sure it feels better when you've got all your guards up, but you can't carry on this way!'

She cocked her head to one side. 'Maybe you should get a job here at the hospital,' she said. 'It seems like you'd have a great time. Anyway, my relaxation thing is starting now. I don't want to miss it.'

Michael grabbed her hand. 'Do one thing for me,' he said. 'When Paul comes this afternoon, you take a long look at him. And instead of just seeing your husband, you remember what you told me about him, about when and how you really met him.'

She didn't reply, but he thought he saw a flicker of emotion cross her face, and he hoped he'd got through to her.

Seventy-Three

'Michael, you can't carry on like this,' Sadie said. It was the next day, and he'd barely slept all night. 'You're making yourself ill,' she continued. 'You're not eating, you won't say more than two words to me...'

He tried to ignore her, but she wouldn't give up.

'Michael, what *is* it?'

'I don't want to talk about it,' he said. He wished she'd just stop. He didn't think he had it in him to explain to her what Tamsin had told him.

'Right,' Sadie said, 'I've had enough of this. I know you're worried about Tamsin but you shouldn't be in this much of a state. I'm going to call the hospital and get them to tell her you can't come in any more.'

'Sadie, no.'

'Then tell me what the hell is going on!'

He looked at her, and saw her face was flushed with emotion. 'You said you trusted me,' he told her, 'you said I would do the right thing.'

'And are you? Making yourself sick with worry—'

'I'm doing my best.'

'Really? What use are you to anyone in this state?' Her voice softened. 'Michael, you're scaring me,' she said. 'I'm not angry with you, it just frightens me to think what must be going on for you to feel like this. Are you worried Tamsin will hurt herself again, is that it? Has she told you she's planning to, or something?'

'No.'

'Is she angry we wouldn't look after Madeline?'

'Sadie, please...'

'I *want* to help you—'

He slammed his hand on the kitchen table. 'Then get off my back!' he shouted. He regretted it immediately, and he saw Sadie flinch with surprise. Then she pointed at her finger at him. 'Don't you dare!' she said, 'don't you *dare* shout at me. You're stressed out, and I get it. I do. But I'm having to look after our baby, and your shop, while you look like you're about to have a bloody nervous breakdown. Visiting Tamsin should not be making you feel like this. Is she blaming it all on you, or something? What is she saying that could make you *this* upset, I just don't under-stand—'

230

'She told me she was sexually abused,' he said all in a rush. 'When she was thirteen.'

Sadie's face turned white and she sat down at the kitchen table. 'Oh,' she said.

Michael sat down opposite her. 'That's what was at the bottom of it all,' he told her. 'All the lies, all the strange things she comes out with. It all stems from that.'

'So do you think that's what she's been trying to tell you all along?' Sadie asked, after a long pause.

'I don't know. I'm not sure she always remembers it. She's tried pretty hard to block it out, and I think sometimes she really does forget.'

'What are you going to do?'

'She doesn't want anybody to know.'

'Is that why you didn't want to tell me?'

'Partly. And I couldn't find the words.'

'Well, you shouldn't have to deal with it all yourself. I'm glad you told me. How do *you* feel about it?'

He stared at her, and suddenly his mood darkened again. 'I can't do this right now,' he said. 'I don't want to talk about it. I can't even think straight.'

'That's because you haven't been sleeping.'

'It was Paul!' he said. 'It was Paul who did it to her. She's going to go back to him.'

Sadie's eyes widened in shock. '*Paul*,' she said. 'Her husband—'

Michael stood up abruptly. 'I'm going out,' he said.

'Where?'

'I have to see her again.'

'Michael, wait—'

She stood up but he brushed past her. His mind didn't feel like his own any more; it felt volatile, dangerous. All he knew was that he wouldn't rest until somehow he'd found a resolution to what Tamsin had told him.

...

He felt sick as he drove. He'd heard nothing from Tamsin, and he felt as if he was being torn apart as he tried to decide what to do. Then his phone chimed, startling him, and when he saw the message was from her, he pulled over to read it.

I'm about to leave to spend the afternoon with Paul at home.

They want to see how I cope with it. I'm going to try to talk to him about what I told you. I remember it so vividly today. It's like a fog has lifted. I don't know how he'll react, but he's my husband and I want to be honest with him. I half expect him to not know what I'm talking about – we never speak about it, and in my head I always feel like he's not the same man. Perhaps he isn't, and I really have lost my mind.

Michael sat for a while in silence. Then he started the engine, and turned the car around. He couldn't let Tamsin go home with Paul. He didn't want her to have to be alone with him, and although he had no idea what on earth he was going to do when he got there, he began to drive towards her house.

Seventy-Four

Tamsin blinked in the sunlight as she left the hospital. It was a surprisingly warm, bright autumn day and it was nice to be outside, but it also felt surreal. Paul held her hand tightly as they walked, and when she got into the car she shivered involuntarily, and touched her jeans pocket where she'd placed the folded-up paternity test letter.

'What's wrong?' he said. 'You're okay with this, aren't you?'

She nodded.

'I've got a surprise for you at home,' he said. He reached across and put his hand on her thigh. 'I've missed you so much. I'm going to make sure you get everything you need to feel better, okay?'

She nodded again, and they spoke very little as he drove them back towards the house.

Once they arrived, Tamsin didn't want to go inside. She froze as they made their way towards the front door, surprised by how much the thought of going another step was scaring her.

'Paul,' she said, 'could we sit in the garden?'

He stopped and looked at her. 'Of course we can,' he said. 'We can do whatever you want. Your surprise is inside, though. Do you want to see it first?'

'Can't you bring it out to me?'

He smiled. 'Not really,' he said. 'You'll understand why when you see it.'

She stayed still, staring at the front door. 'I don't...' she said, 'Paul... I don't feel good.'

'Take my hand,' he said. 'I know it's been a difficult time for you. But there's nothing to be frightened of.'

Tentatively she closed her fingers around his, and she let him lead her inside.

'Upstairs,' he said, 'come on.'

She followed a step behind him, and the air seemed to close in around her. She took a few deep breaths, but it was like she couldn't get enough oxygen. She watched Paul make his way across the landing and she hung back, struggling to move.

'Paul, I'd like to go outside...'

'Here,' he said, and he swung open the door to their bedroom. Tamsin stepped tentatively towards it, with no idea what she would see, and when she looked inside she gasped because it was so different to what she was expecting.

'Paul, it's beautiful,' she said.

Every surface was crowded with candles. The curtains were closed, and the room was like a twinkly cave, with rose petals strewn across the bed.

'I asked Sally to light the candles,' he said. 'She did it just before we got here.'

'It's so thoughtful.'

Paul tried to pull her towards him, but her body resisted.

'What's wrong?' he asked her.

'Paul, I can't,' she said. 'I'm sorry.'

'What's going on with you?' he said. 'You're acting so strangely. Is it that place? That bloody hospital? Have they been putting ideas in your head, saying it's all my fault or something—'

'No,' she said quickly. 'It's nothing like that. I'm overwhelmed, that's all. I appreciate the candles and everything, but I'm not ready to do anything yet. I know you must be disappointed...'

He let go of her and his face softened. 'It's all right,' he said. 'We don't have to do anything. I just wanted to show you how much I missed you.' He ran his fingers through her hair. 'I don't like going to bed without you. I can't wait until you're home again.'

Tamsin sat on the bed and picked up a rose petal. 'Paul, can I ask you something?'

'Anything.'

'What do you see when you look at me?'

He sat beside her. 'I see my beautiful wife,' he said.

'That's all?'

'Why? What more do you want me to see?'

Tamsin frowned down at the petal in her hand. 'Can we go and sit in the garden now?' she asked.

...

They walked down almost to the bottom of the garden, where there was a large swinging bench seat surrounded on three sides by borders filled with shrubs and flowers – many beginning to look a bit sorry for themselves now the summer was over. Tamsin lay along the bench, her head in Paul's lap. Above them the sky was a warm blue. She closed her eyes, and let Paul stroke her hair while she tried to think how to begin.

Seventy-Five

When Michael arrived at the house, he parked his car on the road, and walked up the lawn at the side of the gravel drive so that his feet wouldn't crunch on the stones and alert them that he was coming. He still had no idea what he was going to do. He half thought he'd just turn around and leave again.

When he reached the pond at the side of the house, he hesitated. He felt really stupid. What was he thinking, that he would barge inside and start accusing Paul? There was no way that could end in anything other than disaster. *Paul.* Just the name made his body surge with adrenalin. He could see Paul's car on the drive, and the proximity to him was making Michael feel dizzy with anger. He couldn't seem to think clearly, and no matter how sensible he knew it would be to leave, he couldn't. Suddenly, he was startled when he heard some voices further down the garden. Tamsin and Paul – they weren't inside the house after all.

He made his way towards the sound, and he caught full view of them on a seat amongst the flower borders. Tamsin was just sitting up and Paul was saying something to her. They were too intent on each other to notice him, and he darted behind some large bushes, gradually creeping closer.

...

'Do you feel better?' Paul asked her. 'It seems like you're exhausted.'

'I get tired of having to talk all the time,' she said. 'I've had to repeat the same things over and over. So many people come and talk to me in the hospital – they want to know everything.'

'You'll be away from that place soon.'

Tamsin rubbed her face, and looked out across the lawn towards the house. When she spoke again, it was as though it wasn't her voice.

'I won't be coming back here,' she said, 'not to be with you. Not as your wife.'

...

From his spot behind the bushes, Michael felt a surge of joy at her words. 'Come on Tamsin,' he mouthed silently, 'you can do

235

it.'

...

'What?' Paul said. 'What are you talking about?'

Tamsin looked straight at him. 'Our relationship is over,' she said. 'It has to be.'

His eyes narrowed. 'Is this *Michael?* Has he been coming to see you?'

'It's not because of Michael.'

'Then I don't understand. Is it Madeline? Because you think I was meddling with her things, moving her blanket, hiding her coats, or whatever...'

'You did do those things,' she said. She saw his face and before he could respond, she said, 'And I know why.'

...

Michael watched as she took something from her jeans pocket and showed it to Paul, and he realised it was the test results. He braced himself for Paul's reaction. *Thank God I'm here,* he thought to himself, *if he flips out I can help her.* Suddenly, an idea occurred to him. He slipped his phone from his pocket, and opened up a voice recorder. If Tamsin was going to go through every awful detail with Paul, perhaps he could save her from having to go through it again. He held the phone out in front of him. And hit record.

...

Tamsin watched Paul's face. His expression was grim, and he handed the letter back to her. When he spoke, his voice had an edge of emotion – disappointment, she thought it sounded like. 'Why did you order this test?'

'So you did know that we're related?' she asked him.

'Yes, I knew.'

Tamsin sat completely still for a moment, then she threw the letter at him. 'How could you?' she shouted, 'how could you?'

She stood up and he grabbed her.

'Tamsin, calm down,' he said, 'calm down. Listen to me. Listen. It doesn't matter.'

'How can you say that? I'm your daughter, Paul! Your daughter!'

She started to sink to her knees, and Paul knelt down with her. 'Tamsin, stop this,' he said. 'You're overreacting—'
She took a breath, and then she screamed.

Seventy-Six

Sadie sat quietly in the living room after Michael left, holding Rose in one arm and reading a book with her other hand. She couldn't concentrate. All she could think about was the state Michael was in and the things he'd told her, and she began to feel more and more frustrated and worried, until she went over to the drawer in the sideboard and took out the piece of paper with Sally's phone number on it. She hesitated for a moment, wondering if she was overreacting, then she shook her head. She'd never seen Michael like this before. She had no idea what he might do.

...

'Tamsin, listen,' Paul was saying, 'listen to me.'

She held her hands over her ears, and he tried to pull them away. 'Fine!' he shouted, when she wouldn't let him remove them. 'And you wonder why I didn't tell you? When you behave like *this!*'

Slowly, Tamsin felt her mind clear. She uncovered her ears and fixed her eyes on Paul.

'You're looking at this all wrong,' he told her.

'It's why you wanted Madeline away from here, isn't it?' she said. 'You saw that I was struggling with her anyway, and you tried to drive me over the edge. So that I'd give her up without a fight. So I'd never find out that... that you...'

'I was trying to do the best thing. For all of us.'

'You let me think I'd put a blanket over her head! You changed the washing powder! You hid things, you... she was so scared of me she'd cry when she saw me—'

'She didn't cry because she was scared of you!' he said. 'I gave her a little pinch when you talked to her.'

Tamsin felt a surge of horror. 'You did what?' she said quietly.

'It didn't really hurt her,' he said, 'it just gave her a shock—'

Tamsin drew back her hand and slapped him so hard that the sound seemed to reverberate around her. It took Paul a second to compose himself and she lifted her hand again but he caught her wrist. 'Stop,' he said. 'Stop now. I deserved the first one, but that's enough. I was cruel to you, and I'm sorry. I took no joy in it. It got so out of control, I never meant for other people to get involved, I never meant for people to start saying you were ill. It shouldn't have gone on so long like it did. But I thought if I could just get you to agree to the adoption, everything would be okay again. Tamsin, you can't look after her. You're not capable—'

'You said yourself that you would drive me to rock bottom, if that's what it took—'

'I was desperate. I got it all wrong...'

Tamsin tapped her finger against the ground to mark out her words. She was fighting to keep her thoughts together. 'It is against... the law...' she said, 'us being married, it's against the law.'

'Oh, don't give me that!' he said. 'The law is wrong. It's outdated. There is absolutely *no* reason why we shouldn't be able to get married. None at all. As long as we never, ever have children—'

'But we *did* have a child!' Tamsin cried.

'Because you were too stupid to take your pills properly!' he shouted. Then his face changed. 'Tam, I'm sorry,' he said, 'I'm so sorry. I shouldn't have said that. It was my fault. I shouldn't have put the responsibility on you, not when it was so important. I should have been more careful.'

'It's *wrong*,' Tamsin said, 'it's immoral.'

'It's not wrong. Does it feel wrong? When we're in bed together? Because I've seen your face, I've heard the sounds you make—'

'I didn't know who you were!'

'Really?' he said, 'or was it just that you didn't want to face it?'

'I didn't know,' she said, 'I didn't know.'

...

In the bushes, Michael's stomach twisted. Tamsin was crying, and Paul was trying to put his arms around her but she was fighting him off. He was in two minds about whether to come out from the bushes and pull Paul away from her, when suddenly he saw something. Half hidden underneath the foliage beside him was a glint of metal. He reached out for it and discovered a pair of secateurs with a dark green handle and shiny, mean-looking curved blades. They must have been left there accidentally by the gardeners. He pulled them towards him and held them in his hand. They had a nice weight to them. He found that holding them made him feel better.

...

When Sadie got off the phone to Sally, she threw a coat on, and went out to the car. Her fingers fumbled as she strapped Rose into her car seat, but she knew she had to go after Michael. She didn't know what was going on exactly, but when Sally had explained that Paul and Tamsin would be at their house that afternoon, she knew that must be where Michael had gone too. Finally, she got Rose fastened in safely, and she put Tamsin's address into her phone to get directions. She took a few deep breaths. She could see Michael had lost his judgement. He'd looked *tormented* over the past few days. She just hoped she managed to get to the house before things got out of control.

Seventy-Seven

Tamsin let Paul help her up, and they sat on the swinging seat again.

'I can't be with you,' she said.

He ignored her and instead he said, 'Do you remember the first time we made love?' He looked at her closely. 'No, I suppose you don't.'

She stared down at her lap. 'I remember it now,' she whispered. 'And we weren't *making love*. You weren't loving me. You were hurting me. You were making me do something I wasn't ready to do.'

'Then you obviously don't remember it right,' he snapped, 'but I never forgot it. I remember everything. Tamsin, you're so precious to me. And I feel so privileged to have spent so much of my life with you. To have watched you grow up.' He touched her hand gently. 'I couldn't believe it when I heard what you'd tried to do to yourself, that you wanted to die. It breaks my heart to think that you're not happy.'

'I was a child,' she said softly.

'What?'

'I was thirteen,' she said. 'You were forty. And you... you're my dad. You're supposed to protect me.'

She was still looking down at her lap, and Paul reached out and raised her chin. 'Tamsin,' he said, 'what are you saying to me? I do protect you. Why do you think I put a ring on your finger? It's so you'd feel safe and secure, because you can't look after yourself, you never have been able to. I wanted you to have a home and somebody you knew you could rely on. And as for our ages, they're not important, are they? I don't see your age, or my age, when I think about us. I love the *core* of who you are.'

'Do you say that to other girls?'

'*What?*'

'Do you say it to other teenage girls?'

There was a long silence. When Paul spoke his voice was soft. 'I'll forgive you for saying that,' he said, 'because you're not yourself. Since Michael has been back on the scene, your head's been all over the place. He's no good for you. When I think,' he said, his voice rising, 'if I'd kicked him just one more time I might have killed that little prick—'

'Stop!' Tamsin said, 'please stop—'

He held her hand. 'I'm sorry,' he said, 'I'm sorry. But I don't understand why you're saying these things.'

'You're right that it's because of him,' she said, 'partly, any-way. I told him. I told him all of this.'

Paul nodded slowly. 'I see.'

'He hasn't told anybody.'

'I can make sure he doesn't.'

'I just want you to admit it.'

'Admit what?' he said. 'This is Michael. This is all Michael. I can guess what he said to you, but his mind is in the gutter if he told you that your age was all that mattered to me – that I wanted you because you were young. I wished you were older! I always have. You know I tried to stop myself, you know how difficult it was for me. When your mum came to me and told me about you, I couldn't believe I had a little girl. I was so excited, and happy. She wanted money, she was trying to blackmail me, but all I could think about was how much I wanted to meet you. I came to the flat, and when I laid eyes on you I thought you were so beautiful. You were just this little scrap of a thing, but your eyes were so bright and you didn't miss a thing. You watched me like a cat.' He laughed. 'Then when I asked what your name was, you said, "What the fuck has that got to do with you?"'

'I didn't like strange men.'

His expression grew serious again. 'I never meant to find you attractive,' he said. 'I didn't *want* to, I would have done anything to switch it off. I felt like I was going mad, it made me feel ill sometimes because what I felt was so intense.'

'Am I supposed to feel sorry for you?'

'No.' He gave her a hard look. 'Actually, yes. You have to take some responsibility. It's not like you told me to leave you alone. You enjoyed spending time with me, and when I told you how I felt about you, you said you loved me too. Did you tell Michael that? I bet you didn't. I bet you said it was all my fault.'

'I told him the truth.'

'And what did he say? That you were "too young"? That I *made* you have sex, that you weren't capable of making decisions like that?'

'Paul, I wasn't capable of making decisions like that! I liked you, I *loved* you, or thought I did, but I didn't want to have sex yet. You just told me that I did! Why do you think I made up all the crap that I made up? Because I wanted to escape! But I was a child, and I had nowhere to escape to but inside my head.'

Paul was watching her quietly. 'And you're blaming that on me?' he said. 'You were messed up in the head long before I came onto the scene. You already made up your little stories. You used to tell them to me, don't you remember? I thought it was cute, actually.'

'Cute? You didn't think it was cute, you thought it was *useful.* If I was already halfway out of reality, it just made it easier for you to send the others.'

'You're not making sense.'

'Yes I am. You know what I'm talking about. You know there were other men.' Paul's blank expression infuriated her and her voice rose. 'You know there were!' she shouted. 'You know!' Paul grabbed her and gave her a shake.

'Stop this,' he said firmly. 'Stop it. Are you going to let Michael tell you that you were stupid? For God's sake, you weren't a child! With a mum like yours, you knew fucking everything about everything. You weren't *innocent.'*

'You made money from me. You, mum, and maybe you paid Star off too, to keep her quiet—'

'I don't know what the hell you're talking about.'

'Those men! The other men, I know there were others! I know what you did.' She found her voice was almost a scream. 'I'm not crazy! I know they were real! You made me get rid of my baby, you made me get rid of Bella to protect you and your sick friends. All this crap you say about love and about my age not mattering to you, it's all lies! You say it to manipulate me. You didn't love me! I'm not sure you've ever loved me, I think you just like having sex with young girls!'

Paul nodded slowly. 'Okay,' he said, 'then tell me this. Why did I marry you? If you're not in my... my what? My *preferred age range?'*

'I don't know. Maybe you like the fact I'm your daughter. Or maybe you just wanted to keep an eye on me.'

'How dare you say that? I've done nothing but care for you.'

'You've done nothing but stifle me! And I let you do it. I let myself believe I needed you to protect me...' She stopped and took a deep breath. 'How much money did you make from me?'

'Don't be so disgusting.'

Tamsin closed her eyes for a second. 'You used to tell your first wife you were on business trips, didn't you? When you came to visit me?'

Paul didn't answer.

'Where do you go when you tell me you're on business?'

'You think I go away to have sex with young girls, do you?' he spat. 'How does that work, when you used to come with me on my trips, before Madeline—'

'Not all of them,' she said slowly. 'I didn't come on all of your trips. I only came with you when you said I could come with you.'

'I'm not listening to this. Talk to me when you've calmed down. You're hysterical.'

He started to stand and she pulled him back down. 'You used me!' she cried. 'You took my trust and you used me, and you let other men use me too. And I want you to admit it!'

Suddenly Paul grabbed both of her hands and brought his face close to hers, so close she could feel his breath.

'Paul...' she said. 'What are you—'

'You really want to play this game?' he hissed at her. 'Fine. Maybe what you say is true...' He moved even closer to her, his lips near her ear. 'But I'd like to see you try to prove it.'

...

In the bushes, Michael's heart was hammering and there was a roaring sound in his head. He was gripping the handle of the secateurs very tightly. He watched as Tamsin stood up and tried to run back towards the house, but Paul caught her by the arm.

'No, you don't,' he said. 'That's it for you, is it? You think I'm some sort of pervert? Why don't you say it to me? Go on, I dare you. See what happens.'

The roaring in Michael's head reached a screeching, dangerous pitch. He thought Tamsin would try to get away from Paul, but she stood her ground.

'You know what you are,' she said. 'I don't have to say it.'

Paul grabbed hold of her tightly and she began to struggle in his arms. 'Listen to me carefully,' he said. 'If you tell anyone about this, here's what will happen. Me, and Star, and practically every person who's ever spoken to you in your life will confirm that you are a compulsive liar. No one will be able to find any evidence, and it will be your word against mine. And I will say how you're currently in a *mental hospital.* How I've endured years and years of your irresponsible, childish, reckless behaviour, and in the end it won't be you that anyone feels sorry for. It will be *me.*'

'I've proved that you're my father—'

'And I'll say I didn't know. You have not thought this through, have you, *little girl*? My little *Kitten.*'

Tamsin started to cry again and Michael found himself rising to his feet. Paul had his back to Michael, but Tamsin saw him and she must have realised what he was intending to do, because she screamed, 'No! Michael, no! He doesn't mean it! He doesn't—'

Michael raised the secateurs, and Paul turned.

'Oh,' he said casually. 'I see. You thought you'd come and stick your nose in, did you?'

Michael took a step closer and held up his phone. 'I've recorded everything you said.'

'Is that right?' Paul nodded towards the secateurs. 'I know you're not going to do anything with those,' he said, 'because you haven't got the balls. So I'll tell you a bit more about how it went down, shall I?'

Michael took another step.

'Tamsin… or should I say *Kitten,* was not the pretty little victim you think she was. She was a nasty, dirty little *animal* who couldn't keep her legs closed. Not for me, not for any of them. Perhaps seeing her mum's disgusting habits messed her head up, because believe me, when I came along she *couldn't get enough of it*—'

With one swift movement Michael drew the secateurs back, and before he really understood what he was doing, he'd plunged them into the side of Paul's neck. A split second passed, and Michael saw a look of surprise and confusion on the man's face, but he found himself stabbing Paul again, and again, before letting go of the secateurs like the handle was burning him. He made a noise of horror as he watched the blood spilling from Paul's body, and then the man seemed to crumple before his eyes, dropping to the ground and then falling still.

Seventy-Eight

The next few moments, all Michael could hear seemed to be white noise. Tamsin was screaming. She pulled her top off and knelt beside Paul, pressing it against the wounds, though the thin fabric was nowhere near up to the task.

'Why?' she screamed at him, 'why did you do this?'

He staggered backwards and his phone slipped from his hand, forgotten. Then he heard a sound behind him and to his horror, when he turned, he saw Sadie standing there, clutching Rose to her chest, her eyes huge and frightened.

'Sadie,' he said, 'Sadie, listen to me... Sadie...'

She began to back away and he saw her take out her phone. 'I'm going to call the police,' she told him.

'That's okay,' he said, 'I...' He looked back to Tamsin who was shrieking, and shaking Paul's body to try to wake him up.

'Why are you crying?' he yelled at Tamsin suddenly. 'After what he did to you, why are you crying for him?'

She carried on sobbing, and he remembered something she'd said to him. *Paul is the only man, the only **person**, until I met you, who ever told me they loved me.*

...

Michael felt like he was in a dream while they arrested him. He went along with everything, making no attempt to protest or escape, but he did try to explain.

'I need you to listen,' he said. 'That man, Paul Quinnell, he is a paedophile. Tamsin is his daughter. And he has a daughter with her. You have to understand.' He received little response; they must have thought he was crazy, but he knew they'd heard him. As they moved towards the drive, Sadie suddenly appeared again, her face a mask of tears, and he quickly said, 'Sadie would have heard what Paul was saying.'

He looked at her desperately and she turned to one of the police officers. 'I didn't hear anything,' she said. 'I heard shouting, that's why I went into the garden, but when I got to them Paul was... Michael had already...'

'My phone!' he said, as the memory rushed back. 'I was recording their conversation. He admits everything. It's in...' He struggled to remember where he'd dropped it. 'It's there in the garden,' he said, 'near the bushes. It's somewhere...'

He thought they weren't listening but he noticed one of the police officers disappear around the side of the house.

'I'm sorry,' he called to Sadie, 'I'm so sorry.'

Sadie just stared at him silently and Rose started making a weak little cry. He realised there was nothing he could do. And somehow, the realisation felt like a relief.

As they neared the police car, he felt lighter all of a sudden, like he was floating. He closed his eyes briefly and let the police carry on leading him. Paul is dying, he thought to himself. Paul is dying, or maybe he's already dead, and I saved her. I saved Tamsin. I saved *Rae*. He looked back and saw Sadie and his daughter standing near the pond, but he let his mind just go, let it drift away to a world where none of it had happened. Where his years were just blank sheets of paper, where the night he'd cheated could be rewritten, where Rae hadn't been subjected to eleven more years of abuse and manipulation because of his silly mistake, but where somehow he could still have had his life with Sadie, and his beautiful daughter. He knew it was a fantasy, but he grinned idiotically as he thought about it, as he was placed in the back of a police car, and finally as he watched the figure of Sadie and his daughter grow smaller and smaller, until they finally disappeared; swallowed up by the haze of the warm autumn day.

THREE YEARS LATER

Celeste Hardcastle sighed contentedly and stretched her legs out so they could catch the sun. She was working on a sketch of the garden, while in the distance Madeline was playing with her best friend Freya – some hectic game of throwing balls around and chasing after them with a huge amount of screaming.

Suddenly, Madeline ran over to her. 'Mummy,' she said, 'come and play.'

For a moment Celeste hesitated. She still felt a little strange around Madeline even now, uneasy about what she knew about her parentage, scared about what would happen when Madeline was old enough to understand the things Celeste had told the police about Paul. She'd struggled for a while about that - about what to say to the police. Initially she'd been so angry with Michael that she'd wanted to say whatever she could to get him put away for as long as possible, but then her anger had cooled, and it had changed. It had turned into anger against Paul and about what had happened to her, and she'd told the police the truth, going back right to the beginning when Paul had first walked through the door to her mum's flat.

Michael. Celeste felt a little rush of strength when she thought about him. *I can be a mum,* she told herself, *Michael always believed in me. Paul wanted me to think that I couldn't do it, because it didn't suit him. Now there is no more Paul. And Michael will be okay,* she reassured herself. She felt guilty about what had ended up happening to him, but her testimony, his phone recording of her and Paul's conversation in the garden, and his cooperation with the police had worked in his favour. His prison sentence would make him miss some of his little girl Rose's early years, but Celeste was relieved that he wouldn't miss all of her childhood. And Sadie, though she had been deeply hurt and angry, had seemed committed to standing by Michael. Celeste hoped that Sadie would wait for him. She hoped that they would all have the happy future they deserved.

She stood up, setting her sketch pad aside, and some nerves fluttered in her stomach. The two little girls were both looking at her. 'Okay then,' she said to them, with a glance towards the balls they had been playing with, now discarded at the bottom of the garden. 'I'll play now. What *are* you playing, anyway? I don't understand it at all.'

Madeline giggled, and grabbed her by the hand. 'Come *on,*

Mummy,' she said. 'It's *easy...*'

Celeste took a step forward, and it struck her suddenly how lucid she felt, how rarely now she'd get lost in her fantasies or feel confused. Her face broke into a smile that briefly made her stop in her tracks, and then without any further doubts she let Madeline pull her over to where she was playing her game.

Organisations offering advice & support for the issues covered in The Stories She Tells:

Help for Adult Victims of Child Abuse:
https://www.havoca.org/

National Association for People Abused in Childhood:
https://napac.org.uk/about/

Information about personality disorders and dissociative disorders can be found on the Mind website
https://www.mind.org.uk

A note from the author

Thank you so much for buying *The Stories She Tells*. I hope that you enjoyed reading it.

As an independent author, one of the most difficult things is getting my book seen by potential readers, because if nobody knows about it, nobody will read it.

This is where you can help!

If you purchased this book from an online retailer, please consider visiting their website to leave a rating and review, as even a short review can make a big difference. And if you enjoyed The Stories She Tells, don't forget to tell your friends! I also invite you to join the LK Chapman Newsletter. I send only occasional emails with information about new releases, offers and giveaways - no spam. And you will be able to download a free copy of my short story about a one night stand gone wrong, 'Worth Pursuing' when you sign up!

Visit www.lkchapman.com to sign up to my newsletter

Thanks again for reading.

Other books by LK Chapman

"No Escape" psychological thriller trilogy

Anything for Him

Found You

Never Let Her Go

Sci-Fi thrillers

Networked

Short Stories

Too Good for this World

Worth Pursuing

Acknowledgements

Finishing The Stories She Tells was not an easy process for me. A combination of Chronic Fatigue Syndrome and repeatedly coming down with infections – one of which became serious enough that I had to spend some time in hospital – meant my progress kept getting derailed. At times the pace felt glacial and I struggled to manage even twenty minutes of work while sitting up in bed. Needless to say it wasn't the easiest time for me or my family! For supporting and helping me through all of it and putting up with me declaring over and over that I would never be able to finish the book I have to thank my husband Ashley. He has to put up with a lot while I'm writing! But I did get there in the end.

For her brilliant help with copy-editing thank you to Carrie O'Grady, and for my wonderful cover thank you to Stuart Bache at Books Covered.

Carol and Ben Barbersmith, thank you for your help with proofreading, and thank you to all my friends and family who support me.

Last but not least, I have to mention *THE Book Club* on Facebook. This wonderful group has been such a brilliant and positive place for me as an author, and I've received so much support and encouragement for both this book and my previous novels. The difference this has made to my writing career is enormous, so thank you so much TBC.

About the author

My full name is Louise Katherine Chapman, and I am a psychological thriller author (although I've also written a sci-fi novel!) I
have always been fascinated by the strength, peculiarities and
extremes of human nature, and the way that no matter how
strange, cruel or unfathomable the actions of other people can
sometimes be, there is always a reason for it, some sequence of
events to be unraveled.

After graduating from the University of Southampton in 2008
with a first class degree in psychology, I worked for a year as a
psychologist at a consultancy company. In 2009 I had to give up
work after developing chronic fatigue syndrome (CFS) – a long
term health condition that causes debilitating physical and mental
exhaustion. After a few years I thankfully managed to regain
enough energy to spend some time volunteering for the mental
health charity Mind, and eventually to begin writing. Although
my energy levels are still limited, I am mostly recovered from
CFS and I am so grateful to be able to write and for the support
of my readers.

Mental health is a topic I often explore in my books. I suffer from
bipolar disorder and OCD myself, and I find writing very helpful
and therapeutic.

I live in Somerset with my husband and son. When I'm not
writing I enjoy walks in the woods, video games, and spending
time with family and friends.

Anything For Him

Book One in the chilling NO ESCAPE psychological thriller
trilogy by LK Chapman

How far would you go to win the one you love?

Vulnerable and alone after the tragic loss of her parents, Felicity
finds herself in a relationship with volatile and troubled Jay.

Reluctantly drawn in to a twisted revenge plan against Jay's
former best friend, Felicity soon becomes trapped, and as Jay
turns increasingly controlling and abusive she questions everything he has told her about his past and his former girlfriend
Sammie. But when she wants to expose the truth she comes up
against an even greater threat: Someone obsessed and dangerous.
Someone who has always been in the background of Jay's life.
Someone who will do anything for him.

For more information visit www.lkchapman.com

Lightning Source UK Ltd.
Milton Keynes UK
UKHW011849021120
372665UK00001B/7